Praise for John W. Campbell and *The Moon is Hell*!

"Had it not been for John W. Campbell, science
fiction as a publisher's category might have perished
with the demise of the pulp industry. As editor of
Astounding (later *Analog*) *Science Fiction*, from
September 1937 to December 1971, he demanded
good writing. That is his achievement, and he set the
standard with the better of his own stories. Campbell's
skills are nowhere dramatized more forcibly than in
The Moon is Hell! The First rocketship to the moon
crashes and its crew of research scientists, stranded
on the dead rock, win from the object of their curiosity
food, water, and air. . . ."

—*Science Fiction Writers*

THE MOON IS HELL!

JOHN W. CAMPBELL

Carroll & Graf Publishers, Inc.
New York

Copyright © 1951 by John W. Campbell, Jr.
Copyright renewed 1979 by the Estate of John W. Campbell, Jr.

First Carroll & Graf edition 1990

Published by arrangement with the author's estate and the
Scott Meredith Literary Agency, Inc

Carroll & Graf Publishers, Inc.
260 Fifth Avenue
New York, NY 10001

ISBN: 0-88184-674-0

Manufactured in the United States of America

CONTENTS

PROLOGUE

FIFTEEN MEN IN SHINING, bulky air-tight suits stood beside the great hull that had brought them across a quarter of a million miles of space, and landed them at last on this airless satellite world. Warm golden light still shone from the windows of the giant machine, the greatest rocket ship Earth had ever produced. Harsh, electric-blue sunlight glinted on the jet-shadowed spires of the crater wall beyond. In the near foreground was the cracked, pitted surface of a crater-bottom, scarred and broken by ages-old moon-quakes, fading into a horizon strangely near, made jagged by incredibly rugged crater walls. And above, in a star studded sky hung a blue-white ball of fire, the unshielded sun. There was no air here; warmth was only where the sun was. Night was everywhere, hidden from the blue light of the sun in every shadow.

The fifteen men were grouped about a metal structure they were rapidly raising from a barren, level mass of rock. When it was completed, a bedraggled American flag hung limp in the airless space. In forty-eight hours it would be a piece of white bunting, bleached colorless by the violent light of this place. Later they were to replace the limp-hanging cloth with a sheet of painted metal.

But now they had other work. Dr. James Harwood Garner was the leader of this party of carefully chosen men, and in the name of the United States of America, he claimed the so-called dark half of the moon. Half a world! Millions, tens of millions of square miles of utterly barren surface, surface never seen by Terrestrian eyes, save when, five years before, Capt. Roger Wilson had circumnavigated the moon twice, landing for two brief days on the Earthward side, and had claimed that.

But unlike the earlier party, these men were here for continuous exploration, and not for two days, but for two full years! Their orders read: *"On June 10, the ship will leave from Inyokern, California, Earth, arriving at Luna June 15. One circuit of the satellite will be made, and a landing made as near the center of the "dark side" as possible. Explorations will be conducted and data collected for one year and eleven months. On May 10, 1981, a relief ship will take off from Mojave, California, Earth, proceeding directly to the camp on Luna, landing as near to the dome as practicable. For one month both parties will remain on the satellite, then the return shall be made, starting June 15, and arriving at Lake Michigan, Earth, on June 20."*

This first ship came out, loaded with the tons of supplies and instruments that must last the men two full years. So great was the load of oxygen and food, that no fuel for the return could be carried. Hence the need for the relief ship, carrying oxygen and food for but fifteen days for the total crew of both ships, seventeen men in all. The men were to weigh *"an average of 153.5 pounds. Two thousand pounds of instruments, samples, photographs, and materials may be returned. Under any circumstances the comparative-reading instruments* (instruments whose value was lost if experiments conducted with them on Luna were not repeated with the same instruments on Earth) *shall be brought back."*

From the squat, pointed cylinder, heavy leads were run, while other men set up powerful electric winches. Electric wrenches and tools were brought out. Inside the ship motors were pumping the atmosphere back into the tanks from which it came. Presently the trained crew fell to work, and rapidly the entire machine was unbolted, the gaskets between the plates laid to one side, and the numbered pieces piled in order. Only the low, round battery-house remained untouched; this was the base of the original ship, housing the batteries that would supply heat and light during the two-week long lunar nights. Now the winches began work again, and rapidly the pieces from the hull were transformed into a new shape, assembled till they made a huge, polished dome, with five small windows set in it. Within it were the bunks, stove, supplies, tanks of oxygen and water, air purifiers— all the equipment and supplies of the original ship, converted into this more spacious dome.

Beyond the battery house and the Dome, a series of racks were set up, and on them huge photo-cells that soon began pouring energy from the sun, converted into electricity, into the batteries. Camp was made. Ten hours had elapsed, and now the men retired to the dome, and turned the air from the tanks into it. In another hour the pressure and heat within were normal, and a meal was under way, their first on the Moon.

Sleep now—then the two years' work was begun. It was during the lunar night that most of the exploration was done. *"During the days,"* wrote Dr. Thomas Ridgely Duncan, *"we are constantly oppressed by the monotony. It is a time of rest, and repairing things that need no repairing. The heat from the sun is absolutely unbearable, the rocks are hot enough to melt tin, even lead. The entire world is bathed in burning heat. The suits cannot radiate enough to cool, and perspiration does no good. We are continually subject to sunstroke, and have to remain in the dome.*

"At night the work begins. The sun sinks, and the great barren surface cools. Starlight, far brighter than starlight of

earth, gives a slight general illumination while our suit lamps
supply more. But little battery heat is needed, and wide ex-
ploration is possible. The greatest handicap is the necessity
for eating. One cannot eat in a space suit, and one cannot
take it off. Oxygen supplies for several days could be carried,
but food and particularly water, is the problem."

But explorations were carried on. During the day the
two mineralogists, the two chemists and the photographer
were busy. The little astro-physicist, Melville, was busy day
and night. The magnification possible on the airless moon
threw him into a terrible despondency, because he had only
two three inch telescopes, the greatest weight he had been
allowed, and their light gathering power did not permit him
the magnification he wanted. So Duncan and Bender and
Whisler working together, made a twenty-inch reflector of
fused quartz, and with this Melville succeeded in getting
photographic maps of the famous "canali" of Mars for the
first time, maps that proved them not canals, but tidal
swamps, caused by the cross drag and pull of the two satel-
lites of the planet and the Sun.

The others had little to do during the day. Birthdays
were celebrated; and the Fourth of July, Christmas, Thanksgiving, New Years Day, all were feast days.

Two light tractor-treaded trucks were included in the
equipment. The chassis and treads of the trucks had originally been landing gear for the great rocket, and their engines
had served as air pumps and fuel pumps. Every piece of
equipment had served dually on the rocket. Assembled on
Luna, they carried the men further afield, and did heavy
work.

But *"There is little to do. We know all the motion pic-*
tures now, every move of every film. Only our own new
films are of interest. There is no radio here, since the airless
moon has no Heaviside layer to bring the waves about the

curve that hides Earth from us. We can neither send nor receive from Earth. It is nearly 1500 miles to the nearest point where earth is visible, and therefore reachable. We are thrown back half a century in time to the period when explorers were cut off from other men.

"Our little helmet radios work fairly well up to a distance of about five miles, further if we are atop a ridge. The powerful tractruck sets can reach some twenty miles broadcast from a ridge top. But the curve of the Moon's surface makes real ranges impossible—it brings the messages too far underground."

Cut off from humanity by distance and solid rock as they were, it is no wonder they welcomed the night's work. Most of the exploration was done by foot, rather than tractruck, since men afoot could *"make better time over the incredibly jagged rock, and the frequent chasms. We can leap fifty to seventy-five feet easily, and the tractrucks can't. Future expeditions should develop a mechanical grasshopper, perhaps on the order of an inverted catapult with powerful steel springs, cocked and released by an engine. Nothing else can move far here. Airplanes cannot be used, of course, where there is no air. Small rocket ships can't be supplied with fuel."*

Still the tractrucks could carry the men further, as the hard working explorers needed greater oxygen supplies.

There is little of interest that has not been made public already. Perhaps a few of Duncan's weather reports are most interesting, best give a picture of that cruel, dead world. *"The mercury thermometer was left outside accidentally, and has been broken. We were alarmed at breakfast by an inexplicable* boom *from the Dome walls. We rushed out to see what had caused it, and found that the rising sun had struck the mercury bulb, blackened to register in this airless place,* and had quickly raised it to the boiling point. The explosion had caused the sound."

Again he reports of a lunar pre-dawn. *"Winter here now. We hadn't believed it would make any difference, but apparantly it does. We cannot notice it; it is always cold or hot. Nothing is moderate. The chasms are terrifically deep, and terrifically abrupt. The craters are gigantic, and their walls miles in height. It is either utterly cold or utterly hot."*

The sensation of constant fall, which Duncan mentions at first, left them as they became accustomed to the lesser gravity. Their muscles did not weaken, as had been feared. Instead they grew stronger from the heavy work. Yet the weight charts that Dr. Hughey, the expedition's surgeon, prepared read like kindergarten records. Duncan, in prime condition the beginning of the second year, was recorded as weighing 31 pounds! Dr. Hughey reports he was weighed on a spring balance hooked through his belt, and supported at arms length by one of the men. Yet that means a normal Earth-weight of very nearly 186 pounds.

Then late in the second year came the first fatality. Duncan writes, *"Today we had our first tragedy. In but two months we will be leaving; and Morrison and Wilcott would have gone with us. They were exploring near North Chasm in tracktruck No. 2, and the edge broke away under the weight of the machine. The chasm is over half a mile deep, and they were precipitated to the floor below.*

"The slow fall under lunar gravity was a mockery. Wilcott called the Dome, and told them they were falling! They sent us word where they were, called good-bye—and there was a crash.

"Efforts to recover the bodies were in vain, though Rice, with the aid of the other tractruck and a long cable, succeeded in reaching, and recovering the machine. He says

he will be able to repair it. The two men were hurled free,
apparently, and buried under a mass of rubble.

"*North Chasm has been renamed Morcott Chasm.*"

As the months passed, the time for their release from
voluntary exile came nearer and nearer. As each lunar night
passed they watched more anxiously the dark heavens for a
moving dot of light. Tremendous work had been done; and
now they wanted only to return to the Earth with it's soft,
natural air, winds and rains. But their release was not to be
so soon. Nor for some of them, was it ever to be.

The remainder of this account is from Dr. Duncan's diary,
kept faithfully throughout the two years, and later through
the terrible period of waiting for a second relief ship. It was,
like all their records and accounts, written in chemical pencil,
since ink was either frozen or boiling much of the time. During all the months the expedition spent on the alternately
frozen and baked moon, Duncan missed but one entry, the
last, when his hands could no longer hold the pencil.

Throughout the diary he mentions the men by their last
names. A list of the men living at the end of the second year
is given here.

PERSONNEL OF
THE GARNER LUNAR EXPEDITION

Dr. James Harwood Garner, leader, rocket-ship engineer, astro-physicist, chemical engineer.

Dr. Thomas Ridgely Duncan, physicist, second in command.

Dr. Eustace M. Hughey, surgeon of expedition.

Dr. Robert Kenneth Moore, chemist.

Dr. Warren P. Tolman, chemist.

Mr. Arthur W. Kendall, photographer.

Mr. David H. King, mineralogist.

Mr. Hampden S. Reed, mineralogist.

Mr. Anthony T. Melville, astro-physicist.

Mr. Carl Jewell Long, astronomer, navigator. (Who did much of the work in determining latitude and longitude on the moon, and in navigating the ship, across space. Fort Washington was taken as the zero meridian.)

Mr. George W. Rice, expert electrician and mechanic.

Mr. Joseph T. Whisler, cook, mechanic, lens-grinder.

Mr. Frederick L. Bender, mountain-climber, adventurer, mechanic, amateur astronomer.

THE FIGHT FOR AIR

The Diary of Thomas R. Duncan, Ph.D.

May 16.

King and Reed returned from a last expedition to the south-west. They report a remarkable find, a bed of silver selenide so enormously rich that they declare it could be profitably worked and the silver carried back to Earth. It is an enormous bed of "jewelry ore".

The morning is half over now, and tomorrow the relief ship is due. We are awaiting this release with the most intense eagerness. The moon, for all its terrible harshness and cold and heat has become beautiful to us—a frozen hell, but awesome and magnificent for all that. Most of the men spent the day looking for the relief, and little work was done. We know that it is due tomorrow, and a day more or less means that some accident has happened.

Whisler promises a feast tomorrow. We are all eager for news from home. As we have not even seen Earth in two years, it may have been wiped out for all we know. An all-out atomic war might be in progress, and we would not know.

May 17.

The relief has not arrived this evening. It was to be here not later than the seventeenth. We have air supplies for two months, food for three, and we are worried. Interplanetary schedules are exact, of necessity. The ship should have started at syzygy.

May 18.

Outside, the relief ship lies, a crushed, red-hot mass of broken, glowing metal. It arrived this afternoon, twenty-one hours late.

The meaning of this to us, is terrible. It will be at least one full month before Earth even knows that the relief expedition has failed. It will take at least another for action to be started. And not less than five months will be necessary to build a new relief ship. This means that not less than seven months must pass before we can hope for relief—and we have oxygen for two months more! Food we can cut down on, but oxygen we cannot reduce.

This morning Rice caught a glimpse of it as it came above the horizon, sweeping rapidly up till it was 'new' and dark, a tiny satellite of a satellite. We all saw it disappear below the horizon. We were watching for it when it appeared over the horizon again, rising. It was much nearer and larger, and our spirits rose. It was less than 1000 miles away, and the rockets opened just after it crossed the horizon, with the result that it began to fall rapidly toward the surface. A cheer broke out from the men, and Rice, as radio operator, attempted to establish communication. At 10:55 he received a reply; the ship was less than 300 miles away, settling on intermittent rockets, and coming fast.

We welcomed them, and watched them settle less than a mile from the Dome. They landed with a slight jar at 11:12. Almost immediately the stern rockets broke out, and hurled the ship fully fifty miles straight up, with terrific acceleration. The men were very quiet as we watched. It was easy to understand that the main rockets had in some way been accidentally opened, and could not be shut off.

The ship was finally driven to a height of half a mile by some of the most skillful management of rockets I can conceive. The servo controls failed suddenly, and under the full drive of the main rockets, and lunar gravity, the ship crashed to the plain, now less than a quarter of a mile from the Dome. It exploded instantly. In fifteen seconds it was a white hot mass in which we know the pilots have lost their lives. We could not investigate today, as the wreck was too hot to approach.

Dr. Garner called a meeting of the men shortly after that, and briefly pointed out that it would be over a month before Earth would realize the relief ship had crashed, and at least eight months before a second ship could be built. He asked that suggestions be given in the morning.

May 19.

Temperature: 163 C in rocks.

The meeting was called this morning after breakfast. Moore, in charge of pure atmosphere, advised permanent discontinuation of all smoking, as it consumes oxygen and fouls the air. He has stated that he may be able to get oxygen from compounds in the rocks, though the process will be difficult.

As quartermaster I had to state that the rations would have to be greatly cut down.

Air is evidently the primary problem, as it is impossible to greatly reduce our allowance of oxygen. We will at least have warmth. Water we have for two months, but Moore promised relief on that score.

Rice reports, however, that the batteries which have served us two years under the most extreme conditions, are in danger of breaking down. Originally built for lightness, they may fail, since they have been run continually on what amounts to an overload.

The tractruck has a fuel supply for but sixty hours operation; and in hauling the minerals for extraction of oxy-

gen would be exceedingly valuable. Bender objected to its
use, saying it required too much oxygen; actually it uses less
than men accomplishing the same work.

King and Reed reported the brightest spot in the meeting. There is a large gypsum field nearby, where water can
easily be obtained by roasting the rock. Moore had hoped to
find something of the sort. Electrolysis will furnish the needed oxygen. Demand on the batteries will be serious.

We have spent the day bringing supplies of the gypsum
to the camp, while Rice, Whisler and Bender constructed a
wheeled trailer. King and Reed, after showing us the loca-
tion, started work on the electric roasting furnace we will
need. Obtaining the gypsum is very trying work, as explosives are useless on this airless world, unless very heavily
tamped. We find we have very small supplies of explosives.

It will be difficult to live off so barren a country. One
must work even for the air one breathes.

May 20.

Temperature: 169 in rocks.

Afternoon is coming in the lunar day, and Rice warns
us we will not be able to use the batteries to produce water
during the night, and advises against diverting the power of
our photo-cells. The batteries are not fully charged after
last l-night's (lunar-night's) use. I am inclined to agree with
him, though Bender does not believe it, and has convinced
the others it will be safe, even necessary.

I have made a trip today to Reed's silver deposit. I think
it will be useful.

Nearly ten tons of gypsum hauled today. King advised
construction of roadway, but Tolman, in charge of works,
felt it best to get all the gypsum possible in before night. It
will be difficult to work then; it will be too dark to handle
explosives.

We are all tired tonight, and feeling the pinch of reduced rations. Whisler has been ordered to cut down the amounts slowly.

May 21.

At my suggestion, Garner ordered a roadway constructed to the gypsum mine. I feel it wise, as the tractruck will not always be available.

I have been accused of favoring certain members of the party in the matter of rations. They have been very short and are due to become shorter, and the men's tempers with them. We are working harder than ever before, and with less food.

The sun is approaching the horizon now, and Reed tried out his still today. The photo-cells would not carry the load, and the batteries had to be drawn on, against Rice's protests.

The mechanism is not satisfactory, for though the water comes off readily, it will not condense, surrounded as it is by a world all of which is above the boiling point of water, even under atmospheric pressure.

May 22.

The road has been finished, and late today the tractruck broke down. There is so little fuel left it was decided not to repair it. Another cart was built, and the men are hauling the material. It is fortunate lunar gravity is so weak.

Reed has improved his still, and it works. He was forced to build a shelter which cut off the sun's rays. He says it would be impossible to work at night anyway, to which Rice privately gave a sigh. He seems to love that battery set.

I paid another visit to Reed's silver deposit today, and returned with some samples on a small sledge. I will try to make some photo-cells * with Moore's aid.

---

* The photo-cells were made of silver plates, a layer of silver selenide, and a transparent layer of a second metal. Sunlight falling on these generated a quite powerful current. These had been their source of power during all the past two years.

Food has become a popular subject of conversation. Though they realize the necessity for drastic rationing, and take it in good spirit, all the men are hungry. The tobacco smokers are particularly unhappy. I have taken to chewing a crumb of tobacco occasionally, and find it far from satisfying.

When the call for meals is broadcast we all come promptly. Whisler is being unmercifully kidded, and tonight a mock trial was held in which he was accused of wasteful use of water. The soup tonight was rather thin.

May 23.

It is nearing sunset now, and during the sleep-period tonight the sun will probably set.

A considerable pile of gypsum has been hauled from the mine, and Reed has made a larger oven for use when the sun appears again. He found some large blocks of pumice rock, and has set these up as insulators for his furnace.

Moore and I have started work on the photo-cells. The silver was refined electrolytically, after we reduced it to a soluble compound. We made a crude, small cell, and were delighted—and, I admit, somewhat surprised—to find it worked. Kendall and Rice have agreed to help us.

Pancakes for breakfast, washed down with coffee, at 7:15, and some twelve hours later dinner of vegetable steak and a watery soup. You feel satisfied for the next half hour, till the water is absorbed. There is some complaining from our stomachs, but there is surprisingly little grumbling, though the men are working hard all day, under difficult conditions. Luckily the mine is now under a ledge of rock that shades it, and makes the work endurable.

It seems curious to dig ones air from the rocks.

May 24.

Dr. Garner has detailed Moore, Kendall and Rice to assist me in making the photo-cells. Rice however, spends half his time with his beloved batteries. I can understand his worries, after seeing the cells. They were made, I fear, for light weight, rather than long service. The material has been falling from the plates badly. Rice experimented today with the possibility of rebuilding the plates, and had to give it up.

We are not equipped to resist cold. We have only the thinnest of blankets, for it was not expected that it would ever be cold within the dome.

My stomach is constantly afflicted with an unpleasant burning feeling, and of course the others feel it too.

Temperature outside: –143.

May 25.

Ten large photo-cells completed, and the gypsum pile increased. At my strong recommendation the still will not be used until day. We hope to have a considerable battery of cells by then. Even Rice agrees that the current we are drawing for making the cells is drawn in a good cause.

Very difficult to work glass for cells without gas flame, but the oxygen cannot be spared.

Reed, King and Tolman are working on an electrolysis apparatus for use with the still. Some question as to disposition of hydrogen released. We have all too many empty tanks, and I suggested storing it for possible usefulness. Certainly as well as to release it.

Temperature: –147.

May 26.

About two o'clock this afternoon Melville was brought in in a horrible condition. There was an accident at the mine today, a rock slide, and Melville was buried. Instinctively his arms protected the faceplate, and it was not broken, but a great rent appeared in the leg of his suit, and the air began to rush out. The others uncovered him in a very short time, and found him clutching his leg tightly to prevent the escape of the remaining air. A rope was tied about the thigh, to cut off the leak, and he was hurried back. He said nothing on the trip, and was unconscious when they arrived. They set him down in the airlock as gently as possible, but when they picked him up to carry him in they discovered his leg, the right leg, had been broken off three inches above the knee. The heater wires had been cut when the suit was torn, and without heat from the battery, and the circulation cut off by the air-stop, his leg had frozen on the way back. It was evidently brittle as glass in the cold of the lunar night. Dr. Hughey tied the veins and arteries, dressed the wound, and hopes for the best. No one has had any experience with such wounds. The stump of the leg was soaked in cold water, which had to be constantly renewed at first, as it froze against the flesh. Aside from the small capillaries, burst in the vacuum of space before freezing, the flesh appears normal.

Work was stopped at the mine, and tonight Dr. Garner spoke to us briefly on the dangers, but the absolute necessity of mining. We can only continue the work. The men are greatly depressed.

We have fifteen photocells finished.

May 27.

Melville is conscious this evening, for the first time since the accident. Dr. Hughey has kept him under soporofin, but his stump is thoroughly thawed, and he was allowed to regain consciousness. For some time as he came to consciousness he complained that his foot itched, and tried to scratch it. When he was fully conscious he quickly understood that it was missing, and heard the whole story. He has been very calm, merely saying that as he is an astro-physicist he will not greatly miss it. He wants to help us with the photo-cells, as he says that is the only work he can do now.

He suffers no pain, apparently, and Dr. Hughey says the freezing was so rapid that the tissue of the stump is unharmed. If only he had not been laid down there in the air-lock. But then, no one ever had experience with space-freezing before.

Twenty-five completed photo-cells, now. The work at the mine was resumed today, while Dr. Hughey replaced Rice here on the photo-cell work.

The rations have been reduced to one and one-half pounds per day per man, which will mean about five months supplies for us, in-so-far as food goes. However, we will certainly not die of starvation. Before that occurs we will be too weak to work the gypsum mine.

May 28.

Since the sun has long been below the horizon, work at the mine has become hard, for it is cold and dark. The trac-truck batteries and lights were dismounted, and set up beside the mine for illumination. There is scarcely a score of steel picks left, and Garner is worried about the situation. The steel picks are invaluable to us; and in the terrible cold of the shadowed space, they are, as I have said, very brittle. Kendall broke one today, as he is inexperienced in their use under these conditions. At my suggestion Reed tried something with the cinnabar we found two miles south-west of Fort Washington. It was difficult work at night, in the cold outside, but we could not refine it inside due to the poisonous fumes. Rice, as usual, complained bitterly at the drain on his batteries, and some of the men complained even more strongly at the use of oxygen, but fortunately the work was successful, and two new picks of solid mercury were made. In this extreme cold they are hard as steel, and no more brittle. Further, should they break, the pieces need only be picked up, and brought back here. They fuse together, and can be returned to service in half an hour. They are much heavier, and are very popular for that reason.

Melville is improving rapidly, much more rapidly than we had dared hope, and has been helping greatly on the photocells. He is a skilled manipulator.

In speaking to Dr. Hughey about the chance of stretching our food supplies, he gave as his opinion that it would be impossible to reduce the rations beyond one pound per man per day if mine work were to be maintained, and doubted that that could be done. Privately I agree with the latter reservation. I have been mining the silver only intermittently, but I can readily appreciate the feelings of the miners.

May 29.

Dr. Garner is on the sick list at present, and the men are trying to make him stay there, he claims. Our leader has certainly been leading the men in work, and it has told on him more heavily than we knew. Dr. Hughey has ordered him to rest. Dr. Garner is the oldest of us, and probably would not have been chosen had he not organized the expedition himself.

Forty photocells completed. Fifteen today, thanks to Melville's aid, and the experience we have gained. Dr. Hughey says it is much better for Melville to do what he is able to, as it improves his mental condition.

May 30.

Reed is 28 today. I issued a quart of the Scotch whiskey for him, and some of the men froze it into a cake, with "iceing" of pale ginger ale. Reed insisted that it be cut with a knife of mercury to be in keeping. Needless to say, the "cake" was not eaten, though Reed got a few cold-burns from handling his knife and the "cake."

Work continued as before, however. Another still is being built now, with provisions for continuous process operation. Pumice-like stone cars will be dragged through the kiln, saving the heating and cooling of the furnace between charges. Experiments have to be made, and one mistake almost made was in putting the planned outlet to the condenser at the top. It is hard to remember that such a thing as hot gases rising is unheard of here. ALL gases sink—when they occur. It makes things easier, however. The vapor need only be collected in a funnel-like tray at the bottom.

May 31.

Long has made a proposal. He offers to go to the edge of the portion visible from Earth, set up a heliograph, and signal Mt. Wilson. He feels certain even a small mirror would be visible. He plans to carry a flask of mercury, and freeze his mirror on the spot. Food he says can be carried in the form of canned milk in a rubber bottle, and drunk through a tube. We have all, but Melville and one other, offered to accompany him. Garner has refused his offer, and ours. As the leader he feels responsible, and says the expedition is impossible. He points out the danger of starving and thirsting if the tube is dropped from the mouth while asleep or by accident, since it would be impossible to restore it.

But it might well save a month or more of time.

June 1.

The men are tired nights, and sleep is heavier. In the evenings, however, various amusements are tried. There has been considerable amusement derived from a planetary round-robbin story. Melville left the hero stranded on Jupiter, where the gravity was too great for his ship. Long comes next. He will carry on tomorrow night.

There seems to be a tendency, during the course of the story, for the characters to partake of some very tempting meals. All the frozen fresh meat is gone, and the meat-flour, though nourishing, is not tempting.

More photocells today. We have now a total of eighty-five cells, or one full bank. We will set them up tomorrow.

June 2.

Long disappeared during the night. We all volunteered to go after him, but Garner ordered us to stay. It would be impossible to find a man on this dark lunar surface. The entire country is indescribably rough. Every ancient moon-quake rift is as sharp as the day it was made. We are all hoping for Long, but as Rice said, "It ain't a Long hope and it's a hell of a Long chance." The great circle distance is 1100 miles, probably 1500 across country. It is not difficult to make 300 miles a day here, and under forced marches he will probably make 500 the first day. He took oxygen for seven days.

I wish I could foresee my entry for June 9.

Four new Mercury picks made. They work excellently, but blunt rapidly and have to be re-cast every day.

June 3.

Long evidently took six days rations of powdered milk chocolate and water, as I miss them from my store. Curiously I thought they were there yesterday, and thought he had merely eaten a heavy meal. We do not begrudge him those supplies.

The men are greatly excited about Long, and have been trying continuously to reach him by radio, but he is already beyond range. A month's difference in the arrival of the rescue ship may well mean life to us.

June 4.

It is shortly after midnight, and Rice has reported to me privately that the batteries are failing badly. He says that if they are to last till sunrise, we must lower the temperature of the Dome. They are evidently going to pieces even more rapidly than he feared. Ironical, the beauty of our calculations in making the equipment. This was to have been our last Lunar night, and the failure of the batteries would have been a minor nuisance. As they certainly won't last another night, it's hard to know what it does mean now. As I have said, we brought no heavy clothing, the suits being sufficient in empty space. I have stopped working on the photo-cells, as the others are advancing nicely, and have started on a burner.

The men were told this evening of the probable failure of the batteries. Like good sports they agreed to the change. The Dome will be cold while the men are out working, kept just above the freezing point (we cannot let it fall lower) will be warmed at supper time, cold all night, and warmed in the morning. The saving will really be considerable.

June 5.

Long's birthday. He was 28 today, but not with us to celebrate. We hope he will be here to celebrate Tolman's, the 14th. It will be sunrise, then.

Burner worked successfully. Too bad we can't use it tonight. It will save us, probably.

June 6.

Last of canned milk issued. Last sugar gone, also. The supplies look amazingly low, now that we have cleaned out all the empty boxes which had been saved for possible future use.

I was again accused of favoritism in distribution of food by Bender, today. He is ill-fitted for mining work, and hunger adds to his distaste. I am only surprised none of the others have made accusations, though I deal with all possible fairness.

Very uncomfortable working in Dome with temperature low. Rice says he prefers the mine. We are using the heater at the laboratory end which makes it slightly better.

June 7.

Rice claimed he heard signals from Long. I doubt it, as but five days have passed, and he expected to be gone seven.

There is a great pile of gypsum outside now, and some of the men are saying they can take a rest, since we have enough for now.

It is very cold in the dome during the day, and it is almost impossible to work. But Rice says the batteries may last till the 14th, when the sun rises.

Two full banks of photocells completed, increasing our power generating equipment 50%.

June 8.

Today Rice had to cut out several of the worst cells and cut the heaters in half. They work very poorly, and we freeze all day and all night.

The round-robbin story, which was left off with Long's disappearance was continued. The ship was hurled free by a volcano, and has landed on Mercury. Heat in abundance, and plenty of food, I noticed.

Melville is almost completely healed, and Rice has made him a sort of push-cart on which he can move readily.

June 9.

No word from Long, though we have waited till 12 o'clock, New York Midnight. Garner ordered us to rest.

Two more burners arranged. Rice has made a compact recharging outfit, and Garner has agreed to the plan.

Some fear today the temperature will fall below freezing and burst the water tanks and food tins. It would be disastrous, for they would be lost beyond redemption.

June 10.

Signals from Long! It began at 11:30 P.M., and Rice at once took bearings. The signals were too weak to decipher. At 11:45 they were readable. Long was then twenty-five miles or so from the Dome. He had thrown away everything, except one oxygen tank, almost empty. He hoped to reach the station before it was exhausted.

Rice wanted to head a relief expedition at once, but was ordered to remain at the radio. Bender is leading an expedition commanded by King, carrying oxygen tanks, and a stretcher.

June 11.

The sun rises in five hours. Long is freezing. His battery is exhausted, and his oxygen so nearly gone he cannot work to maintain bodily heat. Distance 22 miles. The expedition has covered five.

Dr. Hughey has made a startling proposal. The expedition cannot reach him in time, and Hughey advises that he allow himself to freeze as quickly as possible! From his experience with Melville's leg he says he feels sure thyradren will restore him to life. If it is possible it will save Long's life.

Long has assented. He has thrown himself into a position that will be shadowed even after the sun rises, and covered his suit with the emergency radiation paint. He has stopped speaking.

Later—sunrise. The expedition found Long, and brought him back on the stretcher. He was frozen solid, and the oxygen and gases in his suit are liquid. The photocells are pouring in power, a great relief after nearly freezing to death. It has been hard on us.

(*Equipped as the expedition was with light summer blankets, working on a starvation diet, stating that it was "hard on us" was a fearful understatement of facts.*)

Hughey had Long brought into the Dome, placed inside a huge coil of wire, and from the main radio set, drew radio frequency current at the maximum power. The body was warmed to 99 degrees in less than five minutes. Artificial respiration with pure oxygen mixed with carbon dioxide was started, and heavy injections of thyradren administered directly to the heart.

The process has been continued for half an hour now, with no results as yet.

Later. Long is alive! He was badly starved, as well as under-oxygenated, and already he has eaten! He is recovering with unbelievable rapidity. He is apparently wholly unharmed. It seems a miracle to us who saw him brought in, a frozen statue, bathed in liquid air, brittle as glass, and as dead! Kendall, worse than any newspaper photographer, has photographs, he says. Long will be interested!

Work continued this afternoon, consisting mainly of setting up the photocells, and starting the furnaces. Everything is working smoothly. Long has not been allowed to speak yet.

June 12.

We were disappointed to hear that Long had been unsuccessful. He stayed twelve hours within sight of the Earth, trying vainly to correspond. Neither heliograph nor radio brought results. Radio, he believes, was interfered with by the tremendous group of sunspots he noticed, and the aurora of Earth was magnificently bright, even from there. He evidently picked an unfortunate moment for his brave attempt.

It was the twelve hours delay which caused his—death, as a matter of fact, though it seems wrong to say that while he sits watching me.

Hughey is writing a medical report, which will explain the case more fully than I could.

June 13.

Work progressing rapidly. Gypsum fed into the furnaces is quickly ejected as de-hydrated $CaSO_4$, the water collected, and taken to the electrolysis apparatus. It is warm and comfortable inside the Dome now, for which we are all thankful, and the work on photocells is progressing rapidly. Another load of silver selenide was hauled over today.

Rice has repaired the batteries to the best of his ability, and they are being recharged for lighting and laboratory needs during the night. The burner heating system is being charged and more burners prepared.

I find in re-reading the diary that I have not described this. Hydrogen and oxygen, derived from water, electrolyzed during the day by our photo-cell power, is stored, and burned together for warmth during the night. The water so formed is collected, condensed, and stored to be re-electrolyzed the next day. It is thus a perfectly reversable action, requiring only the electro-chemical energy from the photo-cells. And our heating plant will be once more free of the batteries' defects.

Long is feeling well, and worked today on the photocells, though he maintained he was perfectly capable of returning to the heavier mine work. Dr. Hughey says that he is best here.

Long tells me he took but one day's supply of food with him. Some one else must have rifled the stores. We all feel hungry, save immediately after meals, but I did not expect that, since our company has been so finely uncomplaining.

June 14.

I made another trip for silver selenide. The lunascape is awesomely wonderful under the early morning sun. Titanic peaks loom up, casting shadows as black and hard as full night. It is a land of blinding light and blinding darkness, with mighty, rugged chasms on every side, and only bare, jagged rock underfoot. The passage from light to shade is accompanied by a sudden fierce chill that seems to bite through in a moment, then the welcome heat of the battery dispels it.

Returning, dragging the tractor-wheeled sledge loaded with ore, the sheen of the dome is a beacon, the only brilliantly metallic sheen in all this land of rugged, waste rock. Not a spindle of grass, no hint of shrub, nor fallen leaf. Not even sand, only jagged, harsh rock.

It seemed vicious to us at first. Now, like the desert to its prospectors, it is beautiful for its fierce harshness, clean and naked and unashamed under a blazing, blue-white sun.

But it is a relief to get back to the Dome. And more of a relief, after remembering the night of chill we have passed, in watching the meters that record the steady, powerful flow of energy coming from the photo-cells.

June 15.

Today marks our second year on Luna.

We had planned to take off today, for the return trip. The crumpled wreck of the relief ship seems to mock us. It has been investigated time and again, and not a vestige of any useful article has been found. The burning fuel destroyed everything.

We have been forced to look for glass-making materials. Our supply of glass is running low, and we need quartz glass for the photocells. The hydrogen has been helpful in making them, for the flame is easier to work with, and Moore and Tolman have installed a recondensation apparatus which collects water from the air passing through the purifiers. It is electrolyzed for oxygen.

More food has been stolen from the storehouse. It is

curious that no one sees this, as it is light at all times now.
But all the men are tired from their work.

June 16.

Fate has turned ironical. Rice, searching for quartz
crystals for the tubes, brought in some magnificent, clear
crystals, and said there was a considerable bed of them,
enough to last some time. Had it been quartz, we would have
been lucky, for the crystals are clear as water. They are diamonds, most of them large as my fist. They are utterly and
completely useless to us, as they cannot be worked in any
way.

No suitable quartz supply has been found.

The gypsum pile is diminishing, despite the continued
activity of the miners, and the oxygen pressure in the tanks
is rising steadily.

I have been interested in the psychology of the story
tellers of the interplanetary round-robbin. The ship has gone
to Pluto now, where it is exceedingly cold, but their power
is endless. Oxygen is found frozen in glaciers, and may be
chopped off with axes or explosives. Kendall, who has been
working at the mine told the story tonight. It's Rice's turn
tomorrow night. He will spend the day searching for quartz,
and I have a half-hope he doesn't find it to see what his story
will be.

June 17.

We should have been sighted from Earth today. Interplanetary schedules are exact, and our non-arrival will probably start discussion.

Funds for the building of a relief ship will have to be
raised by public subscription, to a total of approximately
three millions. I fear it will be slow coming in.

Work continued today hopefully. The oxygen and hydrogen tanks are filling ever more rapidly, for more photo-

cells are constantly being added. Reed is now able to run two furnaces and is electrolyzing faster. The pile of gypsum is nearly gone.

The hunt for quartz has been unsuccessful. The one thing we need beyond all others, the basic need, is power, and without the quartz we will be helpless to install the proposed electrical machinery at the gypsum mine.

Rice carried on the round-robbin tonight, and the interplanetary travellers landed on the warm-belt of Neptune. Neptune's warm belt is caused by its satellite, which is a solid globe of crystal quartz, and which acts as a burning glass to warm the planet.

June 18.

Long has made another proposal, which I can back with my full agreement. Money must be raised by public subscription, and a ship built. The building will take at least four months, and Earth knows we have supplies but for one month more at most. That we have a new supply of oxygen and water they do not know. People will hesitate to give money for a cause lost before it begins. If some word is sent, telling that we have oxygen at least, the aid may be hastened.

His new plan is that twelve men start from the Dome, all but three burdened with oxygen tanks, these three travelling light. At the end of one day, one oxygen-unit's distance, six men will turn back, caching all the oxygen they carried, save one tank apiece for the return. The remaining six will continue, again three heavily loaded, three going light. At the end of that twenty-four hour run, three will turn back, caching all their oxygen save one tank apiece. These will return to the first stop, sleep there for the first time on the trip, then return with one new tank. The remaining three, hitherto unloaded, will sleep at this farthest cache for twelve hours, then carrying four units of oxygen, a small photo-cell bank for power, a convertor-transformer, and a powerful portable radio, will make a dash for the visible border.

If the whole trip be made by daylight, no batteries need be carried, but a second trip to the first cache could put batteries there for emergencies.

The men have all volunteered, and even Garner approves of this plan. Long insists he should go, as he knows the way, and the easiest way. The group will carry more powerful apparatus, and have a far better chance of success.

The second thing of import in today's happenings was the discovery of a great outcropping ledge of crystal quartz. It was discovered by Melville—under the battery house! Rice threatened to tear his hair out by the roots as the Universe's prize ass.

Actually, the reason it had not been discovered was simple. Since we came, an accumulation of battery sludge had hidden it. Our power worries are ended.

Almost equally cheering was the discovery that we had forty pounds more protein flour than I had thought. That is three days added to our lives here.

June 19.

The plan Long outlined has been decided on. At his urgent request, he will guide the party. I have been given command, so I will get my first glimpse of Mother Earth in two years, shortly. Rice will be the third member of the three who make the dash. As he is the radio expert, he is the logical choice. Since all the others want to accompany us, the others are to be chosen by lot. The start will be made the ninth of July, which will give us fourteen days of sunshine, a plentiful margin.

It was noon of the Lunar day, and terrifically hot today. The storage batteries will take no more charge, and have been disconnected. All new photocells were taken to the mine, along with the batteries and motors from the tractrucks, and several other electric motors taken from the rocket ship. The diamonds have proven useful after all. All the empty cans were collected, and the lead and tin melted off. A diamond toothed saw was achieved with the aid of the old tractor belts from the tractrucks. It cuts the soft gypsum with an enormous saving of labor. Carting it back is not easy, however.

The mine power station is not yet self-sufficient, and is drawing on the batteries. New photo-cells will help, however.

June 20.

The long afternoon has begun. Miners are gaining on the furnaces now, and Reed is making a new one, wants new photo-cells.

Work continued as usual.

June 21.

New furnace finished, and consuming more power than cells produce, but new cells coming. The complete heating system was tested, and found to function perfectly. So perfectly the Dome was unbearably hot in no time. Oxy-hydrogen flames are hot!

June 22.

More food stolen from supply house. I will be forced to rig a burglar alarm! It is exceedingly serious, for our supplies are rapidly diminishing, and we are all underweight. (*A strong understatement. At the time he wrote this, Dr. Duncan had fallen from a normal 184 pounds of muscle and bone, to 155.*)

Moore is experimenting with what he calls "edible" acids. Most of the men are claiming them "terrible acrid". I doubt that we could eat the substances, though undoubtedly they have food value. He has compounded them directly from water, carbon dioxide and nitrogen. He claims they will save our lives.

June 23.

Afternoon is well advanced now. We have gained considerably over our uses of the last month, and the oxygen tanks are beginning to show pressure. Water has gained even faster, and a new electrolysis apparatus is being set up. Despite the short rations the men are feeling better as they see the power from the sun wresting atmosphere from this frozen, lifeless world.

June 24.

A two pound can of dried milk is missing today. I cannot understand how these bold thefts are carried out. Nor can I understand how any of the men can do it; they are all pitching in and working without grousing. We are all tired though, when we turn in. There is a distinct rivalry now between the furnace gang, those extracting water from the gypsum, and the mine gang, those extracting gypsum from the mine. The mine gang is gaining now, thanks to hard, heavy labor, and the new machines. Reed demands more power, which we are trying to supply.

Long did the first heavy labor since his death! He went to the silver selenide mine with Rice, and brought back a supply.

Preparations going on now for the dash to the visible area. Long insists the message will come at the psychological moment.

June 25.

The sun is very low now. Tomorrow it sets. Reed has had to close down the small furnace, as the shadow of Garner Crater began to touch the new bank of photo-cells. We will have to move them "tomorrow", that is, next morning.

The miners will be sadly handicapped when their power tools fail them, with sunset. There is still a brisk demand for photo cells however, as both mine and furnaces consume power at a fearful rate. Certainly, on earth, with its clouding atmosphere such power would be almost impossible to maintain with so small a bank of cells.

There has been some discussion of the message we are to send, when we reach the visible zone. Garner points out that possibly only parts of the message will get through. He suggests that it be so worded that even fragments of it will be intelligible and hopeful. It is a wise suggestion, I believe.

June 26.

It is dark now, outside. Dark and cold. After two years, the transition from day to night is still a startling thing, when in half an hour the rocks, blistering hot but a few minutes before, become so cold that mercury freezes, then carbon dioxide, and within an hour oxygen freezes to a liquid. The rapidity with which first the mercury, then the alcohol, and finally the pentane thermometers freeze up, leaving only the metal thermometers, is still a phenomonon to wonder at.

And the heavens, studded so thickly with colored stars, not the great, blurry white things of earth, but infinitely minute pinpoints of red and green and blue and orange! It is glorious, and the light from them is incomparably greater than starlight on Earth.

Our force of photo-cell makers is augumented. Tolman has joined our staff permanently, and is devoting all his time to extracting the chemicals we need. The stocks we used for operations were running low, and now gracious step-mother Moon has provided as liberally as her scant bounty permits, with further supplies. Luna is a single, vast chemical laboratory! The richness of the rocks is beyond belief. Probably the enormous volcanic upheavals of the past brought these substances to the light, and the absolute lack of rainfall has prevented their being buried.

Further argument over message to be sent tonight. I believe it is an important point.

June 27.

The heaters are working nicely. The temperature stays constant with beautiful precision, the only disturbance being a slight, endless hissing, to which we are growing accustomed. Rice, in further protection of his beloved batteries, has rigged a metal stove, burning hydrogen. Whisler was heard cursing him horribly, told to refrain as he was damaging the precious atmosphere, and requested to explain. Rice was over enthusiastic, and had a regular oxy-hydrogen blow-torch for a burner. Whisler tried it out cautiously, but not cautiously enough. It burned a hole through his heavy aluminum frying pan so quickly he couldn't get it away in time.

The stove has been tamed, and works nicely. I agree with Rice that the batteries will be important for light, and for the indispensable electrical work at night, and must be preserved. At least five months more—five nights. Even cooking might wholly disintegrate them. Without their power, our airlock could not function, and the cost in lost atmosphere, when we could no longer pump the air back to the Dome, would be heart-rending.

June 28.

The work at night is even heavier than before. During the day the machines lifted a heavy load from the men, but now that it is night there are no electric hoists to lift the blocks of gypsum sawed out by electricity, and the men are complaining of weakness. I fear they are indeed underfed. For some time those working in the mines have been fed more heavily than those who work inside, since their work is so much more strenuous.

Beginning with tomorrow those who are to make the longest dash to the Earth-side of Luna will be fed more heavily, the three making the full trip getting three-quarters full rations.

June 29.

No work today. We declared a holiday, not-so-jokingly called Collapse Day! The men spent most of the morning dozing. We needed it badly. Extra rations issued to all.

I am too sleepy and too contented to write more this night.

June 30.

Work resumed today.

Rice has shown himself a genius with tools. He is utterly invaluable now. Today he spent the whole time working on one of the fuel-less tractrucks. This evening to the amazed joy of the miners, it ran down to the mine! He has somehow rigged up a valving system so that it works effectively on hydrogen and oxygen, and the exhaust, pure water, is carefully collected and recondensed to liquid. He arrived at the mine to be greeted with rousing cheers. He dragged behind him two sledges, one loaded with two great fuel tanks full of hydrogen and oxygen, and on the other, one of the large motors converted to a generator. In half an hour he had all the electrical mining apparatus going again. It costs us nothing, for the fuel can be reelectrolysed in the day-light period, and burned again that night. Rice is a popular hero, despite the fact that the machines must be run on more or less reduced load. We will need more photo-cells than ever now, but it is an inestimable boon to the miners.

Moore has joined the laboratory staff. Reed was sent out on an exploring expedition, seeking certain minerals at the directions of the chemists. King is hunting in the other direction. I heard him order nitrates, so I suspect we are going to have explosives again, which gave out long ago.

July 1.

The men are glad the hydrogen driven power plant has been built, aiding them so enormously in the hoisting and sawing, even though the saws stop when the hoists start. Rice wanted to fix up the other tractruck, but we need the hydrogen we have for the heating apparatus. The system is working perfectly, keeping us comfortable again, but we cannot spare much hydrogen.

Output of photo-cells greatly aided by Tolman who showed us how to make the metal much more workable. We are turning out twenty cells a day regularly now, but with the consumption at the mine both day and night now, and the furnaces during the day, we need a lot of power. Power has become our chain to life.

The message to be sent has been decided upon. It will read: "Relief ship crashed. Oxygen from gypsum by electrolysis assures supply. Food scant. Help."

We hope the message will get through successfully.

July 2.

Evidently the thief is a heavy eater. Despite the large supply already missing, chocolate has been taken.

Gypsum pile growing rapidly, while Reed and King are back now. The needed nitrogen has been located, and a bed of carbides Moore wanted, as well. The furnace crew is working on new and bigger furnace, still and electrolysis equipment. The Moon's lack of air and water allowed metallic nitrides and carbides to exist in the rocks as stable compounds. They will be a great help.

The mine crew and the furnace gang have been going about with contracts, attempting to contract for photo-cells, as a keen rivalry is developing. Reed swears to destroy the gypsum pile when the sun rises. He will have a good chance as practically all the men will be gone two or four days with us to the visible half. Power is badly needed in both camps.

Electrolysis apparatus has been built beside the mine, for re-converting the fuel for the motor-generator set.

July 3.

Lunar midnight. The members of the dash party are getting larger portions now, and I for one feel new strength coming. I do not tire so quickly now in carrying the loads of silver selenide from our mine. We are using an incredible amount of that substance now. Three new racks of tubes completed, however.

July 4.

Another holiday, with extra rations all round. Nevertheless two more tanks of fuel taken out to the mine. That is the last that can be issued them safely, as the hydrogen for heating is getting scarce. And another frame of cells completed today. Moore has been making an unholy stench with his chemicals, and he drew a prodigious amount of electric power yesterday from the batteries.

July 5.

The packs for the expedition have been made up, and a definite schedule outlined. I will carry the transformer-converter, Long will carry the photo-cell racks, and Rice the set itself. Portable—but not too portable. In the last dash we will each carry four cylinders as well.

Moore's stenches were worse than usual today. He refuses to reveal his aims.

July 6.

I was surprised today, and seriously sorry, to see Moore secretly swallowing something. I can scarcely believe that he has been our thief, yet the stores were tampered with last night most ingeniously, despite a trip-wire I had strung.

We will start in four days now.

July 7.

I have been watching Moore, and today again he drew a tremendous amount of power to run a small furnace. While it was running he went off and again swallowed something. Tonight he pleaded sick, and did not eat. It attracted some attention, as he did not look sick, and when food is scarce, it is seldom refused.

Moore presented the miners with several sticks of an explosive he assured them would work, but must be protected from extreme cold. It has resulted in saving fuel, since the saws are no longer needed so much.

July 8.

The photo-cell frames have been set in place today, five new racks of cells. Three were placed at the mine, and two here. The mine will get one more, and the furnaces one, before leaving. Over 2200 horsepower is available at the mine now, twenty-four hours a day during the daylight period. During the sleeping period all this power will be turned into the electrolyzer.

Without the machines and explosives, I am afraid little mining could be done, as the men are greatly weakened.

July 9.

The final selection of the party has been made. Garner, Moore, Whisler, Reed and Bender will turn back after reaching and establishing the first cache, Tolman, Hughey, Kendall, and King will turn back at the second, while Rice, Long and I go on. Only poor Melville will be left behind altogether. We are turning in unusually early, for a long sleep. We start three hours after the sun leaves the horizon. Thermos bottles of hot chocolate have been fixed in the suits of Rice, Long and I. The others must go hungry altogether, though water is the greatest problem.

July 10.

We have stopped at the first cache. Garner, Moore, Whisler and Reed and Bender will return. The sun is up, casting long shadows over everything. We have covered a considerable distance I feel sure, so far with no accidents. We had to skirt several craters, and finally descended into this one. Tremendously high walls ring it, but Long showed us a pass. A second, smaller crater within it is the marker of our cache. By turns we have roasted and frozen all day, particularly on the pass, as it was largely shaded, which means cold here. The moon is a vast frozen hell. The crater tips flame in all directions like motionless, frozen tongues of fire, jagged and broken, a hell frozen in an awful cold, the very light frozen in the flames, where the sun touches them.

We are ready to start.

July 11.

We are nearly exhausted for want of sleep, and from the continuous labor. It will be worse returning, with four days without sleep, and practically without food. Tolman. Hughey, Kendall and King have it even worse, I fear. They have just left us, to make their way back over all the distance we have come, with scarcely the chance of a rest, no food, and little water. They will not have slept for four days when they reach the Dome. Sleep for us in our suits.

Later. Twelve hours sleep, a quarter of our chocolate, still warm, and now on our way. It is eternally magnificent, never beautiful. It is as magnificent as the Grand Canyon of the Colorado made six thousand miles wide, six thousand long, and ten miles deep, with ten times the color. But it isn't beautiful, it's stern and harsh, and horribly, bleakly dead. It makes me think of a skeleton lying in a cave, its skull crushed, and a stone ax beside it. It seems to have died violently. We are oppressively alone here.

Time to go. Four oxygen tanks, besides the load we have carried, which was little. We are fresh from sleep now, to make the attempt!

July 12.

We have camped. The photo-cells are sending their power to the set correctly, and the convertor-transformer is working smoothly. We cannot test the set, as our suit-sets won't pick up its wave. It seems to be okay however. Rice is sending the message. New York now.

The Earth is immense above us, reddish-green in color, turning slowly, majestically as we watch. It looks wonderfully beautiful and familiar to us, and terribly far away.

Later. Sending again. Chicago now, with all the power we can get. The aurora is small, so there is hope.

Still sending. No lack of power, apparently. Let us hope some station receives this.

Long has contributed a surprise. He produced a can of aluminum paint, and has selected a broad, flat spot on the rocks. He is painting a message in symbols ten feet high. Mt. Palomar could easily read it. But there are some 3,142,000 square miles of rock visible to Mt. Palomar.

He has finished. "O_2 from $CaSO_4$ send food," he has written. No more paint.

Denver now below—or above us. Telescopes show cities clearly, even some bigger buildings visible. Tremendous magnification possible, but light gathering power of our little telescopes limits it.

California now. When it passes we can send only to Hawaii, the Philippines and Japan. Opportunities poor. We think it best to start back.

Rice has produced another triumph. He had an electric clock device rigged that will keep the set transmitting toward Earth as long as the set operates. It is Sun-powered, of course. There is small motion across the skies, so there is no need to aim it carefully! The set, worked automatically, and powered by the photo-cells will continue to send a code message.

We are leaving. Rice and Long object, but I have ordered them back. We will be exhausted when we get to the first cache, and tired men make for dead men. There are too many opportunities for falls into chasms.

July 13.

Back at the second cache with a spare tank of oxygen. We have decided to carry it; though it increases our load it may save us. We can move more slowly, and not force ourselves so heavily. Leaving at once.

July 14.

First cache. Exhausted. I wonder that Long ever made it the first time, despite his use of anti-fatigue capsules. Last chocolate gone. Terribly thirsty. Twenty-four hours more. Going on at once.

Later. More than one hundred miles from the Dome, and Rice has had an accident. Fell into chasm. Miscalculated his leap, fell seventy feet, the rope joining us caught, held for a moment, and sawed through on some outcropping quartz crystals. Irony! Two weeks ago he was searching for them, today quartz hurled him another hundred feet and broke his leg. His arm is badly bruised I believe, but his face plate is unbroken. He has an extra oxygen tank, thank God. He is conscious—communicating by radio. Long will stay here, I am going on to the Dome.

Reached the Dome. Very tired, but ate, and drank a little water, while Moore, still working with his brews, started out to the mine to get the men. I will have to lead them back. They are coming now. Dr. Hughey will go with us, though he can do little till we bring Rice in, and get his suit off.

Taking ropes, block and tackle, extra oxygen.

Five hours to get back to Rice. He is still conscious, but weak. His suit is uninjured. Poor Long had gone to sleep.

Rice said he had been unable to keep awake. Too tired to stand, and as soon as he sat down he went to sleep. Rice couldn't sleep. The men have reached him, but cannot move him, as he is in pain. Dr. Hughey going down the ropes. He came prepared—brought a tank of CO_2 as anesthetic. Hughey reached him, substituted CO_2 for oxygen. His fatigue will keep him asleep now oxygen tank has been reattached.

Long won't wake—just mutters and tries to brush us away. He will have to be carried. I'm afraid I would too if I hadn't been writing. Starting back at last.

July 15.

I fell asleep on the way back, and Kendall, King and Reed had to return and hunt for me. Carried the last ten miles. I've slept nearly twenty hours. Still sleepy.

July 16.

Half the day gone, and routine is at last restored. Rice's leg was not badly broken, and has been set and bound up. He is working at the photo-cells with us again, sitting before a low bench rigged on two chairs. Twenty cells turned out today. Gypsum pile diminishing rapidly. The water made by the heaters last "night" has all been broken down, and the fuel for the motor-generator at the mine has been regenerated. Oxygen tanks showing steady pressure gain.

We wonder what success our trip had.

(As the world knows, the trip was successful in the extreme. As the men realized, the work of subscribing to an apparently lost cause, that of rescuing men probably dead already, was going very slowly. So many scientists stated positively that it was impossible to secure air on the moon, that the people would not subscribe. The news-bureaus were broadcasting news continually, of the probable plight of the men, and there was much speculation as to whether the ship had crashed before landing, or when starting back to

Earth, or whether it had wandered off into fathomless space with all aboard.

The message did not get through complete, and even the fates seemed to be against the men, for the automatic transmitter failed after but a few hours operation. It was afterwards discovered (by the Thurston Expedition in 1994) that the intense heat of the sun's rays had melted the sealing compound of the transformers and caused a short circuit. The only parts of the message that did get through read: "Relief——crashed——ox—en——gyp—m——electrolysis assures supp———food sc—t——help" As even this came only a few letters at a time, despite the fact that almost every amateur and professional operator was tuned to it after the messages started coming, it is understandable that a terrific debate began. It was almost impossible to determine where, in the message, the letters received belonged. Some maintained that the "ox" was part of some such word as "box", while others declared it was the far more important word "oxygen." For nearly a week the discussion went on as to the placing of the letters. Then finally the claim of James R. Caldwell, an amateur radio operator of Sucasunna, N. J., was printed in the New York Herald-Tribune. He had made phonographic records of the messages as they came, and by careful timing, transcribed the words as "Relief (ship) crashed. Ox(yg)en—gyp(su)m (by) electrolysis assures supply. Food sc(an)t. Help."

Immediately scientists who had stoutly maintained that air could not be obtained on Luna, rushed to his defense with explanations of how oxygen could be obtained from gypsum by baking and electrolysis, and that that would assure a supply.

But long before this important point was settled, the rush of subscriptions had begun, because the men had sent a message of some sort, proving them alive. The interpreta-

*tion of the message, and a very fine imaginative account of
the hardships the men must have met to send the message,
written by Thomas W. Hardy, of the San Francisco Times,
and widely re-printed, sent the subscriptions up rapidly.
Within two weeks of the receipt of the message, orders that
had already been filed, were being filled, workmen donated
their time, Universities their instruments and laboratories.
The work, terrific though it was, was being rushed ahead at
maximum speed.*

*A telescope manufacturing corporation in Chicago sent
one of the largest donations, explaining that the tremendous
increase in sales made them feel it only right. Everyone was
watching the moon.*

*Then Mount Palomar, Flagstaff, and Sydney Observa-
tories announced the discovery and confirmation of the sign
on the moon almost simultaneously. A photograph taken at
Mt. Palomar even showed the tiny, square point of the radio
set! The oxygen from gypsum was confirmed. The excitement was world-wide, and the works in the Mojave Desert,
California, were besieged. Daily bulletins of progress were
published in papers. And, more important, the necessary
funds were collected. The amount was passed, by thousands
of dollars, before the subscriptions could be stopped. These
extra funds permitted the building of the famous detachable
tanks, the fuel tanks that were dropped shortly after leaving
the Earth's atmosphere, or better, blasted away, leaving a
great amount of weight behind.)*

July 17.

Moore has been thrown out of the Dome. He has retired in disgrace to the privacy of the battery-house. His
fumes became terrible, and tonight the men rebelled, particularly as he will not say what he is doing.

More cells made today, and another bank installed at
the furnaces. The batteries fully recharged now, and the

heater-tanks refilled. At the mine, their tanks are full, and they demand more. Two were shipped down, after being cut from the dome. They are being mounted permanently at the mine, and King contributed several hundred gallons of water. Rice is sadly flat on his back, but was finally put in a suit, at his and the miner's insistence, and is directing the work on the second tractruck. Tonight they will have full power, and even search-lights. It is a race against time now. The food supplies are dwindling. Rations are so low now, that it is impossible to cut them while the men work.

King is running all his furnaces for de-hydrating the gypsum during the work period, and doing very little electrolyzing. During the sleep-period, since the furnaces must be shut down, he turns all the power into several big electrolysis tanks. It means a few hundred pounds of oxygen each lunar day.

It is surprising the interest we take in these things. Each group inquires at night what progress has been made, and bantering rivalry masks a deep interest and sympathy with the problems arising.

July 18.

The sun is sinking now, and the cell-frames have been moved so that no shadows will strike them till the last possible minute. Another frame of cells will be filled tomorrow.

Under Rice's able direction the second tractruck has been converted to hydrogen operation, and a second generator mounted. Trials showed perfect operation.

The air in the Dome is better since Moore moved out.

Further inroads on the supplies. The thief must be storing them; no man could eat so much, it seems to me. Nearly three pounds of chocolate gone.

But I found in reinventory that I had made a mistake. We have fifteen pounds more dried milk somehow mislabelled "soap powder." A very welcome surprise.

July 19.

Another cell bank mounted at the furnaces, though the miners claimed they needed it to fill their big tanks. They already have enough fuel to operate both engines all night, since the machines were partially shut down most of the lunar morning.

Rice blasted Moore this evening, with a torrent of anger. Rice's nicely charged cells had been drawn upon again, and had to be re-connected to the charge line. It seems Moore needs more power than the charge-current allows him. He wants some more carbides, and promises explosive in exchange.

July 20.

Rice's batteries charged again, and King reports great progress. The water tanks are completely filled on the North side. The oxygen tanks on that side are three-quarters full, and the oxygen tanks on the South side, which had been emptied, are now half full of hydrogen.

Rice has given as his expert opinion that if Moore persists in drawing on the batteries at night, they will be so discharged as to endanger our lighting. Without light we should be distinctly unhappy. Several of the men are studying different lines nights now, to "give their minds some stretching" as they say. Their bodies get sufficient, I imagine. The labor in the mine is lightened, but by no means light for men in their condition of semi-starvation.

July 21.

Another trip to the silver mine. Also another bank of cells arranged. The furnaces got this, since it is really too late in the day to help the mine any, and their tanks are nearly full anyway.

Moore turned out a gray powder today. Explosive, he claimed. Finished the process on a rock outside the battery house, after shading and cooling the rock. He carried it to the mine himself. It was super-successful. It pulverized the gypsum for five feet around, and cracked it for many more. Miners say it is useless to them as it is uncontrollable.

July 22.

Melville has started a new entertainment for the evenings. He is giving a short course in astro-physics. The sun is exceedingly low now, and tomorrow at about five P.M. sets. The stars are visible now, of course, as they are at all times, but tomorrow he will give demonstrations.

King will follow his course, with a course on mineralogy and geology. Moore on Chemistry. I on Physics.

Moore turned out another batch of explosives. Commandeered some of Dr. Hughey's gelatine capsules, and filled them. Detonated electrically they worked fairly well, a super-powerful explosive that works here on the airless moon and cracks the gypsum to fragments. Moorite he calls it, and we agree. Di-nitro-acetalide and a certain catalyst. The catalyst is his secret, and absolutely necessary.

He will need a power board himself now, to manufacture the stuff! The Lunar Power Company (unofficial title of our group) is being over-worked. The Lunar Mining Company, Satellite Smelting and Reduction and now the newly organized Interplanetary Explosives all demand more and bigger power boards! Temporarily both Smelting and Mining will have to sacrifice power to the explosives. King claims Mining gets the benefits, and should make the sacrifice.

July 23.

No power now. The burners are on, working effectively. Melville gave an excellent lecture tonight, interesting to all.

The entire smelting crew will join us tomorrow in making cells.

July 24.

The two power plants at the mine permit continued work at full force. Fuel will readily last till dawn.

Moore is working at something else now, he says. Has apparatus to turn out his explosive all set up. Will require 400 horse continuously day and night tomorrow, to make less than one pound of explosive a day!

Unprecedented number of cells made today, a total of forty-two.

July 25.

Fifty-four cells today! At the present rate neither mining nor smelting will lose power to the explosives.

The thief had given us a rest, but last night stole four pounds of fats, principally lard and hydrogenated cottonseed oil. He apparently has hesitated over my arrangements, but figured out a successful system to elude them.

Conversation tonight centered about the message sent to Earth. We wonder if it was successful?

July 26.

Fifty-five cells, apparently, is the maximum number we can make. A trip to the selenide mine brought in a considerable quantity of material. The men have settled down, and know the work now.

Moore demanded a supply of carbides and nitrides and also sulphides if possible. He has been reducing sulphur from the gypsum, a difficult and power-consuming process. King knows of a sulphide bed.

Moore is working on something other than explosives, but refuses to say what. Admits the malodorous compounds he made were not explosives, but goes no further. Considerable curiosity. A mystery, no matter how slight, is a matter of comment. The food thief has been privately figured out by everyone here, though no accusations have been made, I am thankful to say.

July 27.

Food stock inventory taken today. The result is rather disappointing. Due to the fact that all of the men are working heavily, an absolute minimum ration was one and one-half pounds of food per day per man. If we could lighten the labor somewhat and make machines, deriving their energy from the sun, do it, we would be able to conserve our food. As it is the men are terribly underfed.

(Although Duncan does not mention it in his diary, the miners and the smelters, during the daylight periods, received twenty-four ounces of food, while the photo-cell workers, with the exception of Melville and Rice, received but 20 ounces.)

We have enough food to last till October first at the present rations.

I am working on the possibility of a cableway. I am afraid it is impossible, though most of the men's work now consists in dragging the heavily loaded carts to the Dome. It was suggested that work might be saved if only the oxygen were carried here instead of the heavy calcium sulphate, that is carry on reduction at the mine. It is not practicable, as the heavy tanks needed to convey the oxygen more than offset the gain.

July 28.

Moore has been observed by several of the men eating something in a surreptitious manner. They want to accuse him. I am convinced that the thief is storing his stolen food, and Moore, although he does appear to be eating, may merely be chewing something. Bender in particular insists he be accused.

July 29.

Fifty-six cells. We will have a great increase of power tomorrow.

The lights failed this evening, and Rice succeeded in repairing them with Bender's help. One cell had gone completely to pieces, and broken the circuit. The sensations of sitting in the eerie dark, lit only by a slight glow from the hydrogen burners convinced us that we cannot get along without our batteries.

Moore lectured on chemistry tonight. I was greatly interested, particularly on his talk on the chemistry of digestion. It makes me curious, and if my guess is right, I feel heartily ashamed of my suspicions.

July 30.

The lights failed again tonight. Rice says that next night they will not work. The cells are terribly weakened, and he insists that Moore's work during last day did much to hasten their dissolution. He is working on something to replace them. Making an attempt to construct a steam engine! His only materials are oxygen tanks cut off for cylinders, and food cans, braced with metal for pistons. If it works, Rice is a genius. But I admire the man's determination. He has drawn up, with my help, a diagram of a three cylinder wabble-plate engine. It is a known, but little-used type—but the crank problem, hardest of all, Rice says is eliminated.

July 31.

Rice working on his engine. Only fifty cells today.

The lights are yellowish already. I fear that before dawn they will be useless.

A vial of vitamine concentrate stolen from the food lockers. The man is certainly storing food. Vitamines are being supplied and the concentrate is neither tasty nor filling. The men are distinctly enraged over this systematic thieving.

Dr. Garner's forty-second birthday, and celebrated with a large issue of alcohol.

August 1.

Lights failed twice during the day, and once after the miners returned. The filaments are distinctly orange, and the voltage has dropped from 100 to 85. Rice spent the day on his engine, with interruptions to fix the batteries, and install some sort of a circuit breaker, though Lord knows the current the cells will give is little enough. We have to use suit batteries to test the photo-cells now.

I lectured tonight on modern conceptions of space and time.

August 2.

I understand now why Rice installed the circuit breakers. Somehow a cell blew up, and short circuited the line. Before Rice could repair it, only twenty-one cells were left in working condition. The others had been wholly destroyed. The filaments will scarcely glow at all. Moore made a gas mantle for us, and with three of these over hydrogen flames, we get some little illumination. Only twenty-two photo-cells today.

August 3.

The Dome is very weakly lighted, and practically no work can be accomplished. But twelve cells today, and the men went to work at the mines. I am helping Rice with his engine. My admiration for the man grows! It may work. I only hope so! It was most depressing tonight, in the faint light, the eternal night outside, and that terrible, frozen hell of jagged, black rock under unwinking stars that seem somehow more remote and unfriendly, than Earth's.

The thief took advantage of the darkness. My new burglar trap was avoided with amazing skill, and ten pounds of protein-flour taken, but five had to be left behind, to avoid the trap. It did some good anyhow.

August 4.

Dark, flickering shadows. We cannot use more mantles, as they require the oxygen of six men, give little light, and the water is recovered in only a very small proportion.

No photo-cells today. I sat up and watched the store-rooms for three hours, but could not remain awake longer. No food was taken.

August 5.

The suit batteries are giving out now. The men complain their batteries will not stay charged. They are being used in relays, charged from the generator for half a day, used the other half. Eventually we will be forced to stop work at night.

No lectures. It is too unpleasant sitting in the dark after all day in the dark. It is amazing the effect light has on us.

August 6.

Sunlight! The cells are all set up, the various machines humming, and power flowing in. The furnaces are going full force. The sun is life itself to us!

Rice's engine is progressing. I am becoming more and more hopeful, and the men also, though they still kid Rice about it. It is a sorry looking piece of apparatus, with tin cans and oxygen tanks, pipes for valve cylinders, and welded cables stiffened into a solid framework for support.

Twenty-three cells made today. Moore is at work on his explosive, and has the process almost entirely automatic. King brought nearly three hundred pounds of sulphide ore for him.

August 7.

I have set a trap that will work eventually. We can wait

now for our food thief, inasmuch as he is storing it! I hope
he returns!

Moore's explosive in action. It has doubled the mine
production, and King and Reed are hard put to even keep
up. They have enlisted Bender to aid them and their crew
of two, Tolman and Whisler, to aid in constructing a new
furnace. They demand power.

August 8.

New furnace completed, and power in demand. I have
advised storing water, and electrolyzing none till power equipment is made. Moore's explosive wonderfully efficient. We
cannot realize its power here. I believe it will astound Earth.
A tiny capsule breaks the rock so finely that little or no crushing need be done for the furnaces.

The thief has returned. He has stolen my bait. We need
only wait, and let nature take her well-known course.

The men have openly accused Moore, Bender making
the accusation as spokesmen. But four men backed him, however. Moore smiled at the accusation, and refused to explain
his eating beyond saying he was chewing some chemicals. I
believe him right, and my guess becomes an hypothesis.

August 9.

Engine being assembled. It is a weird thing! I wonder
if it will work for more than a turn or two, despite the mar-
velous skill Rice has shown in working with it. He welded
a piston ring about each can, after building up the inside
with silver plating. The inside of the oxygen tanks were
similarly treated.

Another bank of photo-cells built, and set up. Our clock-
work that keeps the cells facing the sun is overloaded. Rice
to the rescue—with an electric torque amplifier. I believe
that Rice is an assumed name. The man must certainly be

an inventor of note, else necessity is a mother like unto a termite queen, laying her egg each second.

August 10.

Moore deathly sick tonight. He barely succeeded in attracting our attention. Dr. Hughey gave him an emetic, and he seems better. My bait contained an emetic. Now was Moore the thief, and was he made sick by that? I doubt it. My hypothesis advanced to a theory, though hope does not rise.

Explosive making entirely automatic, and Moore works practically all day on his experiments. But one-half pound of explosive used each day. There will be a generous supply tonight, for one pound a day turned out. It is amazing what man can do in the face of such an environment. Engine largely assembled. Tests tomorrow.

August 11.

The critics were dumfounded today. I include myself. Rice's engine was the event of the evening. It is really an internal combustion engine of a sort, as the hydrogen flame which runs it burns in the water of the boiler. It is 100% efficient thus far, and the real test came when the pressure mounted. We all expected a terrible creaking and groaning and hissing of escaping steam. It ran with the smoothness of a sixteen-cylinder automobile, with scarcely a quiver, and without more than a faint hiss of valving steam. It develops nearly twenty horsepower.

Another cell bank installed, for the furnaces. The mines demand more power, and get the next. Moore now has sufficient power.

August 12.

Engine placed, and set up complete with dynamo, a converted motor, in the battery house. The batteries will still be used, with some alterations and repairs, to level out line surges, Rice says, as they might well be serious. Also, in case of temporary breakdowns, exceedingly convenient.

Miners maintain they haven't sufficient power stored to last the night. Reed claims they don't need as much, with Moore's explosive. The explosive is being delivered now in cartridges of lead. It can be pounded, burned, will not explode; will explode when wet, if the proper stimulus is given. Wonderful stuff.

However, more power for miners tomorrow.

August 13.

The thief returned, and Moore was subject to another attack, particularly as he has been eating little at the tables recently, saying he is sick, and yet is not losing strength. I am still waiting for the proof I need. I feel convinced Moore is not our thief.

Power board installed at the mine. New cell bank also, amid rejoicing. Some power is now always going into electrolyzers. A new electrolyzer was needed as well, which Rice made. His generator set is complete, and on a ten hour test today, worked perfectly.

Another load of silver brought in, three sledges of it. Should last all night. Our photo-cell market is approaching saturation, however. Mine needs no more power, Moore has enough, he says, but *may want more later*. This interests me.

Only the furnaces still demand more. The miners, with explosives and machines, are getting well ahead of them.

August 14.

Miners again complained of suit batteries. Rice has been working on them today, repairing them for the work tonight. They are the Renolds-Wirth type of dry storage battery, most suitable for work where they may be turned upside down. Tremendous hydraulic pressure needed to make them, which Rice cannot supply, and therefore they cannot be duplicated. Night work may have to be stopped. This would be exceedingly serious.

Oxygen supplies on hand for three months now, water for five (convertible to oxygen, of course) and the oxy-hydrogen supplies for heating and running Rice's engine.

Moore asks for very large supplies of carbides and nitrides. Also suggests continued building of phofo-cells as "power may be needed later for new processes." I become hopeful.

August 15.

Miners ending open cut work, and constructing a tunnel. Plentiful supplies of cement on hand now. They want to make an airtight tunnel that can be heated at night, avoiding use of defective batteries. Walls of tunnel could be completely coated with cement, and an atmosphere of pure oxygen at three pounds pressure used. Leakage would be small, work faster because of removal of hampering suits. Water needed for making cement, however. Open discussion, all miners in favor, suggest a small furnace and recovery plant at opening of mine, to supply this water, and save double haulage.

Batteries for suits in hopeless condition, Rice agrees, and votes favorably. I am for it. Garner against, as he says danger of an explosion opening a rift into space, and letting atmosphere escape is too great. Miners promise locks and bulkheads. More argument tomorrow night. It means new demand for power. Miners will have to stop work tonight, due to bad batteries.

August 16.

Tunneling plan accepted at last. Preparations under way now, with Reed and King working at new furnace and still. Demand for at least 1000 horsepower. Fortunate that we have plenty of metal from the ship!

Sunset in three days. I made two trips to the silver mine,

and returned almost exhausted. Pains and swelling in my limbs. Dr. Hughey diagnosed it as over-exertion and under-feeding. I doubt it, myself, as all of the men are under those conditions continually, particularly the miners.

August 17.

Furnaces completed at the mine, and cementing begun. Very difficult work under space conditions, but finally a close-grained cement was achieved, and a doorway fashioned. The space-door escape for the ship has been installed at the mouth of the tunnel. Air purifying apparatus is being made by the two mechanics and the two chemists. Other work partially halted. The entire apparatus will be made of silver and fused quartz, as these materials are most easily obtained. It seems peculiar that the vast iron beds we discovered are worthless because of silver beds nearer, which can be worked more readily. Silver is cheaper than iron!

Three men made the trip with me to the silver mine, and we brought back nearly six tons of "jewelry ore." But fifteen photo-cells made today.

August 18.

After a series of experiments, Dr. Garner, whose experience with rocket explosives has taught him much, has made a table of strengths for Moore's new explosive under space and air conditions. Exploded in space, it is of course, soundless. In air it's explosion is so infinitely sharp and sudden, that the effect is peculiar, but one explosion wave reaching the ear, and the echoes producing all other sound, the result being a dull rumble that continues for some time in the dome.

Door set at the mine, electrolysis apparatus and air cleaner arranged, and the first tunnel section charged with air. A heater was also installed, and for the first time the men took off their suits outside the Dome. Air loss trivial, and working conditions highly satisfactory. The tunnel was at once lined with concrete, and a lock built, and pumps installed. Three pounds pressure of oxygen feels just as the Dome atmosphere of fifteen pounds of mixed oxygen and nitrogen, once one is accustomed to it.

August 19.

Work resumed on routine now, production at the mine slightly increased. Miners feel much better at night, say the work far easier, since their limbs are not hampered by the suits.

Demanding power for daylight work. They will run on the tanks tonight. They will be handicapped, since one of their oxygen and one hydrogen tank must be used for heating and breathing. Less power tonight, but the explosive will help.

August 20.

Night again. This barren world is most awesome at sunrise and sunset. The great globe of the sun is harsh blue, and takes an hour to sink through it's own diameter, behind the near horizon. Meanwhile the indescribably jagged, rugged country, with it's million craters, and it's billion spires of rock, is set off like a world made of burning candles. Each spire-peak is blazing in the sunlight, each base is black with the night of space. And frozen, unwinking stars illuminate them dimly.

Heaters on now. Miners report the mine comfortable still. They are aiming downward, hoping to reach a level of stable temperatures in the rocks, where night and day do not effect it.

The furnaces are deserted, and their forces have joined the photo-cell makers. Thirty-seven cells today.

August 21.

Sixty cells today. Miners overjoyed with new conditions,

and report rapid progress. A new bulkhead has been erected. A cableway has been installed in the mine, hauling the loaded trucks back and forth, from the working level, to the lock, out to the roadway. The bulkhead doors are plates taken from the ship. There are but five left now.

Moore extremely, but not dangerously ill. His stomach was terribly upset, and he vomited for several hours intermittently. I feel sure I know what he is doing, and the man is a hero. Unfortunately the moon supplies no guinea pigs.

August 22.

Sixty new cells. At this rate we will readily supply the mine.

The miners are beginning to feel the pinch of the lessened power. It has been decided to take down two of the big tanks from the Dome, and give them the needed power. The men are certainly doing their utmost for the group.

Rice's engine and generator are working perfectly. It requires some ten minutes to start it in the morning, but in the meantime the batteries can carry the load. One light burns all night, instead of the former eight. I am expecting the thief.

August 23.

Expectations fulfilled. He stole four pounds of dried egg.

Another sixty cells. The miners, and everyone else, took the tanks down to the mine today, and both engines are running. The place is well lighted, and the smooth, concrete walls, gentle incline, and mild temperature makes one homesick. It seems so entirely mundane, so like the entrance to a moving walk, that it is almost impossible to realize it is the Moon we are under instead of Earth. The gravity to us seems normal.

The new mine seems so deserving of a name we have

decided to call it Times Square, as Kendall insists the passage exactly resembles that at Times Square.

August 24.

Times Square's main corridor has been branched, and while one tube slopes sharply down, and to the right, the other bends left, and continues level. Thus the party is separated into two groups, and a single calamity will not be so apt to kill all. It is safer. A bulkhead was installed in each corridor immediately after the separation.

Sixty more cells. And Moore came in tonight slightly drunk, and with a breath that almost caused us to put him out. But it didn't smell of alcohol. It smelled like nothing so much as chocolate! Moore does not talk, when drunk it seems. He only repeated, "Jush one li'l glassh." If he's right, and I suspect he is, from the look of wonder on his face as he says it, it's potent. I wish he would talk.

August 25.

Moore presented the camp with a 500 c.c. breaker of a nauseous looking liquid that smelled like chocolate, with something else. He measured out ten c.c. to each of us, and explained it was a concoction that he had stumbled on, and that this was the cause of yesterday's downfall. It tasted horrible, but did not burn the throat. In thirty seconds I felt ready to carry the Dome over to the mine and save the Miners' work. Apparently the others did also.

I hope Moore discovers a less wonderful but more practical decoction.

Sixty cells again today. We are all practiced now. Rice's engine working smoothly, and the light makes us much happier. It is very slightly subject to fluctuations, but quite steady.

August 26.

King and Reed have a new job on hand. They are mak-

ing an apparatus for constructing bulkhead doors. A regular
smelting furnace will be used, and silver metal cast in the
needed form. Oxygen consumed in some quantity, but that
must be borne, as the bulkheads are needed. Four more, at
least. After that, bulkhead doors will be moved from points
no longer endangered, to the working zone.

Sixty-two cells. Half the power banks will be installed
at the mine, and half at the furnaces. No smelting can be
done before daylight, of course. The selenic acid formed
when the silver is reduced is being used in the electrolysis
vats as an electrolyte. We use everything now.

To Whisler's delight, he is permitted to use the electric
stove again, which is much more readily controlled, and with
which he has worked now for more than two years. Rice's
engine gives plenty of power. For our purposes the apparatus is 100% efficient. What energy is not converted to electricity becomes heat, and we use the heaters that much less.

August 27.

Sixty-one cells. Rice, Bender and the miners are working to move the mine generator plants, the tracktruck engines and dynamos, into the mine. It will conserve fuel. This
was my suggestion, after considering that last statement of
last night. Heretofore they have been outside, and heat was
lost as radiation.

Gypsum is being brought out at a far greater rate than
ever before, for the lighting is less given to black, dangerous
shadows and brilliant spots. The explosive too, is more effective in air, and gives off no noxious fumes.

August 28.

Moore has made a request for *Platinum!* Poor old Luna
is stumped, I fear. She has been unfailingly generous with
her scanty wealth, so far, but platinum is so heavy that she

is not likely to possess any. King and Reed will be sent out on exploration.

They were gone all day, with the result that we made only fifty-four cells.

Whisler's birthday, and Moore turned up tonight with a modification of his famous J.O.L.G. (Just One Li'l Glass). It was smoky rose colored, with an odor of chocolate, and a strong lemon flavour. It was as stimulating as ever. Moore forbade all alcohol as they would react. Whisler appreciated the honor done him, and received fifteen c.c. of the liquid. Later he must have felt fifteen c.c. too little (it looks so tiny) and had a glass. I had to cook tonight.

August 29.

Rice's engine shut off for half an hour tonight for an examination for wear. The batteries could not carry the lighting load for even that time, and only one dim light over the engine remained. The machine showed no wear whatsoever, and continued to function smoothly when restarted.

Our clothes, of which we could not bring an excess, are beginning to wear out. Unfortunately, as I am bigger than any of the other men, I have not been able to get any substitutes.

Garner has a few things that poor Morrison never got a chance to wear out. No serious problem, however, as we scarcely need clothes, save space suits, and those are equipped with plenty of patching and repairing materials. The miners show most wear.

No platinum reported. Only fifty-five cells.

August 30.

I paid a visit to the mine today. I honestly envy the miners. The tunnels are smoothly walled with fine-grained concrete, and now Moore is turning out a rubber-like paint which makes them absolutely air-tight. They are faintly grey-white, and brightly lighted by lights strung along the roof. Little cars, rolling on small wheels, and pulled by cables, run up and down the corridors, dragged by the cable-way. The bulkhead doors work efficiently, and easily. The end of the working, the jagged, grey gypsum, alone leaks air slightly, but only slightly, as it is fairly solid rock. Tiny capsules are used now that merely break off some fifty pounds at a time. They are not dangerous, and the work proceeds rapidly.

One corridor, as I said, slants down, to the right. The angle is rather steep, and lines in the cement permits easy traction. The other group, working in the left tunnel, have widened their tunnel to a large room, and are putting in concrete pillars. In here the two generators have been installed, and the main powerboard. Several slabs of gypsum have been sawed out to form benches and even chairs, surprisingly comfortable, rounded out by careful sawing. Rice constructed a small stove for them, and they have been getting coffee, and serving hot coffee occasionally. The men are in much better spirits since they went underground.

Little or no heat is required from the burners now in this section, as the engines supply plenty. The condensers act as mufflers, and there is practically no noise, save a steady hum. The engines have been wiped and polished till they shine, and the rough parts painted. The fuel gas and oxygen tanks have been left above, as they could not be brought through the tunnel, but holes were drilled directly through the rock, to the tanks, and pipes lead down. The electrolyzer for the mines is also down here. I was much interested, and greatly intrigued. Some of the men want to carve the walls, while they are at it. Moore has offered colored paints, instead.

The room is almost finished, rectangular in shape, and but one corner remains to be completed. When this is done, both gangs will again work on the same tunnel, driving downward. The gypsum mass is immense.

August 31.

Fifty-two cells today, and King finally found a platinum supply. But it is hard to get, a few small nuggets of platinum, osmium, iridium and paladium combined. He brought back about six pounds (earth pounds) of the nuggets, and Moore will have to separate it. The task is terrific, as the metals are almost absolutely insoluble. Moore and Tolman are both working on it.

September 1.

Sunlight in two days. Reed says he'll need it, as the gypsum pile is growing apace. Demands two thirds of the power units, on the basis that the miners work twice as long as he can. The miners have a contract from us, however, which they insisted on earlier, and I realize, as does Reed, that their claims are just.

Sixty-three cells today. Moore working on separation. He has all the acids he needs, fortunately, but the task is not easy. I wonder what he wants the platinum catalyzer for. I noticed that his wedding ring was missing, some days ago. That was platinum. He must consider it important.

September 2.

Our thief was at work again, and got away with a supply of coffee extract.

Sixty-one cells. Sunlight tomorrow, so the morning, before sunrise, will be spent in placing them in banks. Moore has asked for two banks, from the miners. Though the miners need the power he has been given them for his excellent service in their behalf.

September 3.

Daylight. Both mines and furnaces opened with a roar today. The exhausted fuel tanks at the mines are filling rapidly, and our fuel tanks here are filling. The engine gets a rest, and Rice is going over it carefully. There is a vast sup-

ply of gypsum on hand, but a new furnace has been constructed, and the pile is diminishing rapidly.

But—so is the food. We have enough for only two
weeks more at the present level, but the rations are being
cut, beginning today. We all feel the familiar burning in our
stomachs tonight. But one pound of food per man today.

September 4.

Power flowing in rapidly now. Men complaining about
making more cells, as they say we will no longer have use
for greater power. I could only reply that more power
meant less work. Moore has privately asked me to supply
power in quantity soon. Asked today for more mineral supplies.

Visited the mine during daylight. Cool and comfortable,
particularly in the lower levels. Even the upper, lounging
room is cool enough, since it is nearly two hundred feet
under the surface, and the surface is largely pumice stone.
A steady breeze is maintained from the lower levels.

Upper room complete now, and lower tunnel nearly five
hundred feet below the surface of the cliff, three hundred
beneath upper room. It has been driven rapidly, and rather
narrow. It descends quite sharply. Today a new branch was
started, going toward the heart of the cliff, on a level. A
small platform-room, with level floor, was made, and the
tunnel turns off, while the main tunnel continues straight.
Bulkhead doors rather far between.

September 5.

Miners in particular complain of growing weakness, and
pain in limbs.

I am working in the mine for a while now, while Kendall takes a rest. It is very heavy labor, particularly moving
the stubborn carts back to the Dome. The road is smooth
now, but not too level. Fortunately the mine is on a higher

level than the Dome, and the downhill track is loaded, the uphill pull, empty.

The lower branching tunnel is being driven straight in. Long, who has been a civil and mining engineer among other things, is in command of the mining groups. He wanted me to take charge when I came, but he knows the plans, and finally agreed to continue. He explained that he hopes to make a large room so far down here that night and day will make no difference. That heating will be unnecessary. Then he plans to move the engines once more, and bring them down here. He even suggests moving the camp here. But not too hopefully, for the great load of oxygen tanks, water tanks, and other apparatus is beyond our strength.

My limbs are very sore tonight.

September 6.

My theory was right! At last Moore has talked. He presented Whisler with a 500 c.c. beaker of a peculiar smelling liquid, rather thick, and tarry in appearance, and told him to put it, with one can of peas or some similar vegetable, into a pan with sufficient water to make soup for all, and season it heavily. Whisler did as ordered. The odor was rather awful, the taste nothing to boast of. But within ten minutes of eating we seemed to feel new strength coming back. Moore explained that the stuff was a synthetic protein and fat mixture, exceedingly nutritious, mixed with some of the stimulant stuff he compounded before by accident. However, it requires tremendous power to make the stuff, and needs cells. He will be unable to make any at night, for we cannot supply enough power then.

He is working on flavor now. Admittedly the flavor is very bad. It has no vitamin content, and our vitamin concentrate is almost exhausted.

He requires enormous power, since he must use acetylene as the base of his synthesis. This he makes from his natural carbides, but there are a number of complex reactions, all taking power, after that. To get sufficient to make his product for thirteen men, two meals a day, will require far more power than we can readily supply at once, and we have an immediate need for the food. Fortunately we can reduce on the production of water and oxygen temporarily, and turn Reed's power over to Moore and Tolman.

September 7.

Again today the food supply was generously helped out by a portion of the sticky, tarry liquid Moore is producing. We are all helping Moore set up the complicated apparatus he needs—and also mining our food supplies! Food and air from the rocks! Man has conquered this frozen hell, and is living off the most inhospitable territory ever touched. I believe that with men like these we could have wrested a living from cold, frozen Pluto itself!

Already we feel new strength. The almost pre-digested protein material that Moore made up flows into the blood stream almost as quickly as water, and the small portion of stimulant added raised our spirits.

The flavor is still vile. Whisler is cloaking it as best he can with tremendous quantities of clove, onion-flavor extract, pepper and celery-seed. But we who have so recently felt our limbs bloating and aching horribly from over-exertion and under-eating can forgive the flavor as we feel the new strength!

The mine is at present almost deserted, everyone helping Moore and Tolman. Enormous retorts of fused quartz must be made, and the Dome is stiflingly hot now, for the sun is beating down on it and enormous oxy-hydrogen flames are needed to fuse the refractory quartz. It is fortunate we have so huge a reserve of hydrogen!

September 8.

Last of Moore's already-prepared supply of food-stuff gone, but the new apparatus has begun functioning, and by the day after tomorrow a plentiful, steady supply will be coming in. Moore has three distinct chains of apparatus: one synthesizes carbohydrates, simple sugars, the second modifies part of this product to proteins, and the third makes fats.

Photo-cells in even greater demand than before now, and as the construction work has been finished, the men will start work on new cells for the furnaces.

I have not stated that the food-making apparatus—since the tiny battery-house was too small, and the Dome already crowded—has been set up in the great lounging room, as Long calls his upper cavern. It will be moved later to a deeper level.

September 9.

Work on photo-cells today, both the furnace crew and our regular crew, and we turned out sixty-nine cells! We are all feeling more cheerful, I believe. The great racks of photo-cells that have stood just beyond the dome, are stripped to a bare few that are used mainly for cooking, and a little electrolyzing. Moore needed nearly all. They have been carried down, and are now set up near the mine.

Moore brought up some carbohydrate material, already made. Glucose. We had sweetened coffee again, and the glucose was clear, clean, and crystalline. It had no flavor save sweetness. Protein and fat processes are slower; they will be ready tomorrow, however. Our natural food supplies are down to a few pounds of flour, a little bacon, a keg of cottonseed oil, and six tubes of vitamin concentrate. One small can of dried egg, half used, and a third of a can of dried milk also left.

September 10.

Soup tonight, rich, and highly spiced. Whisler found a can of sage, and that stuff would drown any flavor. This food is certainly highly nourishing. We are all gaining weight again, with astounding rapidity. Dr. Hughey says that is because of the extreme digestibility of the foods.

Moore has made an astounding proposal. He wants all our old, worn-out clothes! He says he will make them into bread. As they are nearly all cotton or linen, cellulose products, starch will be easy. That is an original use for old clothes. I have heard of men who were forced to eat their clothes, shoes, sleeping bags etc., but not in the form of bread!

Seventy cells today, and a new power bank!

September 11.

The food-liquid has been vastly improved. It is a milky fluid now, and almost odorless and tasteless, only a slight acrid taste, something like lemon. The first of our old clothes are back, in the form of a starch that made the soup thicker, and less watery looking. Whisler produced a "vegetable" dye, and colored it red. The menu announced it as purée of tomato! It didn't taste like it, but it was good, we all agreed.

Plenty to eat again, and we all feel better. The knowledge that we have an inexhaustable supply of food, water and air is tremendously heartening. If it takes a year to build the relief ship, we will be comfortable.

Seventy-one cells today, and another completed power-bank. The fuel for the light-engine completely hydrolyzed, and the mining engine fuel prepared.

Moore reports that he will have enough food to carry us over the night.

THE FIGHT FOR FOOD

September 12.

Another completed bank of cells today, and all the oxygen apparatus operating now. The gypsum pile is getting ahead of the furnace crew. The miners have driven their tunnel in, and are now carving out the great lower chamber. It will be thirty feet high, or I should say, low, since they are cutting downward. It is to be one hundred feet long, and sixty feet wide. A second tunnel is being driven that will meet the floor level of the completed room. A larger reducing furnace has been set up at the mine, to supply them with the oxygen they need to maintain pressure in the constantly enlarging tunnel system. Several empty tanks from the Dome are to be moved up there soon.

I am beginning to wonder if Long is not insidiously getting his way! The food plant, the mining, the reduction apparatus, tanks—in the end everything may be moved there, and with no loss, either. The temperature in the lower rocks is constant, and about equal to that of Earth. The tremendous influx of heat during the day is about equaled by the efflux at night, and through the many layers of rock becomes equalized.

September 13.

I am drawing entirely from one oxygen tank, and pouring the incoming gas into another partly filled. Long wants another tank, and it has been decided finally that we will move to the mine! The empty tanks are heavy, but our strength is almost completely returned now, and with winches we can handle them. They are being placed in a pumice-stone house built in the shade of the cliff. Motors, valves, many other things are being moved. A general exodus is in progress. The new photo-cells are being installed above the mine, and Reed has built four new furnaces for reduction of gypsum.

The great room has not been finished as yet, but thanks to the removal of the necessity for carting the material outside, much faster work is being done.

September 14.

Another bank of cells, and today the great room was roughly hewn out altogether. The saws are at work, and the concrete pillars, reinforced with silver bars made from our mine, are being put up. The entire surface is to be smoothed over with concrete. Power in plenty now, since no more heating is needed. Rice's engine has been moved up here, ready to be put in place. A second, smaller room will be hollowed out to hold all the engines. Since the mining must be done anyway, a third room will be prepared for the chemical synthesis room.

September 15.

Last needed batch of photo-cells prepared, and a final bank installed at the mine. The batteries have been left at the Dome, and we are still sleeping there. By night we will move in. Everyone working at the Castle, as we now call it. The room has been cemented, and painted with two heavy coats of Moore's rubbery paint. Lights are in place, and bunks of concrete set up, waiting matteresses and blankets from the Dome.

A small alcove to one side, with the electric stove, is the kitchen. Greater room and comfort very welcome to us. We are all working hard, and tremendously interested. Melville is now working in the Commissary department, since the photo-cells are no longer being manufactured.

September 16.

The batteries moved today, and all sleeping equipment. The Castle is our home from now on. The old Dome is a deserted ruin. The last air tanks and water tanks have been moved, the water tanks being set up in a special, hollowed cavern near the surface, with thermostatic devices to keep them at a temperature at or near 35° F.

I have already gained thirteen pounds! All the other men have gained similarly. And there is plenty of food for tonight. Moore has laid by quite a stock.

The Castle is complete. A regular elevator service to the opening has been established, and one of the carts will draw us up any time, though, save for the furnace crew, few of us need go.

Messages have been left at the Dome telling where we are, and how to enter, if the relief ship comes when we are all down under. At night, I suspect, we will scarcely leave the Castle.

September 17.

Night now—but how different! There is no temperature change. Rice's engine is supplying all the light and power we need now, while tomorrow the big engine will again be started, and the new engine and power room down here will be fixed. The descending passage will be widened, and the big engines brought down. We have plenty of piping to carry the fuel leads down here. Though the engine room will be nearly seventy-five feet higher than we, the power room itself will be right next to us. The entire Castle is well lighted, and the joy of being able to walk about for hundreds of feet without a space suit is absolutely indescribable. Like describing harmony to a deaf mute.

Kendall, who is something of an artist, has by means of the movie machine, projected a scene taken on the surface, and with colored paints Moore gave him, he is painting it on our wall. It is beginning to shape up excellently. He proposes to do several. It does improve the blank, grayish-white walls.

September 18.

The temperature has not fallen by more than one tenth of one degree; our ordinary thermometers do not register it. It is perfectly comfortable here, with no heating. The work on the power room today required the use of the big engines, and it has been made warm up there too, and the engine room itself is quite warm.

The new engine room has been almost half completed, as almost everyone was helping in some way, Rice controlling the engine, his leg almost completely healed, Bender working the cable-way for us, and the others blasting, or loading, or installing piping or electric leads.

Rice's small steam engine runs all the time, and runs perfectly. It supplies light and cooking heat.

Rice, by the way, has installed a shower bath in a small alcove he demanded for an unrevealed purpose when the Castle was being dug out. The water is collected, filtered through crushed gypsum, and run through the electrolyzer. We bath in it, then breath it! But it makes us feel free to use all we wish, since none is lost. After the dusty work, it feels very good.

Moore has been adding various things to his food-syrup. It has acquired a flavor today. Like his chocolate-smelling stimulant, but it tastes of chocolate, with some vanilla. Not at all unpleasant. He has also added calcium-and-iron containing compounds, and one with some iodine. Magnesium also. And every day we are growing stronger, and eating more of our old clothes as a fairly tasty bread. These will give out soon.

September 19.

The new engine room complete, with just sufficient room to contain all three engines, and leave room to walk. A small tank has been used as a pressure-reducing valve, and the smoothness of the engines aided. Hitherto the high-pressure gases were admitted to the cylinder, allowed to work the machine half a stroke on their compression, then exploded. The engines ran rather unevenly, with considerable wear. Now the gases are expanded and released to fire at once. The efficiency is actually greater, and the wear reduced.

Rice's engine and one of the big engines have already been placed. The other engine is still above. The power room is being cut out.

September 20.

Power room finished today, and the switchboard moved. Lights failed for a period of some five minutes, till the new connections could be made, and our Castle became a thing of gloom and shadows. It became a tunnel in the ground, instead of a home. The absence of light would be worse here than in the Dome.

But the lights were soon on, and Rice's engine functioning again. The switchboard was re-connected, and the lower engine in the new engine room started. This evening everything has been moved down, all the batteries placed in the power-control room, and the second big engine in place.

Regular mining will start again tomorrow.

September 21.

The tunnel is being driven downward further, partly out of curiosity as to temperature conditions. With our new feeling of security of food, water and air, our scientific spirit of investigation is returning. The rocks are being watched

for possible fossil or bacteriological signs. Only very slight
appearances of possible water action noted. We suspect that
Luna lost all her atmosphere and all her water long before
the present crust was stabilized. With no stripping action of
flowing water, and no upheavals, on a perfectly isostatically
balanced land, there is little chance for geological exploration, save by tunneling.

Moore is asking for further platinum supplies for cata-
lysts, as he is making his apparatus 100% automatic. He is
working on other elements now. We will need phosphorus
and potassium, sodium, other elements than the carbon, hydrogen, oxygen sulpher and nitrogen of his simple food-
syrups. He is still working hard at making vitamin concen-
trates. Hughey is helping him now.

September 22.

A large pile of gypsum has accumulated outside the entrance, beside the furnaces. A mechanical-electrical device
has been rigged now to dump the trucks, so that no one need
leave the Castle. We are amazingly comfortable here. Slight
cooling felt now, but the heat of the engines working all day
dissipates it. The bulkhead doors to the upper lounge and
corridors have been shut, and the lights turned off, as it is
cold up there now. We can, if need be, heat it, of course.

We have burned no fuel whatsoever for heating tonight.

Reed, King, and I made a trip to the phosphate field
King found last year, and brought in a load of the material.
We are going to make a trip to the platinum field tomorrow,
also to the Dome on the way back, and bring in a load of
quartz. Kendall is leading some men to the silver field.

September 23.

Four pounds of mixed platinum-iridium-osmium brought
in. A fortune on earth, and we shall certainly have to collect
these materials when the relief ship comes. Half a ton of

silver ore, and several hundred pounds of iron ore. We need new picks for mining. Unfortunately Wilcott was our metallurgist, and King and Tolman will have to do their best to take his place. Tolman advises separating the iron electrolytically, and getting it pure, making the alloys up by percent in that way. We have no chromium and can't make any good rustless steel, but an ordinary carbon-steel will do. We may try alloying some silver for toughness.

Moore gathered up several reams of old paper, some old books we no longer need, and from the Dome some wooden furnishings. Promises other foods. Hughey says we may be afflicted with serious bowel trouble since our synthetic foods contain no bulk whatsoever. One hundred percent digestible.

September 24.

More mining. It was quite cool last evening, and during the night, since the engines hadn't been running all day, while we were mineral hunting. Better today.

Moore wants a larger laboratory, or another one, really, and a separate power board. Rice is aiding him in making his apparatus purely automatic. It is constructed of gleaming silver and quartz; some tubes, handling particularly violent acids or bases, he has made of the osmiridium alloy. Now he need only put his acetylene in one end, and get sugar automatically.

We are making him a larger room across the way from the main living room, with a considerable tunnel leading into it, so temperature in his room can be controlled separately.

September 25.

Kendall has been at work all along on our walls and has some really excellent scenes done. The room looks amazingly home-like. The rugged lunar peaks, with men in space suits in the foreground, a rising sun tinting the craters, and the dome off to one side. It is very beautiful to see, when in our well-warmed, well-aired Castle.

He suggests that we use this as the Hall, and have individual rooms below. It is rather wearing on us, to have to turn out the lights and be quiet when the others want it. It removes individual freedom, and has caused some friction. Since we must mine anyway, I think it an excellent idea.

September 26.

Finished Moore's new laboratory in record time. Every one mining, and the machines working splendidly. We have the explosive under such excellent control now that we no longer need do any mechanical crushing of the rock.

But one man needed now at the Locks, and one at the engines. With plenty of food, and an occasional dash of Moore's stimulant, marvelously effective, yet evidently entirely harmless, and entirely non-habit-forming, we are all well. To people who have not felt the hunger and weakness we did, that means little.

September 27.

Moore's separate room being prepared first, in honor of his magnificent work for the group. Roughly hollowed today. Finished by tomorrow noon.

Sunrise in three days, and we will scarcely know it.

September 28.

Moore's room finished, equipped with bookshelves, bunk, a stone desk, and cabinet or locker, with a blanket for curtain. Kendall is enjoying himself putting pictures on the walls. The room is at the greatest depth we have reached, nearly seven hundred feet, and it is fairly warm even now, but an electric heater, for mild warming, and a powerful gas heater have been installed. Rice has been busy all day making silver tubing for the gases, and silver wire for lighting and power.

September 29.

Moore has moved in, and is much pleased. The room has been decorated with a very clever symbolic picture of the chemist with test-tube in one hand, and a loaf of bread in the other, and some more conventional lunar scenes on the other walls.

Tonight finished Long's room. As the author of the idea of living underground I felt he deserved it.

Kendall busy now. He insists the work is recreation anyway.

September 30.

Sunrise and power flowing in in plenty. The furnace crew busy on the accumulated gypsum, an enormous pile representing the entire Hall excavations, practically, and all the other excavations, but the four new furnaces are making progress. Reed insists we haven't enough tanks to contain it, and I agree, though we may want both the water, the oxygen and the hydrogen. The trouble is that we have two tanks of hydrogen for every one of oxygen.

October 1.

My room completed, supposedly in honor of my leading expedition to earth-side, inventing photo-cells, and half a dozen other things.

Kendall has presented me with one of the finest pictures he has yet made. He is extraordinarily skillful now. It shows Earth just peeping over the horizon, the sun shining on it. and on Luna, and three men grouped about a radio set, looking at Earth. Another is a scene in the Dome making photo-cells.

Garner is to have the next room, and should have had one sooner, as the leader of the expedition, but he has insisted that service in time of stress or something like that should determine the order.

October 2.

Reed has asked that after Garner's room is finished, the work of room-making be delayed till night, and immediate work begun on a water tank. He is rapidly filling the tanks now, for he has an unprecedented amount of power. Some of the men, myself included, have been whiling away time evenings, when the work is done, and there is little but talk to do, making photo-cells. Two banks were completed, and with all the other power thrown in, he has far greater power. All needed fuel has been re-electrolyzed, and nearly all tanks completely filled.

Moore announced making of vitamin A concentrate, an important step. More coming, he says.

October 3.

Garner's room completed, and at a new lower level, a very large room begun. It will be the new water tank, and a swimming pool combined. Water will be electrolyzed frequently to destroy germs. When needed for oxygen it can be electrolyzed, and be perfectly pure. Will be extraordinarily large.

October 4.

Reed crying for room. His furnaces now held up. The gypsum pile has indeed been sadly assaulted. He has emptied two hydrogen tanks, and is filling them with oxygen, releasing into space the hydrogen simultaneously produced. It looks strange, glowing in the brilliant, hard sunlight, and quickly disappearing as it expands infinitely.

October 5.

Reed certainly has a fast working outfit. One of the huge oxygen tanks full already, as most of the power is being turned into his electrolyzers. He is consuming water now.

The work on the tank room is progressing rapidly,

however, as everyone has pitched in. It will be made in two sections, one a shelving section beginning with a depth of three feet, shelving to ten, and a larger section forty feet deep, and thirty wide, fifty long. Around the entire pool will be a shelf, or bathing platform, ten feet wide, with a roof seven feet above it. There has been some discussion as to evaporation under the low air pressure and what swimming will be like in this world.

The evaporation will not be increased, as air pressure means nothing, of course; only water vapor pressure. Swimming will be curious, though we will sink as far in this water as in any at home. We are lighter, surely, but so is the water.

The shallow section will be filled first, a dam across it being left that this may be done. It is almost finished now, needing only the rubber paint.

October 6.

The shallow section is being filled, while the work on the deep section is continued. Water coming in at a surprising rate, down the long silver pipe to the surface.

Temperature down here has risen only half a degree since sunrise. The Hall has had a rise of three-quarters of a degree. Absorption is slower than radiation, or the lag is greater.

October 7.

The men have been split into two mining crews, one continuing work on the water-room, one working on the living quarters. The furnace gang is continuing operations at the surface. The furnaces are almost wholly automatic, save for loading, and Rice has taken one of the plates from the Dome, made it into a scoop, and rigged a loading machine for them which Reed runs. The cement is being stored outside in the sun, to complete drying. It is ground electrically now. Formerly much of the grinding was by hand; most of

the time, however, we collected only the dust that had filtered through the piles naturally.

We are watching anxiously for the relief ship. It should
come in about two months now, but there may have been
another under construction, Garner insists.

(*As a matter of fact, the relief ship was even then approaching completion, far ahead of the time the men felt they
could expect it. Indeed, ahead of the schedule of work laid
out. But, like all the efforts to relieve the expedition, it was
handled with consummate blundering. When the ship was
actually completed, near the end of November, it was suddenly discovered that there were no other trained rocket
pilots on all Earth! They had to be trained in the new relief ship! The inevitable result was that in the first week of
December, the ship crashed heavily, fifty miles from Mojave.
It took nearly two weeks to move equipment to it and set it
up, and a month and a half would still be needed to repair
it.*)

October 8.

The pool room finished, and electric lights strung. Two
very powerful bulbs have been fixed in water-proof cases,
and sunk at the center of the deepest part of the pool. Kendall is already busy. Bender objects that the little man is
wasting energy that should be usefully spent. Garner says,
and I agree, that the relieving effect of the pictures is well
worth his while. The color and knowledge that that barren
rocky, jagged world is merely pictured, gives me, at least, a
feeling of security.

The very last scrap of natural food, save spices, and a
can of tomato catsup, has been used now. They have been
put in with the artificial foods occasionally, and now the last
has gone. But barren, alternately baked and frozen Luna is
supplying us bountifully from her rocks themselves.

Moore made vitamin C today, and that has been added.

Also, he has made a curious, greyish cake, which he asked us all to try. It was rather tasteless, sweetened, and not unlike an ordinary cake. Evidently some form of baking powder has been used. He advised against chewing it too vigorously, and gave us each but a little.

Tasteless as it was, it was a welcome relief, as the continual soups, though nourishing, pall. They leave your stomach empty quickly. This stayed with me an amazing, almost annoying length of time. We learned it was made with ground pumice stone, a starch-flour made from paper, wood, and cotton, and his food-syrups. I don't know that I want any more. Reed calls them "stoneage cakes."

October 9.

The shallow part of the pool is full, and water is already flowing over the dam, into the deeper part. For the first time since we left Earth, our bodies were immersed completely in water! It was curious. The room has been fitted with an entrance at the top, about fifteen feet above the surface of the water, and a ladder (of silver, by the way!) leading down. Diving from this level, we float down, and strike the water with a curious reluctance. We scarcely sink beneath the surface, and bob up languidly. The rapidity with which we rise or sink is changed due to lesser gravity. Our entire swimming must be altered. The water is salt, that it may be an electrolyte. A current is passed through it at night, and the liberated hydrogen and oxygen collected, and burned back to water. The combustion is underwater, which tends to heat it slightly. It may be an efficient heat reservoir.

October 10.

Vitamin B_1 announced tonight, in considerable quantity. We will have the entire group soon, Moore promises.

We are all working at the rooms, and a considerable number are housed now. Rice has his. I think his should have been third made, myself. His work in making the engines work on hydrogen and oxygen alone made these comfortable tunnels and rooms possible.

The Hall is largely cleared now that the bunks have been moved out. A great stone table occupies one corner, at which we eat now, instead of the light metal one, which had a tendency to wobble when leaned on.

The course of lectures is going to be continued soon. Slides and diagrams are being prepared for projection. Kendall left one space on our Hall wall blank, and has painted it with a silver suspension, and it fairly glows under the lights.

October 11.

Another bank of cells installed, and the power going to Moore now. He says he can use any power we can give him, so the pastime of making photo-cells will be taken more earnestly hereafter. Several benches have been made for that purpose, and materials laid out.

With nightfall, when going is easier, he wants us to bring more limestone. He doesn't need it just now. Rice has made a practical heater for the suits at last. It has a jet of oxygen and hydrogen enclosed completely in a tank of water, within the suit. A double valve maintains the proportions, though the flow of gas can be adjusted. A small crank-magneto device is carried by one of the party going out, and passed around, that connection can be made, and a turn of the crank sets off a spark that ignites the flame. Heavier than the battery, but the best we can do. Our last trip last night was bad, as we returned terribly chilled, with useless batteries. Unfortunately we will have no more radio communication.

October 12.

Night in two days now. Swimming after our work takes away much of the tired feeling that comes to us. The last of the rooms has been completed, and each with its solid gypsum easy chair, covered with a padding of rubber paint a tenth of an inch thick (which isn't half as uncomfortable as it sounds) its book cases, bunks, wall decorations and small chair for visitors, all well lighted by a roof light, and a floor lamp (a silver tube, set in a block of rubber-paint covered gypsum, with wires running up the shaft) is an exceedingly homelike, and comforting dwelling. I honestly believe we will be sorry to leave this place now! I know I will.

The deep section of the pool room is acquiring a layer of water at an amazing rate. Garner says no more mining need be done at night, day mining will suffice, and scientific work can be carried on at night. We will be returning to the old work, with the actually welcome variation of something to do by day. And day will no longer be hot and blistering.

October 13.

A shower has been installed in the ante-room to the pool, to wash off rock dust before swimming. The gypsum is not removed by electrolyzing, and has slightly clouded the clear water. That water is more precious than silver or gold to us.

Three feet deep now in the larger, deep part. Today we mined a new tunnel downwards. It is mainly exploratory. No signs of fossil life. Rice objects to such deep workings, as the engines must be used at night to lift minerals from this depth. He has been reminded we won't work tonight. Wants to make a vehicle now!

October 14.

Night fell late this afternoon. The power has ceased flowing in, and the water has stopped trickling down to the swimming pool. The swimming pool has been decorated with Earth scenes, the only room of the Castle that has earth scenes portrayed, and even here not all scenes are terrestrial. All the rooms are decorated now, to Kendall's annoyance, I suspect.

Rice's engine can scarcely handle the load now, when all the lights down the long corridors are on, the Hall, the different rooms, and the pool as well. He is increasing the boiler capacity.

Tomorrow we start exploration again.

October 15.

We worked all day bringing in loads of limestone, carbides, nitrides and phosphates for the foods. Mining our food! Also some more quartz was brought over, and a number of metal plates from the Dome, which is rapidly being dismantled. Moore is extracting sulphur from the gypsum, with fair success. Perhaps those compounds have lain there undisturbed for two or three billion years!

Rice's heater is effective, and not hard to manage, though less convenient than the battery heaters, and tends to localize it's action, making the body part too warm, and the legs and hands cold. It was a comfort to return to the Castle, and relax in our own private rooms, well lighted, and home-like in appearance. We have become so thoroughly accustomed to the three pounds pressure of oxygen we scarcely notice the diminished pressure.

Rice has asked us to spare temporarily the electric heaters, as his engine cannot carry the load now. We have been extravagant with light, as it improves the place immensely, and the load is far greater than it was at the Dome.

October 16.

Tired tonight. I, with Reed and Bender, visited Morrcott Cleft today, and descended again to the bottom. We carried the almost useless batteries for lighting, and explored one of the deepest parts. Little of interest, but brought home some specimens Reed believes to be radium salts, or uranium at least. Of little use to us now, but may be of considerable import. It took us nearly all day to descend and climb back out. Very hungry, and Moore's soups and cakes never tasted so good before.

Rice has disconnected his engine, and is working on it, one of the big power engines working tonight. He is making alterations for higher power and greater pressures.

October 17.

Rice's engine fixed up now, and generating nearly fifty horsepower. He attached a larger dynamo, and his engine, which was, as I have said, far better made than we thought, was strengthened here and there by welding, the boiler capacity increased by inserting another burner, and the pressure rose considerably. Since the burners are inside the boiler, burning in the water itself, there was no question of tube area to consider. The gases have been stored under one ton per square inch pressure, so the fuel enters readily.

The electric heaters, sending their infra-heat rays, bake out the chill of our legs and arms quickly, and the power is welcome, though we need little extra heat here.

We have been looking further in the Morrcott Cleft, and the samples Reed brought in were uranium ore, of quite exceptional richness. The deposit seems large, too. Also, a considerable bed of lead was found not far away, alloyed with silver. We will try tomorrow at a different point. It seems that by blind chance we struck an area of Luna that is very heavily mineralized, or else all Luna is a gigantic mine of a thousand ores. Aluminum in abundance, beryllium ores scarce and widely scattered, and plenty of nickle, iron, and cobalt. Certainly, with such living places as our Castle, it would be easy to establish a civilization here, with Luna supplying both food and air!

October 18.

Further explorations in the depths of the Chasm revealed traces of gold shortly before we left. We did not investigate. I fear that both Reed and I have little respect for gold; here on Luna we have learned to judge metals and rocks by their usefulness, and gold is useless beyond all others. Bender, however, was wildly excited. He wanted to load himself with the heavy stuff.

We brought back considerable lead, as it may be very valuable to us. We have none here, and with lead, the precious batteries can be replaced with lead-acid type. Bender was finally induced to carry back a load of the highest grade rock, by telling him it was far more valuable than gold. He was wild when, on getting back, he learned the heavy stuff he'd carried was lead!

October 19.

A regular expedition was made to Morrcott Cleft today, with sledges for transportation of rock. Reed and I descended and loaded the lead ore on a net, while the others raised it to the sledges.

Reed is separating the lead tomorrow. Rice agreed to make batteries, suggesting that we use silver battery cases plated with osmiridium alloy, as they would be stronger, and less subject to breaking than glass or quartz.

Queer how our ideas are reversed here. Iron is valueless, silver valuable because of it's usefulness, availability and workability, osmiridium only because of it's resistance to corrosion, lead more valuable than gold!

October 20.

Further exploration today. Tonight Rice announced the first lead-acid battery was on charge. Unusually tired tonight.

October 21.

The night is half gone. Moore has introduced Vitamin

G and F into the diet, and has at last succeeded in making a solid organic compound, impregnating it with food-syrup and serving it. It was far better than his solid rock cakes of a few days ago. He says it is pure wood soaked with pre-digested meat and sugar. Anyway, it's good, and it's filling.

October 22.

Kendall had developed some pictures taken while the Castle was being made. They were very interesting to us. Also some pictures taken in the Dome, and now we wonder how we got along without the swimming pool, and the free movement we have here.

Rice working in secret now. He has even made a room for himself to work in, way up near the top of the gypsum cliff. It is entered from outside, through a lock of it's own, but draws power and heat and gases from the main Castle. His workshop, private! He's taken a lot of plates from the Dome, by his own efforts, and we all wonder what it is he's doing. He isn't saying. Almost all day we can hear the big power engine running if we happen to come in.

October 23.

King located a new platinum deposit not far from the old one, probably another branch of it, but much richer. He brought in nearly seven pounds this evening.

The first of the lead-acid batteries will be tried out to-morrow.

October 24.

King has made another triumphant discovery, a very rich tungsten deposit. He plans to try working it for some metal which Rice wants. This will have to be done by day-light, however.

October 25.

A trip to King's tungsten mine. No wonder it was called "heavy stone." It is! We brought back nearly a ton of ore however, hand picked, at that. We carried several blasting capsules, and obtained quite a fair collection.

Reed and I will help King set up a reduction furnace tomorrow.

October 26.

The tungsten furnace was completed, and turned out a small sample piece. It requires a lot of electric power, and we had to use both big motors, and draw on the lighting circuit as well to get the needed power. The metal comes out a small ingot, fused together all ready for shaping.

October 27.

No new discoveries. The expeditions are filling in the few blank spots on the map of our immediate (two hundred fifty mile radius) vicinity. All very tired at night.

October 28.

Sunlight! The power is back, and today we rested half the day till the sun actually rose. Then to work, and mining begun. The photo-cell workers stopped today however, for making more cells. The tungsten furnace needs power, and they are never amiss. The mining, at Rice's request, is being done in the form of a tunnel leading from the upper lounge to his workshop, so we will have under-ground communication. He wants a lock installed in the upper end of the tunnel. He is very mysterious. But he has made us a new tool. He did it during the night. It is a huge, round metal frame, spun rapidly by a fairly powerful motor, and set with a number of diamonds. It eats into the rock with amazing speed, as the rock is soft. Then one charge of explosive, and the sawed section comes out, leaving a neat round hole, the size we want the tunnel. The progress is so fast we won't want to make any more rooms, I fear. Kendall suggests, however, that we make a library, as long as we *must* dig.

October 29.

The tungsten furnace has been at work all day long, and several ingots have been made. The gypsum reduction has been slowed by this new work, but a steady trickle of water has continued to the pool, and nearly all the fuel used during the night has been restored.

October 30.

Rice has revealed his secret to me, for help. I am honored indeed, and have assured the men that photo-cells will be badly needed, so even more work is being done on them. He is making a small rocket car for exploratory work! It is capable of carrying only three passengers, and fuel, with oxygen and hydrogen tanks for breathing, and for running his generator.

His fuel he says will be oxygen and hydrogen, and he has completed the entire hull. He used girders from the old ship, plates from the Dome, and windows from the Dome. His rockets will be made of tungsten, lined with iridosmium, far better than the tubes of the "Exelsior" that brought us here. They will be infusible and non-corrodable. His combustion chamber will be made of an alloy of tungsten-silver-iridosmium, principally tungsten.

Most interesting of all, however, is his new motor. It is a turbine type, burning hydrogen and oxygen, and making steam from water simultaneously in the jet chamber. The combination goes to the turbine, and exhausts into a condenser in the ship, which will serve to warm the machine.

The rocket car will be used first to go to Earth-side of Luna. It is rapidly approaching completion. We have only one draw-back, the use of water, or rather, hydrogen and oxygen with no chance of recovery, since the rockets throw it out, to be lost forever.

We are designing the controls now. As tungsten is produced the rockets will be installed.

October 31.

The miners have reached the workshop, and the main driving rockets have been installed, after hours of the hardest work with the tungsten. The furnaces are now ahead of the miners in the gypsum consumption. Water in the pool, four and a half feet deep.

The miners are starting on the library, which will be quite unnecessarily large, of course. Another group drilling a tunnel back into the wall of the Cliff, and angling downward, starting from the branching point where the corridors part to go to the upper and lower lounges.

Moore introduced another vitamin today, so that now our diet is practically complete. The last of the woodwork of the Dome and the last spare paper used up, so in the future all our food will be wholly artificial.

November 1.

A set of heavy tungsten-steel springs was placed on the bottom of the rocket, for landings and take-offs. The take-off will be a vertical rise on the lower rockets, till free of the ground, then a drive forward. Several heavy gyroscopes from the *Excelsior* placed today as well.

We estimate a cruising range of several thousand miles, in fact infinite distance, as we can achieve orbital speed about the moon for long distances very readily. But it couldn't make the trip to Earth.

November 2.

The men have been trying to find out what it is we are doing in the workshop, asking a great many questions. We are filling the fuel tanks now, and Reed wants to know what we are using all the gas for. He is running his electrolysis outfit again, at full capacity, and very little water is going into the pool. The front braking rockets, and the steering rockets have been installed. By night the ship will be finished.

We had all the parts, practically, on hand here to begin with, and so made very rapid progress.

The library has been finished, and Kendall is at work on it. The tunnel leading back into the hillside is being driven on, and a new continuation of the lower mine tunnel, running horizontally however, is plunging parallel with it. In the end of the lower tunnel, a room is going to be made, nearly one hundred feet below anything else, and here will be a food-syrup storage room. We dislike to have aimless tunnel made, as it would bring to our Castle the air of a mine once more, something we have attempted to avoid.

November 3.

Lower rockets completely installed, and electrical ignition system arranged. Fuel pressure up to full value. Little more work to be done.

A number of frames of photo-cells have been set up, and despite the almost constant use of the tungsten furnace, the power is nearly up to what it was before its installation. The mining machine Rice made has permitted the miners to keep two furnaces going, and the fuel we drew to fill the tanks of the ship, has been replaced. Six feet of water in the deep end of the pool-room.

November 4.

Rocket complete save for furnishings and paint. Metal chairs with spring seats and backs being made now, spot welded together. A small power board has yet to be installed.

Tomorrow the ship will be announced. Moore has been taken into the secret.

November 5.

The ship is completed, and has been announced. The interest shown was amazing. It has been agreed that Rice, Long and I shall make the trip back to the Earth-side, as Rice built it, and I aided, while Long knows the way best, and can locate us. Navigation will be important, I suspect, from a few miles above the surface.

The food storage room has been begun, and at the end of the upper tunnel leading into the wall of the cliff, a new tank room will be built, with tanks we build ourselves. The great use of gas for power as well as breathing, and the storage of the more voluminous hydrogen has crowded even our great tanks. The tanks will be made of tungsten-steel, with welded seams, tested for one ton to the square inch. There will be two tanks, one twice the size of the other. Our pumps are almost worn out, and Rice will have to build new ones, which he says he can do. He will use the rollator type, as it is easiest to build.

This will be the rocket-fuel room, principally.

November 6.

Rocket completely equipped, and tomorrow a trial will be made. The workshop will be evacuated after the men enter the ship. The Dome radio set has been moved down here, and with spare parts Rice installed a similar set in the ship. I will control, while Rice keeps in touch with the Castle, Melville at the set here.

Food storage room finished, and equipped with large quartz jars. The food supply has been put in these. A pasty mass which is the wood-like stuff with which Moore makes his famous cakes, has also joined several large jars of peculiarly colored liquids.

Seven feet of water in the pool tonight.

The work on the gas-tank room has been started. The method is new, several tunnels close together being bored, and then joined. It will be thirty feet long, thirty wide, and eight high.

November 7.

Rocket tested! It worked beautifully. The three of us

entered, closed the doors, and the hangar was evacuated. The doors opened electrically, and the ship was hauled out on a cable. The rock had been leveled, and just outside the shop, I turned on the lower rockets, very gently. The machine trembled, and seemed to jump slightly on it's springs. Then more power, and it rose up, with slight shiftings of the gyroscopes. A tail blast drove us forward, and out over the cliff. With half power on the lower rockets, we soared rapidly, and the tail rockets were turned on one quarter. Quickly we gained great speed, and the Dome flashed back in a moment. We were wearing space suits in case of accident, but we soon took them off. In a minute and a half I cut off the bottom rockets, then some ten miles above the surface. The ship dropped slightly, and yet before we sank to five miles, we reached orbital speed, and I cut off the driving power. We were far beyond our widest exploration range already, and Long was snapping pictures industriously, while Rice talked with the Castle.

I let the machine coast for several hundred miles, using no power whatever, then finally turned in a great U, and headed back. We had passed into the dawn section, and turned back to the evening region. We will readily reach the Earth-side. It has been decided to wait till the third of December, when Luna will be at last quarter from Earth, and descend. In the meantime Tolman is going to refine several pounds of magnesium, and mix it with a quantity of silver oxide as a flash-light powder to attract attention. He will make nearly fifteen pounds of the mixture.

We landed safely three hours after starting, and the ship was safely returned to her shed with the cable. Landing is accomplished by verticle descent, somewhat difficult as the ship has a bad tendency to sway, despite the gyroscopes.

Throughout the trip, the generator set worked perfectly. We used nearly three thousand pounds of water, however. We will use less next time, as I know the ship better. All the men feel it was water well spent. The tanks have been refilled.

November 8.

All helped make photo-cells today, or set to work in the gas-tank room. Rice and King are working on metal, however, and tomorrow an expedition will be made for iron ore.

The rocket was carefully gone over, and found in perfect condition, save for slight burning of the landing springs on my slow take-off and landing. The lower rockets, jetting the hot gases, burned them slightly.

November 9.

Five tons of iron ore brought in. Very heavy labor for all of us. We have been working very hard, and seem to have been losing weight slightly. Moore is increasing the food allowance.

Reduction will begin tomorrow, and be rushed to completion in two days if possible. We need only a little, really. Several new banks of photo-cells installed, and we have plenty of power.

November 10.

The tank room is completed, and all hands working at reduction. We will work all 'night' as the sun shifts continuously, and it would mean a delay of two weeks if we waited. One hour rest now for supper.

November 11.

We are all exhausted. The iron and tungsten have been refined, and alloyed, however. Night. Sleep at last!

November 12.

Work going on today on the tanks. The tank-room is completely finished, and heavy concrete bases arranged. These tanks will be spherical, and the gases will be stored under a pressure of two tons to the square inch! Rice is working on plans for his new pumps to handle this greater pressure. The tanks are being made in eight orange-peel sections, which can be carried through the corridors, and welded when in place. A temporary crane has been arranged for handling them. For testing, they must resist a pressure of three tons to the square inch. Today Reed and I ran a test on our alloy, made of electrolytically refined iron, tungsten and graphite, fused electrically, and found that the tensile strength was very high, nearly 175,000 pounds.

Diagonal cross-braces, on all but the bottom and top sections will be installed, slightly reducing the volume, but greatly increasing the bursting strength.

Four sections were made today.

November 13.

Six sections made today, and Rice has completed the welding on one tank. He is annealing it now with his torch. The welding was done after the room had been evacuated, working in a space suit, to prevent oxidation of the metal he was working on, and minimize air-bubbles.

Rice, Long and I leave for the Earth-side tomorrow.

November 14.

Morning—ready to leave now. The doors into space are open, and I am at the controls, rockets on at very low intensity to warm them slightly. Taking off.

Circling now at orbital speed. Beyond radio-range of the Castle. Long reports trip more than half completed. No control needed. We will go well beyond the marginal region of the earth-side.

Earth rising! Great reddish-green sphere, nearly full. Atlantic Ocean and corner of North America visible. Stopping to land.

Landed. We ate in night region, with earth at half above us. Rice is sending to New York, while Long, in a space suit, is placing the magnesium flash charges. They will burn one minute each, with tremendous intensity. We must cover our eyes while they are being fired.

Rice has sent now for five minutes. New York in dark or night portion. Long about to start first magnesium flare.

Light blindingly brilliant while flare burned, which seemed far longer than one minute. Rice sending again. The motor-generator supplying power. Message: "S O S S O S Garner Lunar Expedition. Air supply plentiful. Food supply artificial—synthetic food. No immediate danger. Watch Magnesium Flare."

Since power is nearly eight times as great as when we made our last attempt, I feel sure the message will get through. Clouds over Chicago. Rice repeating message.

Denver in view now. We have a receiver aboard that can pick up signals of the same wavelength we are sending, and the ship acts as antenna. Hoping for message. Rice sending with beam on Denver. Second flare to be started soon. Rice sending notice of flare.

Second flare gone.

An answer has been received. It is fragmentary, but tremendously encouraging. The first word from Earth in over two years! Message follows: "Signals re - - - ved—not com - lete. Relief ship - uilt but - - - ly damaged in crash to - ay. Repairs being hastened. Watching for f - are." This message was repeated several times, with subsequent filling in of missing letters, and extension. We learn that the relief ship built has crashed due to lack of competent rocket pilots. Kingsbury and Wilkins were both killed recently. This is bad news, as it will be some weeks before the ship can be repaired, and at least a month or more before any man can attempt to cross space in her. We have sent our messages through saying we will be safe until that time. We have also announced that we have built a small rocket ship, and can travel about on the Moon, but cannot leave her, though the trip from Luna to Earth is far easier, due to Luna's lesser gravity. It has been agreed that this spot shall be watched for our return with further messages.

Rice has set up a powerful spotlight, run by our generator. Mt. Palomar has turned the great 200 inch telescope on us. Light signalling being attempted.

Signals more legible than our radio! California under perfectly clear skies. Third magnesium flare to be set off now. We will go out while it is burning, and attempts will be made to see us by its light.

Back in ship. Plates were taken.

We were clearly visible!

We are returning to the Castle. Long messages have been sent, telling almost the full story of our expedition, the light signals coming through clearly, in even smaller telescopes, many amateurs reporting visibility with reflectors as small as 15 inches. California passing out of sight. Very tired now.

(*The excitement on earth, created by this expedition can be imagined. The news that the marooned men were living now in a comfortable, well aired tunnel system, with plentiful supplies of artificial food and water and air, with a rocket ship they themselves had built, all this served to whet the interest of the world.*

The announcement of the discoveries of huge diamonds, platinum deposits, silver and especially uranium convinced thousands on thousands that after all, this expedition had been of more practical value than they had been willing to admit. They could not realize of what enormous value the expedition actually had been, nor that Luna was merely a way-station to Mars, to Venus and the rest of the Solar System. With the Castle as a base, within three years an expedition was to leave for Mars, their rocket refueled on Luna, from the rocks of Luna. Already free of the dragging hand of Earth's heavy gravity it was to establish new history. New history, but even now the Castle was establishing history, and while thousands watched the Moon for further signals, thousands sent in more funds to reconstruct the damaged rocket, and rescue these men. The news of the complete (apparant) triumph of men over the awful desolation of the Moon alone was enough to inspire men of gentle, kindly Earth.)

November 15.

Landed back at the Castle without the slightest trouble, shortly after midnight. We descended at once to the hall, where the men were all waiting. We had been in wireless communication for more than fifteen minutes, as we decelerated for landing, and they knew most of the story, yet it was after one thirty when we finally went to sleep. We had been gone but one day, instead of the seven that our last trip took, and we had been far more successful. The entire trip consumed but eight thousand pounds of water. Energy means nothing to us, only water.

The time saved on the trip means little; important are the vastly greater results, and the wonderful ease with which we accomplished the long, long trip. Never again will a Lunar expedition have the troubles of exploration we had. Hereafter, while they cannot bring ships and fuel with them, they will make them here, and explore with ease.

Today we have worked on the great gas tanks, and the two hydrogen tanks are completed, and ready to be filled. Several sections of the oxygen tank are ready.

The rocket ship has been completely re-charged.

November 16.

Dr. Hughey and Moore are both worried. All of us have continued to lose weight gradually but steadily, despite the large quantities of energy we have absorbed in our foods.

Though eating over five thousand calories per man per day now, far more than necessary, we continue to lose. All known vitamins have been made, and are being included in the diet. Also we are getting plenty of calcium, magnesium, iron, iodine, aluminum and other metals and non-metals. Moore is really worried. This has not been publicly announced. I have sacrificed one of my few remaining shirts, and Garner, Hughey and Moore as well to make some more of the natural-base starch, as Moore calls it. We will watch results.

The tanks are completed, and the heavy, hardened silver pipes installed. The pumps are under construction. Despite the numerous electric motors with which we were originally equipped, we are having trouble now to make them go round. The powerful motors in particular are in demand. For these pumps we need plenty of power, and we have had to take one of the cable-way motors for this purpose. The cable-way motor is being replaced by a small steam engine, electrically heated. Rice is making that too.

Tomorrow an exploration expedition of five men will be crowded into the rocket, which can easily bear this load, and we will visit Long Crater for active research. This is the great crater with a smaller one within, which we passed in our trip to the earth-visible side of Luna on the first, foot trip. We believe that the great crater, erupting first, hurled material from great depths to the surface, then that the second, smaller crater brought material from still greater depths when it threw up material.

I will be in control again. Reed, King, Tolman, and Bender will make up the party.

November 17.

We started this morning quite early, and reached the crater in less than fifteen minutes. A successful landing was made in the reasonably smooth plateau of the inner crater, and the work begun. It was a typically meteoric action. But it must have taken place untold millions of years ago. When the Moon was young, this crater was formed.

Mineral hunt highly successful. We brought back a collection of slightly radio-active rocks we found near, hoping to get an age-determination from these samples, by analysis of radium-lead-uranium percentages.

Sulphur in abundance. Also selenium, tellurium and some phosphorus. Metals seemed scarce, though traces of gold were found.

The ship was moved about one hundred miles to the wall of the greater crater, and examination here disclosed plentiful minerals, including a wealth of chromium and copper, in different sections. King picked up what he believes is an emerald, but may merely be colored quartz.

Rice had finished making the parts of his pumps, but wants some mercury for them. We will have to get that tomorrow.

November 18.

Collected mercury and refined it today. Several pounds, and enough for Rice's purpose. The heaters in the Castle feel good after the cold expedition!

The pumps were assembled and installed tonight. Other apparatus for tanks not quite complete, but by dawn will be fully prepared for filling.

The converted shirts were served tonight. We will watch for results. I, and the other men felt unusually lazy after the meal. Going to sleep now.

November 19.

Exploration work today, as usual. The tank room is fully equipped, and I am helping Rice with his new steam engine. The boiler is amazingly tiny. He already has a condenser and injector attached to his little spherical boiler. A small electrical heating coil rapidly boils the water. He has the boiler wrapped in powdered pumice stone for insulation. A pressure switch turns the heater on or off depending on the steam pressure. As a result he uses a heating coil about five times as powerful as necessary. It is another three-cylinder wabble-plate engine of about forty horsepower. It's starting torque will be very high. He is making the parts for six such engines now!

I have been immensely surprised, and so have Hughey and Moore, to notice that with a startling rapidity, in a single twenty-four hour period, the men have visibly gained pounds! We are convinced that there is some subtle vitamin-like thing in natural substances, that is, organic substances, that makes it possible for accretion to take place. While it is evident our foods supply fuel for our bodies it is also apparent they can't supply repairing materials without the aid of that mysterious something in organic foods. Even organic foods that have been changed from cotton to starch. Then, like vitamins, this something can force the inorganic foods into the body.

November 20.

The effect of the starch has worn off, and the men are rapidly losing that gain. Unless a constant supply is kept up they will starve with plenty of food! It has been announced publically, and shirts, trousers, everything have been contributed. We now have one suit of clothes apiece.

Another trip to the message relay point will be made tomorrow.

Rice's new engine is complete. He has tested it, and it works perfectly. Several other engines are assembled, and need only boilers to put them in operation.

November 21.

We left in the rocket early this morning, taking off easily, and landed without trouble at our previous position, as determined by Long. The Atlantic coast of North America was in view, and we commenced simultaneous signals with the spotlight and radio. Soon we were in communication again.

We sent several straight messages, and finally sent a code message Garner had prepared, directed to his backers. This was repeated to us from Earth, and found correct after some trouble. In English it read: "Artificial food lacks ability to support life. No natural food left. Slow starvation. Appears unknown vitamin-like substance missing. We are using cotton, converted chemically to starch. Supply nearly exhausted. Advise doctor with rescue ship."

A further message sent advised that the rescue ship be designed for the use of regular rocket fuel on the way here, but equipped to use oxy-hydrogen, since that would supply sufficient power for the return. Thus fuel for the round trip need not be carried. We can supply it!

But we hope the ship comes soon.

More cotton starch tonight.

November 22.

Exploration has been given up finally, and mining will be resumed. We are preparing a great hangar for the rocket ship. This will be built in the face of our gypsum cliff, with two of Rice's engines to haul it in after landing. More photocells being built as well. Today work was begun on the tunnel that will reach down to the new hangar. Our little rocket has been fully recharged, showing a use of 8200 pounds of water. Dawn, day after tomorrow.

November 23.

Bank of photo-cells completed today. The tunnel is

being lead from the swimming pool, and will be ten feet by ten feet. The larger it is, the more gypsum we get.

November 24.

Dawn this afternoon, and power in plenty flowing in. The furnaces are started, and are roasting the gypsum. The new tanks are getting their first charge, and the gases used for the rocket are being replaced. Despite these drains, the pool is gaining again.

November 25.

Another bank of cells. Twenty pounds pressure in the new tanks. Eight feet in the pool, and most of the gypsum mined last night gone. The new tunnel is driving on, however, and rapidly enough now to supply the furnaces.

An addition had to be made to the power board to carry the increased load of new cells. We are making rapid progress now on the tunnel, and the furnaces. At night the electrolyzers work, for it is night with us, but day without. This too is pleasant, to have dark when you want it. The ceaseless glare of lunar day was annoying, nerve-wracking. The pleasant, cool dark makes for better sleep. We are gaining weight once more, but the supply of materials is diminishing. Beyond them there is no more.

November 26.

Ten and a half feet in pool, and the new tanks now have fifteen hundred pounds pressure. All other tanks full. The regular water tanks have been emptied, and are being filled with hydrogen and oxygen. A small pressure-pool tank alone remains, and that is refilled from the pool when necessary. It is large enough to last all night, however. All four furnaces working. The men have completed the tunnel and are commencing work on the great hangar. New tank rooms will be hollowed out near it, and the suggestion has been made that the rooms themselves simply be lined with plates of metal, and these welded. The rock could carry the strain instead of the metal. I believe it would work, with some modifications.

November 27.

Bender was cruel today. He pointed out that the 26th was Thanksgiving. For the first time in three years we overlooked it completely. But Moore says we'll make up on Christmas. He will try to have solids for as then!

Twelve feet of water in the pool, and the new tanks now have a full ton pressure, half pressure.

The great room is being done in a new way. A slanting tunnel was drilled upward, till we were at the top of the far side of the room, then turning, tunnels were driven that will be the upper edges of the room. Now we need only cut out the block below, and within, and the ten foot tunnel becomes an entrance to the floor. Often previously we have ended up with an entrance near the roof, since we cut downwards.

November 28.

Moore has been giving us nearly 7000 calories of food per day, and with the life-vitamin of the converted cotton, we have been putting on weight at a prodigious rate. It does not seem to strain the digestive system, probably because the food is practically all pre-digested. But now the last of the converted clothing has given out. We can spare no more. We have but one blanket apiece, shoes, one pair of socks, one shirt, one pair of heavy trousers, and whatever woolen material we may have had, which was little, most of it being very heavy duck, or broadcloth shirting. Wool, Moore says, does not adapt itself to his processes.

Tanks have ton and a quarter pressure, pool now up to thirteen and one half feet. All other tanks completely filled. We are trying to have enough hydrogen and oxygen on hand to make the return journey fuel immediately available.

November 29.

The tank-rooms beside the hangar-room are completed, and work has been begun on the metal inner sheathing. It will be half-inch tungsten-carbon-silver steel, welded. Concrete will be poured in all around the tanks in a fluid state, and allowed to harden, filling any small cracks, and perfectly distributing the pressure to the solid rock. The hangar room has been roughly bored out now.

Fifteen feet of water in the pool, one and a half tons in the new rocket-fuel tanks.

A great increase in power since this dawn, for photo-cells have been turned out rapidly. Melville is in charge now.

Moore and Hughey devoting most of their time to the work on the few scraps of life-materials they have. Attempts were made to ferment or mold some of our artificial food, on the basis that the molds would be life, even though unpleasant. Our Castle is absolutely hygenic, so much so that no trace of any mold has been found! All our food was brought canned, or treated to make it proof against molds and bacteria. None now to be found, save a few disease germs that can be depended on to be present. Apparently these are too high a form of life, for they will not live in our purely artificial mediums. Even a disease might mean life!

Another trip to message relay point, soon, with coming of night probably. All too busy now.

November 30.

Sixteen and a half feet of water, one and three quarter tons of pressure in the tanks.

Hughey and Moore are preparing a statement of our artificial food supply, and the results observed. This will be sent to Earth when we next go to the message relay point, and fourteen days later we will return, for a statement from the scientists on Earth. Perhaps they will be able to suggest or discover something. Our present situation is rather less pleasant than we had thought. It was hoped that we could live here indefinitely, but unless we can discover the new life-vitamin, it will be impossible. Hughey says that two months is the absolute limit for us now. That allows of only simple starvation, but as many other deficiency diseases, beri-beri, scurvy, pellagra and such, do not act as simple starva-tion, there may be more serious complications. No one knows. Hughey is asking that it be tried on laboratory ani-mals, of which we have none, such as white mice and guinea pigs, which live more rapidly than men.

The hangar is being finished off. It has been partly ce-mented. As gypsum is a necessity to us anyway, rooms are being cut for living quarters of the crew of the rescue ship, four rooms, larger than ours, arranged for double bunks in each. But four men are expected, however. These rooms are half way between the Hall and the Hangar, on the same level with ours, but on a different corridor.

December 1.

Some of my books on Physics, and Melvilles on astro-physics are being sacrificed. A curious dinner! We are be-coming bookworms and moths! Moore has promised us some unusual flavours, at any rate.

The four furnaces are all running at full capacity now, and the cableways are almost over-crowded with cars run-ning up and down, heavily loaded. Rice has made four new ones, despite his many other tasks, using the metals we re-fined. They are much larger, and barely get through some of the smaller tunnels.

The pressure in the rocket fuel tanks is up to a full two tons this evening, and Rice reports that the first of the new tank-rooms is completely welded, and the concrete poured. Day after tomorrow gas may be put in it.

The new quarters are being cut out rapidly, and now Garner has suggested that since this Castle of ours must some day be the base of a greater, and better equipped expedition than ours, we might cut even more rooms to supply them. We must have more gypsum in any case. Two larger store rooms will be cut soon, down near Moore's present store-room.

It is pleasant to think that we are preparing for the future in our Castle in the rocks. And I believe we will have nothing to be ashamed of in either workmanship or equipment. Rice in particular can point with pride to his engines and his tanks, his silver tubes and power lines.

December 2.

The hardest job of all was done today. The great Hangar was cut off from the rest of the Castle by the newly installed air-lock, and the passage to the Outside was cut. The passage has been driven half way, and the huge, heavy airlock for the ship placed. This has been made of plates from the dome, brought over recently. The hinges were the greatest trouble, but Rice made them. Moore supplied us with artificial rubber to face the doors for seating. Now they are completely installed, thanks to the numerous winches that Rice set up. They have been tested, and found air-tight. A pump of the rollator type, driven by one of Rice's steam engines, will pump the air back into the hangar from the lock compartment in a very short time. Later, when electric motors are available, the steam engine can be replaced by an electric motor. Power lines have been brought down, of course.

Tomorrow the remainder of the entrance tunnel must be finished.

December 3.

Outside the sun is beating down with tremedous intensity. This evening Kendall projected pictures taken during the entire period, beginning with our take-off from Earth, and ending with some taken this morning, while the tunnel outward was being made.

The cable-way to haul the rocket into the Hangar has been completed, and a considerable area just outside levelled off with blasting, which churned the rocks into a sort of gravel, and which levelled itself fairly well needing only a little work.

December 4.

The tank-room near the rocket hangar is being filled for the first time. Only one foot of water into the pool today. The four dormitory rooms have been finished and work now going on in the new store rooms. Kendall has been busy decorating the new dormitories, and the hangar room.

We gained nearly two pounds apiece on the books. Moore took advantage of the natural starches the sacrificed books provided, to give our weight another boost.

December 5.

Sun sets tomorrow afternoon, and this afternoon announced that Tankroom No. 1-H had been lined, and was ready for service. The H or hydrogen tank rooms are just twice the size of the O or Oxygen tank rooms. No. 1-O is already showing twenty pounds pressure, despite it's size. No. 1-H now being filled. Twenty-three feet of water in the pool and the deep, dark water looks good to us as we look down at it. The lights under it, when turned on, make it glow like a huge jewel. It is all that to us! The thought and labor it represents means a great deal.

December 6.

Kendall has finished decorating one of the dormitories, and the hangar, such parts as he intends to do, are done. One wall has two panels, two scenes, one from space just after leaving Earth, one just before reaching Luna. These are excellently done, but the former looks more interesting to us!

The two store rooms are finished. Work begins tomorrow on the new series of dormitories and a laboratory, all to be on a newly driven corridor, extending beyond the back wall of the Hall. A new door will be driven, much to Kendall's disgust, through one of his scenes. This will be a ten foot corridor again.

December 7.

Evening now, and we are back at the Castle. The little rocket functioned perfectly. We landed at the relay point in time to be visible from Eastern Europe this time, and gradually all of Europe and the Atlantic came into view. We left again when California was well visible, and part of the Pacific.

All signalling done by the new spotlight, much more powerful than our other, but radio was worked in conjunction with it. The long articles were sent twice through, and repeated back for corrections. The greatest difficulty was encountered with some of Moore's complex chemical formulas, particularly as they were necessarily structural formulas, and the empirical formula was useless. My chemical learning was slight, but it helped.

Hughey's work was not difficult, but remarkably long. Rice's fingers were sore and stiff when the signalling was all done.

We also sent accurate descriptions of our Castle, and the new Hangar, and instructions on operating all the machines in the Castle. The new relief ship will have spring landing gear like our small ship, and be equipped for landing on it's side, instead of the base. It's exact dimensions were sent, it's mass, and it's fuel requirements. There was

some question as to the possibility of our obtaining so great
a supply of hydrogen and oxygen. It will require little more
than we now have on hand. It is agreed that we will return
in two weeks.

Williamson, in charge of the relief rocket, reports a
minimum of six weeks for repairs and equipment, and the
pilots will absolutely have to have a month's training before
setting out on their trip. That is two weeks longer than
Hughey allows us of life. We will have to live an extra two
weeks despite medical knowledge. It would be foolish to
leave Earth before the rocket pilots knew the handling of
their ship, for it, like the first relief, might be wrecked, and
the further wait would certainly be fatal. I have taken the
responsibility of assuring them we will be able to survive.
Garner approves, though Hughey does not, claiming that it
will be impossible. There are four other lives on the rocket
to consider, however.

The rocket while being repaired, is being re-designed in
part for the return trip on pure oxygen and hydrogen, a less
efficient but more easily obtained fuel than our Garnite.

Mining was continued, and the work on photo-cells.
Another of Rice's engines will have to be installed for the
new tunnel cableway, and an automatic switching device
would save the time of one man now needed to change the
cars from one cable to the other. Rice and Bender are at
work. I am sure they will succeed.

Reed started work on a new furnace.

December 8.

The new cable-engine installed, and operating. Rice
tried out an automatic switcher this evening, just before we
quit work, but it failed miserably. He will try again.

The new tunnel has been driven far enough, and rooms
will be cut. Three men on a photo-cell detail now.

December 9.

The switching device worked this noon, and another man is working on the mining now. Reed has finished his new furnace, and it uses tungsten-steel heating wires, forged at home. It has a much greater capacity than either of the other four.

The gypsum dump is growing at an astonishing rate. It seems impossible that so little water is obtained from so much gypsum.

A trip was made today to our diamond mine for more cutting stones, and quite a collection was brought back.

Rice working on the steel lining of the other tankrooms.

Kendall decorating tunnel walls now. I am surprised he has any more scenes to show; but he has, a constant variety. They are really helpful, for it makes this Castle of ours seem more of a castle and less a buried dungeon.

Despite the two powerful tractruck engines, and Rice's original generator engine, the electric power system is sadly over-burdened nights. Rice may work on a turbine generator when his present job is completed. Our main difficulty is that only the two big generators are available, the two used on the rocket coming here, and neither of them will handle much more. Rice is promising to enlist my help.

December 10.

Rice has finally finished all the welding on the tankrooms. There are two oxygen tanks and two hydrogen tanks, each of which should resist a pressure of three tons per square inch, or probably better if need be. That will be easy enough however.

Rice has been talking to me tonight. He suggests we make an electric power plant of our own. I say the labor will be too great, but Rice insists that labor is our best relaxation anyway, and we won't be able to delude ourselves we have any more mining to do soon. We can get pure iron easily, and he can make silver wire to wind it, and with Moore's rubber insulation paint it would be easy. A neat job it won't be, but it will work. It sounds worth while. I agree that our mining is partially in response to the demand for something to do besides sit and think.

December 11.

The men have agreed. All other work will be suspended to haul the iron, tungsten and silver Rice needs. The old power room will be large enough, but a new casting pit will be needed. I am to work with Rice. We did not mention that this work is merely to keep us occupied.

December 12.

Very tired tonight. We brought in several tons of iron, other parties bringing in silver and tungsten. Moore had sacrificed several of his books. "The work I'm doing isn't in any of them anyway," he said, as though excusing a fault. We have very few books left now.

December 13.

Work on new casting pit begun. The turbine housing has been laid out.

Work progressing rapidly.

December 14.

We gained half a pound apiece thanks to Moore's books. The converted starch appeared in the form of a mashed potato, or at least it was so labelled.

Apparatus entirely laid out on paper now, and the turbine castings arranged for, the heavy generator castings are almost cut out in mould form. The hardest work will be making the armature. The field coils will be wound on solid metal, but the armature *must* be laminated. The laminations will have to be rather thick, but we are using almost chemically pure iron, a thing very seldom obtained on earth. Actually, on thought, I found I had never before seen absolutely chemically pure iron. It always has some carbon, or phosphorus or sulphur or nickel—something with it. We are ready to begin with daylight. Back to mining for now.

December 15.

Rice and I working on silver drawing. The wire is drawn, then passed through the rubber paint, and reeled on our now empty wire reels. Rice himself was cutting out commutator bars. We have discovered no mica, and the insulation of these will be a problem. Bender is aiding us, and keeps shaking his head at the disgraceful lack of appreciation we show in putting silver to work. He thinks we should be mining silver and gold bars, I believe. In fact he asked rather disgustedly why we didn't use gold instead, Rice answered smilingly that it wasn't as good a conductor, and too soft anyway.

The silver, by the way, has been hardened with a small amount of iridium-osmium alloy, which is exceedingly *hard*, but also *hard* to get hold of. However, we needed only a little for the commutator bars. All other work had to be stopped while this alloy was fused, as the furnace drew an outrageous amount of current.

December 16.

Moore has promised us a bakelite for insulating the commutator bars. This solves the last problem. He says that phenol and formaldehyde are easy to make.

The mining crew has cut several rooms now, and a great mass of gypsum is ready for the furnaces. The photo-cell crew has set up no less than seven new frames.

Sunrise in three days.

December 17.

Rice is working hard at an attempt to make good bearings for his machines. He says making the shafts will be the hardest job of all.

I have returned to the mining crew.

We are losing weight again, and it has been decided that the last books must go, save the treatises on metallurgy that are left us, since our metallurgists are gone. A last attempt at "weight lifting," as Hughey calls it, will be made.

December 18.

The converted starches today, and heavy meals. Sunrise tomorrow afternoon, and tomorrow we will again get converted starch. This will be practically the end of our supplies of convertible materials. The sheets even, and towels have been taken, and locked in the food lockers! It reminds me again of the thief who stole such considerable supplies of food last fall. I believed, and still believe he hid them. I wonder where they are, and who he was?

Moore, by the way, is the one who was stealing soap recently. All the soap mysteriously disappeared. He presented us with some artificial soap, equally effective as a cleanser, and explained what the peculiar flavor in our soup had been.

Tomorrow we return to the message-relay point, Long, Rice and I. We hope there will be useful information awaiting us. In the meantime the others will begin the reduction of the metal. The ore will be placed in Reed's furnaces, a current of hydrogen passed over it, and the water resulting from the reaction collected.

December 19.

Midnight. We have returned with rather discouraging news. The scientist of Earth have tried and failed. They said that Moore was a genius—which we knew—and that they had had great difficulty in carrying out some of his reactions. Moore has explained (I should say apologized) that he has space to evacuate into, and can work under conditions they cannot procure.

But their experimental animals all died. They ask us to report again in two weeks, the 27th. We shall. All the news of Luna and Earth exchanged. Earth interested in our work apparently.

(*A mild statement. Earth was wild, fought for it, demanded it. Inventors were struggling to perfect a radio wave that would go around a corner, and reach the camp itself. Any newspaper would have paid a fortune for it.*)

We returned rather late, with a great bulk of messages, but little help. Dr. Garner's sister sent a long message, and Laura (*Dr. Duncan's younger sister*) sent me a message. Most of the men have no living relatives.

Moore said there was little helpful material, and some that he already knew from experience was wrong. Also some brother chemist suggested that we grow mushrooms. I wonder why he didn't make it chickens?

Very tired now. We all tire easily on these artificial foods.

December 20.

Tired again, but this time from work in the reduction of the metals for our generator. The metal is all prepared, and the heavy castings have been poured, and are cooling slowly. The men working in shifts, as we want to finish this job before night overtakes us.

December 21.

The shafts have been cast, and are cooling. Tempering tomorrow. Nearly the whole day purifying the iron for the laminations.

December 22.

Laminations being cast now. The shafts finished, save for grinding. Rice tempered them by plunging them red hot into the Pool. He rigged a hoist to handle them. He has a lathe, and diamond tools and polishing materials to cut them!

December 23.

Rice has cut the shafts, and the laminations are completed. The men are now coating them with a first coat of rubber paint, after rough grinding them fairly smooth. The job will not be an easy one. An inverted winch will have to be our press—and not too good a one.

December 24.

Christmas Eve—but it isn't going to be much of a celebration this year, I fear. There are no normal organic materials left that can help us any.

The inverted winch press performed as I suspected—lacking any rigidity, the pile of laminations repeatedly slipped. It was luck rather than skill that none of us was hurt when the laminations skidded. Five tries led to no results. Work was knocked off until a suitable jig could be arranged. Having no timber to knock together, we must make a metal frame. Having no supply of bolts handy, it will have to be welded. And the laminations *must* be aligned accurately— and even so I fear that there will be a wild wobble to the mass when it is rotated.

Bender decidedly unhappy at the moment. Our soups— may I never have to eat another!—contain some of Moore's stimulant, which he had warned us did not mix with alcohol. Bender felt that Christmas Eve called for a drink. He raided Moore's laboratory supplies for alcohol. The mixture resulted in a violent illness combined with an extreme chill and uncontrollable trembling. He was extremely angry with Moore for making it impossible for him to celebrate Christmas Eve in traditional fashion.

December 25.

Our third Lunar Christmas.

The ancient songs sound better in our Castle than they did in the Dome—and Moore achieved the near-impossible. The dessert for Christmas Dinner was a real gelatine-like substance of excellent flavor. The protein material was solid—somewhat more so than necessary or intended, perhaps. but even though it was somewhat rubbery, the presence of solid food gave a festive air to the occasion.

It was a case of "We shall rest, and faith we need it!" today. Practically nothing was accomplished; the pool was overworked, and the most active group was assembled in front of a board King fixed up out of a mixture of pumice dust and plastic goo, engaged in throwing darts. It is surprisingly tricky; however accustomed we are to lunar gravity in our two-plus years here, we still can't overcome the trajectory habits of the previous years in Earth's heavier field.

King, naturally, won. He's been throwing darts at that board since he made it a week ago, it seems.

December 26.

Laminations in place. Winding begins tomorrow. I will be in charge of this, Rice assembling his turbine now, and the compression chamber, as he calls it. It will not be a true boiler. The feed will come from the rocket-ship fuel tanks, as the largest high compression tanks.

Reed and King back at their furnaces, eating into the great pile of gypsum accumulated, refilling all our gas tanks, and pumping into the huge tank-rooms. No water going to the pool now, as all is needed to fill the tankrooms.

December 27.

One coil wound, and our backs, hands, and arms are aching terribly. I thought this silver wire soft till I tried bending it snugly about the armature and field coils! I can scarcely write.

December 28.

Field done. The work was easier today, as we have learned more. The plastic varnish is drying on it now. It seems an unwieldy piece, but looks efficient. One gang was busy tearing out the tractruck generating system, and this evening we moved the new generator frame in. Rice has placed the bearings, a babbit metal of his own composition. He gathered all the old cans at the Dome to secure the tin and lead. The armature is well underway.

December 29.

Generator completed save for brush assembly! The turbine case has been placed, and aligned. Rice is so uncertain of his shafts that he has a universal joint between the generator and turbine, both machines mounted on very stiff springs.

The crew has returned to mining, and I to Rice's workroom, where the turbine is being assembled. We must finish it before the sun sets, or we will be quite literally powerless.

Tankroom No. 1-H and 1-O show 800 pounds each. The full charge will be 6000 pounds, however. It is rising at 600 pounds a day now that the full power is turned into the operations there. Hitherto our operations have consumed a good deal.

December 30.

Turbine assembly set up in power room, brush assembly placed on generator, and connections to power board bus bars made. Only the compression chamber to be attached. Test tomorrow evening. We are calculating on 2000 horsepower. All apparatus in place this evening, only adjustments to be made. Rice claims less than thirty seconds needed to get up to full pressure in his compression chamber and ten to bring the apparatus to speed.

December 31.

At eleven o'clock this morning the test was made before the assembled company. It took just twenty-five seconds to get up pressure, and in thirty the speed had mounted to the value we wanted. The voltage was five higher than we had planned, and then the load was put on. We were cutting it in on the electrolysis apparatus for load. The machine slowed, but quickly picked up as Rice's automatic controls increased the fuel. By some freak of good luck, it did not quiver, or move, it was perfectly vibrationless, and remarkably quiet! With our crude equipment, that was necessarily chance.

The full load was applied gradually, and when a full 2000 horsepower were being generated the voltage was at just the point we wanted with the brushes set as they were. We could still advance these slightly, and finally we got 2300 horsepower without undue heating. The generator is a huge success!

A fan is attached which maintains a circulation of air through the power room, and carries the heat to the higher passages which tend to grow very cold toward dawn.

January 1, 1982.
New Year's Day.

In frank assessment, I can't promise myself another. But equally, I can see that the men have accomplished truly worthwhile things here. If only Hughey and Moore had small experimental animals to work with, we might be able to find out something about this mysterious living-matter unknown that we are lacking. But, when we came, we did not foresee the need for biological experiments!

Today was a semi-holiday; some light work that the men felt had to be done, or wanted to do, was accomplished, but actually we've been playing the part of kids with a new

toy. Every one of us was very directly responsible for the
success of the new generator, and none of us quite admits
that it was more luck than skill that made the armature balance so perfectly. So today the new turbo-generator system
has been working, but we haven't.

We can't seem to get enough rest to dissipate the feeling of lethargy, however.

January 2.

Mining resumed. Our production is falling off, as we
are growing weaker. The last of the books, the last of the
clothes, bedclothes, and towels have gone. We are sleeping
on our pneumatic mattresses alone now. There is nothing
more we can convert.

Nevertheless, a considerable amount has been accomplished, and the tank-rooms are up to 2700 pounds now. The
pool has not gained more than two feet, as nearly all the
water has been converted directly to gas.

January 3.

Tank rooms now up to 3300 pounds. We have been
mining steadily, and making some photo-cells. We are weakening rather rapidly now; most of our fat has gone. Despite
the fact that we are consuming more than enough energy,
we cannot even retain our weight. Apparently it has never
before been known how rapidly the human body wears out.

January 4.

We go to the message-relay point tomorrow, and I am
retiring early. I am exhausted, though I have not worked
very heavily today. But 500 pounds gain in the tankrooms,
making a total now of 3800. Still 2200 pounds more to go
for No. 1 group.

My face is hollow, and cheeks sunken, as with all of
us, save Bender who seems to be weathering the storm better. He is on the photo-cell detail, though on the 23rd he

went after silver ore. Our limbs are all well rounded, heavily flushed. They are swollen, but give a deceptive appearance of health. We are wearing only woolen trousers and woolen socks, with our thick rubber shoes. These cannot be converted anyway. Everything that can be is gone. Cuts and abrasions are curiously slow in healing, frequently tending to grow larger instead of smaller.

January 5.

We have returned, but our landing this evening was poor. The sun has set, and it may have been shadows from the floodlights, but I think it was principally because I was very tired, and sleepy. The heavy undercarriage springs were broken, and the hull slightly dented. A sharp bit of rock broke a small hole in it. Rice thinks he had best repair it. Bender, who is the strongest of us now, will help him.

There was no help waiting us. Earth has learned only that the animals all die—and can give us no details of the death. I think they can, but our request for full accounts were answered by saying that the information was not to hand.

(*Duncan was correct in his belief. Dr. Hugh R. Monroe who did much of the hurried work was actually with the operators, but refused to send the requested information.*)

The rocket ship is nearing completion of repairs.

There was little news.

January 6.

The power of the new generator is making itself felt. We do not feel comfortable if the temperature falls below 80° F. and we have large heaters set up near our work to keep us warm. The machines are doing more and more of the work, and we are doing as little as possible now. When the room we are now working on is finished, we will cease work, save during the day of Luna. This will be finished tomorrow.

We have enough water stored in the pools and tanks now to supply the fuel for the rocket's return. The reduction to gas requires no labor.

January 7.

The mining work is finished. It will furnish a supply for two days at the furnaces. After that only electrolysis will be attempted. There are enough electrolyzers now to consume all the power of our photo-cell banks, and the power needs of the Castle will complete the load.

Moore says he has enough food-syrup on hand to last the rest of our stay here, but will continue work for a while next lunar day.

We are starving now, but curiously we don't feel hungry, only very tired, and arms and legs and backs ache. And thanks to Moore's stimulants we feel happy.

January 8.

Garner, Hughey and Moore and I were called into session today in Garner's office. Did I say that Garner's room had a separate office connecting?

The discussion concerned Bender. He is as strong and active as ever, his face well filled, his legs and arms are not swollen, but growing fatty. Hughey and Moore agree that this can only be because he is getting a natural food supply somewhere, which, with the food-syrup he is getting with us, is rapidly increasing his weight. Garner has asked me to watch him for the source of his supply. We are all agreed now that Bender was the food thief.

Tonight I thought I saw a thoughtful, calculating look about him as he surveyed us one at a time. Poor Melville was lecturing on astro-physics. With least body material to use, he is, I fear, failing rapidly. His leg stump is badly swollen. I wondered what Bender was thinking of. Later he steered the conversation around to the value of the metals we have been using here, and the diamonds. It was agreed among us that diamonds would be worthless, for if such as these were brought to Earth, the entire diamond market would be broken. The osmiridium alloy got the vote as most useful discovery—in financing other expeditions.

January 9.

I failed in my watch last night. Bender's room is far away from mine, and I could only see the light shining from his doorway from my room. I was sitting in the dark and fell asleep. I was very tired.

I have enlisted Rice who rooms next to Bender. We are convinced that Bender brought the stolen food in from the Dome, or wherever he had cached it when he went after the last load of silver. He will be sent after another supply of silver tomorrow, and his room will be searched.

January 10.

Bender grumbled at the trip, but as the strongest of us had to go. A careful search revealed nothing whatsoever in his room, and it would be impossible to hide it on his person. The room is too bare to allow of any hiding places. Kendall's pictures are intact, and assure us that the walls have not been tampered with. Bender is becoming surly and arrogant.

Rice reports he saw nothing last night.

January 11.

Bender was violently sick today, and I told the others of the trap I had set last fall when food was being stolen, a large portion of a sickening compound Hughey gave me. We know it is Bender now, but can do nothing. He is stronger by far than we are. I have a plan I shall suggest

tomorrow morning. We must get that food. Bender knows
we suspect him now.

But he is safe in laughing at us. We have no guns, save
a Very rocket pistol for signalling. No weapons whatever.

January 12, 10 A.M.

The plan has been proposed and accepted. Rice disconnected the lock feed wires, and now entrance cannot be
gained from without till we restore this power. Bender is
outside with 12 hours oxygen in his tank, so he believes.
Actually he has but one hour's supply. Garner, from inside
the lock is pushing notes through. We have demanded that
he tell us where the stolen food is, and told him of the
tampering with his tank.

He threatens to destroy the photo-cell banks. He hasn't
oxygen enough to climb to them and back to a lock.

10:30 A.M. Bender cursing us, and refuses to tell where
it is. Says he's going to keep us from it. He wants enough
of us to die off so there'll be load capacity enough on the
rocket ship to carry back precious metals. If he is the sole
survivor, as he hopes to be, he will claim the mines. At least
he can take thousands of dollars worth of osmiridium. Calls
us fools and insane to take loads of instruments back when
we could take precious metal to outfit half a dozen expeditions. Only reason he joined was to get a share in the mines
he had heard would be found, and when he learned we intended to turn all the mines over to our backers and keep
nothing for ourselves, he began to steal the food, hoping
he could live to file a claim.

10:45. Oxygen giving out. Bender is weakening.

10:50. He has told us where the food is, *inside* his
pneumatic mattress, and demands to be let in. Investigating.
He told the truth. Almost the whole hour had passed, and
Bender was unconscious when brought in. The food has

been put in my care, and I have hidden it, telling only Garner and Moore where it is. Moore says by conversion he can get more out of it than nature put in. We don't need it's food value now.

Bender is raving; he threw us off when he regained consciousness. It seems he intended to come in before he became unconscious, and re-capture the food. Bender must be eliminated. We are not safe.

January 13.

Moore took but one pound of food, but by conversion made it work wonders. We have each gained half a pound already. Bender is watching me closely. It makes me feel very uncomfortable, as he is much the stronger.

Garner got some of the food out today while Bender trailed me up to the rocket-hangar. This is unendurable.

January 14.

Bender has found the food again. Now we do not know where it is, and he refuses to leave the Castle, naturally. He will scarcely leave his room, and forced us to bring him Moore's food syrups as he doesn't feel safe he says when too many of us are around him. If we did not he would naturally take more of the natural food he has. We are desperate.

January 15.

The suspense and troubles will end tomorrow.

January 16.

Bender has been executed. Rice re-arranged the switch-board wiring, and inserted a radio interrupter-transformer capable of delivering 5000 volts, in such a way that grasping the main circuit breaker would be fatal. Then he cut the rheostat to dim our lights, cut it up, then down, and gave a scream. The lights remained dim. He lay down on one side,

Hughey and Garner pretending to work over him, while I went to call Bender as reserve electrician. He kept his eyes on us and reached for the circuit breaker.

He has been buried half a mile from the Castle on a low ridge. It was heavy work for four of us to carry him, despite the lunar gravity. We will have to find the food now.

January 17.

The food was easily found today, and natural rations resumed. We are all much depressed by what has happened.

Melville does not seem to be recovering properly, and Hughey is much afraid.

January 18.

Shortly after two o'clock this morning we were wakened by a weak cry from Melville's room. We found his bunk soaked with blood, flowing freely from his stump. Hughey did everything in his power to check it, but tourniquets would check it only temporarily, so long as they were in place. A tourniquet was maintained, but Melville had lost too much blood. He died shortly before seven o'clock. The membrane covering his wound, the new flesh, had been dissolved away during the period of starvation.

He has been buried on the highest peak of the Cliff above the Castle. Only two days ago we buried another of our party, the man responsible perhaps for Melville's death, and struggled under his weight. Melville was not a heavy load.

January 19.

Sunrise tomorrow. No more mining will be done. We spend almost all of our time lying on the pneumatic mattresses in our rooms, and bathing in the heat of the electric radiators. We seem to have no energy, but we should improve soon. We have gained over a pound apiece now.

January 20.

Sunrise this afternoon, and all the electrolyzers were started. Reed, King, Rice, and I worked at the furnaces, and succeeded in getting what gypsum we had mined into them. Now the electrolyzers are drawing solely on the water from the pool. The pressure in the tankrooms is rising steadily.

The natural food Bender had stolen is almost completely gone, but one more meal can be served, and we have gained back but two pounds.

Moore has gained four pounds, as I gave him an extra ration of the natural food without his knowledge. We must have his help.

January 21.

Tankroom No. 1-O and H are full, and the second group is being charged. All the fuel used during the night has been restored. Moore and Tolman are working together now to make the last steps of the food processes as automatic as possible, and I, with Dr. Hughey and Rice, am learning how to operate the mechanism. It draws an enormous amount of power. Moore says we must get more materials at once, while the new strength we have gained from the natural food is with us.

January 22.

We made a trip to the carbide mine today, and brought back nearly a ton. It was all the six of us could do to haul it back, yet tomorrow we must get nitrides. I am exhausted, my muscles ache painfully, and a tremendous feeling of lethargy overpowers me. All the men are extremely lethargic.

January 23.

Only three quarters of a ton of nitride ore could be brought in, as King fell down on the way back, and seemed to hurt himself seriously. He could not walk, and ore was dumped off, while he was put on our sledge.

Our crew cannot make the trip next time, our legs are painfully swollen, and Dr. Hughey forbids it. King he says is suffering from a torn muscle. It has, apparently torn itself in two. It is extremely painful, but the pain is rapidly diminishing. King is under an hypnotic drug now. His leg, which was injured, seems sunken, and Dr. Hughey is fearful.

January 24.

A second crew of men went after the nitrides today. Moore and Garner were not permitted to go, and as that left but three, I went with them. Hughey, Rice, Kendall and myself. Little Kendall had a hard time of it, but did his best. We returned safely with half a ton of limestone, to find King awake and comfortable. On examination Dr. Hughey told us that the torn muscle had been entirely dissolved away! A most horrible form of cannibalism! The body is feeding on itself, any injured member will be removed almost at once by the starving tissues. King says he feels much better. But his leg will be practically useless, as it was the great driving muscle of walking that was torn.

January 25.

I remained at the Castle today, in charge of power and equipment with Reed. The pool has fallen nearly five feet, but there is a pressure of one and a half tons in the tank-room. The other has a full two tons now.

The mining group, Rice leading them this time, returned with phosphates and some magnesium. The load was light, but all were exhausted, their legs swollen with the work.

Dr. Hughey says the great danger of our diet is that while the engine has plenty of fuel, and plenty of steam-pressure, it has lost strength in the pistons and boiler. In other words, while we have energy enough, our bodies are too weak to handle it. He advises reduction in our diet, and this has been done.

January 26.

Rice has broken his bad leg once more. It suddenly gave way under him while he was going down the corridor, and he fell forward heavily. He caught himself with his hands, and scratched them slightly. Dr. Hughey says this is dangerous. Rice has been put to bed, and his leg is in a cast. It cannot knit till he gets natural food, but it is in the right position.

Rice has been our mainstay so long we cannot afford to lose so generous and wholly helpful a companion.

Dr. Hughey is more afraid of the small scratches. He has covered them, after thoroughly washing them with antiseptic, with collodion.

Garner did not leave his bunk today. As the oldest of us he is suffering most. Hughey says quite seriously this may help him, if he ever gets food in time, because it is dissolving the excessive deposits of lime that age has given him.

King seems to be getting along all right.

January 27.

King died early this morning. About three thirty he called to us, and we found him in agony. His injured leg was swollen horribly, and a purplish-red color, the skin distended like a bag. The leg muscle had evidently permitted a hemorrhage, and the blood had filled his leg, draining the body. He was very weak, and there was no way to revive him. A stimulant would simply increase the hemorrhage. Blood poisoning was apt to set in as it was. Dr. Hughey drained the leg, after applying a tourniquet.

About eight o'clock King died. He has been buried beside Melville.

We begin to understand what it was the doctors of Earth refused to send us, the information on our probable manner of death.

Hughey has ordered an absolute minimum of movement, lest more torn muscles result.

January 28.

Four days to sunset. The rocket ship relief will be due February 19, Long thinks. That is 22 days. Except for injuries we should be able to live until then.

The tankroom No. 2 registers three quarters full, and some eight feet of water remain in the deep end of the pool.

We are doing almost nothing, and since our energy-diet has been reduced, the lethargy, when motionless, and the feeling of abundant energy when moving has left us. We are more normally weak.

The indefatigable Rice, not to be handicapped by the broken leg, has been working several days in his workshop, moving in a wheel chair, and has at last produced a tiny steam driven automobile for himself. He is working on more. Despite Hughey's dire predictions, and thanks to his care, Rice's scratches have not grown, although neither have they diminished in size.

January 29.

Rice has presented me with one of his little steam driven cars. Moved by a tiny two-cylinder steam engine, carrying oxygen and hydrogen fuel tanks, they save enormous labor in moving about the all too extensive halls of our Castle. Where once we gloried in this freedom of movement, now we curse it, for the journey from the Hall to our rooms is long. The cableway is long since gone, and the car can move up and down easily. It will carry two people, and I act as ferryman frequently in bringing the others up, while Rice does the same. I use two tanks of each fuel (hydrogen and oxygen) a day.

January 30.

Hughey has asked Rice to stop his efforts. They are too dangerous. He has made three cars in all now, and just before evening finished a trailer one of the cars can draw.

The tankroom registers nearly full pressure now, and all fuel tanks for tonight are full. The tankrooms represent our homeward trip, and we watch the gauges with anxious hope.

More and more we appreciate the delicacy of Rice's work, as the invaluable machines continue to function wholly automatically.

January 31.

Sunset tomorrow, and we believe the tankroom pressure will be nearly up to normal.

Tolman has fallen into a stupor from which we cannot rouse him. He did not wake this morning, and has not wakened yet. Hughey fears it is the end. He has been injecting glucose and protein solutions directly into the blood, to supply the necessary energy for his heart-beat. He says it may be possible to sustain life even longer in this trance-like state, but he is doubtful.

Our mattresses have been moved permanently to the Hall that we may be together. No longer does any of us want the solitude of our rooms.

We have not left the Castle now in six days, save for funerals. All machine controls are inside.

Moore says he has enough food-syrup to last at least three months on hand.

February 1.

Tolman is still alive, breathing very slowly, very evenly. Rice is resting quietly on his couch. Whisler was not energetic enough to move today, so wholly lethargic that for the second time in nearly three years he failed to get our meal.

Moore has stopped work, but his machines continued functioning until sunset, turning out food that does us no good.

I acted as cook, to the slight extent of getting supplies from the storeroom on the little steam car. We all feel sharply hungry, as none of us is able to prepare a meal in safety. We are no longer attempting to control the machines, they do much better when left alone. We could hear the turbine start automatically shortly before sunset, and the lights flickered a moment at the change over. The pumps stopped presently, and I went down to see the tankroom gauges. Thirty eight hundred pounds in each of the number two tanks.

Rice and I have been preparing a written account of everything about the Castle, with detailed instructions on handling it in case of emergency, but with a preface advising that it be left strictly to itself. It is strange to think that these machines we have made with our own hands in our own Castle, wrested from the lifeless surface of the Moon, will continue to maintain the correct oxygen pressure, the correct temperature, keep all the tanks full and the air clean, the passages lighted, long after we are gone!

Hughey has, with Moore, prepared a report on the probable best treatment for us when relief comes, with instructions as to what will be found in each of the numbered food-syrup jars. These documents will be left in the air-lock chamber. Instructions for operating the lock have been painted on the door.

Night has fallen now.

February 2.

Today was Tolman's last day. He woke this morning about eleven, dazedly. He thought it was the thirtieth, and complained of pains in his abdomen. They got worse presently, and by noon he was writhing horribly. About two o'clock his abdomen collapsed on itself, and he went into a coma, and at 3:45 was dead. I have prepared a cyanide capsule for myself, and several of the others have, after seeing poor Tolman's death.

We were too weak to transport him to Cemetary Crater, so he was carried on one of the steam cars up to the little rocket hangar, and there we left him, the air being pumped back into the Castle. In the vacuum of space his body will be preserved for burial when the Relief brings help.

Our hair has been falling out for some days, and now we are all almost entirely bald, even eyebrows have gone. Our fingernails and toenails have also begun to drop out, and the quick of the finger, ordinarily protected by the nail, is exposed, and makes every motion agony.

February 3.

Our leader is gone. Garner, the originator and inventor of our ship, the man who gathered us together, and who's foresight kept us so comfortable here for the two long years of exploration, died this evening. He did not wake this morning, but about three he woke, complaining of pains in his abdomen as did Tolman. At three thirty-five he took the cyanide capsule, and died almost instantly.

Our party is dwindling rapidly. Hughey, Rice, Moore, Whisler, Long, Kendall and myself alone remain. We do almost nothing. We have taken to smoking again, occasionally, and get no small comfort from it.

But with Garner gone, we feel our expedition is doomed. He had cheered us up consistently.

He has been laid with Tolman in the Rocket hangar.

February 4.

No food today. We do not need it, really, and we were too weak to get it. Even the operation of the steamcars seems beyond our strength. Hughey says it makes little difference.

The steady, smooth purr of the dynamo in the power

room makes us wish we too, were machines. Its enormous power, and our wholly diminished strength contrast so.

Very difficult to write. All my finger-nails gone.

February 5.

Our teeth have been loosening for some days, and two of mine came out today. The gums are bleeding and I cannot stop it. It is slow, but steady. Hughey says it will be fatal, but he cannot reach me as he is across the room.

February 6.

Long's gums bleeding also. Weak. No more.

Thomas Ridgely Duncan

This marks the end of Duncan's diary.

EPILOGUE

On January 30, against all advice, the Relief ship had taken off from Mojave on the long trip, after less than three weeks of training for the pilots. It shot into the heavens with all its power, striving to gather it's utmost speed before the detachable fuel-rocket tail was dropped. At a height of one thousand five hundred miles this was blown off, and hurled back. Now the main body of the rocket began to spout flame, and the ship continued on. Straight into space they bored, and five days later they were circling the Moon, in a steadily diminishing orbit, turning and moving with the utmost care as they accustomed themselves to the machine and the lesser gravity. They had located the Dome, and as they flashed around the satellite they sent back word to Earth. Then the door of the famous Castle was discovered, and radio messages sent. This was late evening of February 6, 1982. They received no answer, and realized that the men were either dead, or so nearly so as to be unable to reach the apparatus. They strove desperately to reach the surface. Yet it was nearly noon, February 7, that they landed, a mile and three quarters from the Castle, on an open space, the abandoned road to the Dome, actually.

Hurriedly the men prepared to start, each loaded with his space suit, two tanks of oxygen, batteries for heating and light, and great quantities of food and medicines. They were: Rocket Pilot Donald Murray, Rocket Pilot James R.

Montey, Rocket Engineer and Mechanician Bruce Mac-
Gregor and Dr. James Caldwell.

They reached the sealed door of the airlock, hurriedly
glanced at the instructions, which they had already memo-
rized from Rice's messages sent over a month ago, and entered. The manuscripts inside were at once picked up, and
glanced at before any move was made to enter further.

Would the inner door open? The outer door was opened by hand, but the inner door operated electrically, and was
controlled by the pumps. MacGregor threw the lever. The
lights flashed on, and at once air rushed in, their distended
suits relaxed somewhat, and the men rapidly released the air
in them till they breathed the pure oxygen under three
pounds pressure that was the Castle's atmosphere.

The inner door swung open! A lighted corridor extend-
ed before them, branching ahead, bathed in white light from
a dozen electric lights fixed in the ceiling. The air was clean
and sweet, and from somewhere came a low, smooth drone,
a generator, and the soft sugh-chugh-sugh of air purifiers.
But no other sound!

Caldwell halloed. No answer! Their hearts sank, as
they ran forward, and turned down the corridor they knew
lead to the main Hall and the men's quarters. New tunnels
branched, tunnels not mentioned in the message sent, and
five precious minutes were wasted when they turned off into
a wrong tunnel, lighted like the others, that had thrown
Rice's careful directions askew.

They found the right one, and hurried down. In the
Hall they stopped. Seven emaciated caricatures of men lay
on seven pneumatic mattresses. A thin trickle of blood seeped
from the mouth of each, and from each finger end. Aghast
Caldwell went to the nearest, Rice it was, and listened. Living! He called out quick orders, and these men, who, when
not learning to subdue the treacherous rocket that had

brought them, had been studying the little guinea pigs, starving on artificial foods, set to work. They knew what to do even better than Dr. Hughey had. Since the last message had been exchanged, the hitherto unguessed vitamin-like RB-X had been discovered, in every form of living matter, and now armed with this they fell to. Quickly Caldwell examined. One—two—three—seven! All living now. But would they survive,

Hughey opened his eyes inside of three hours, Moore responded next. One by one—till only Whisler was left. He never opened his eyes again. Rice was last to revive, Kendall barely pulled through. But at last all were awake.

Then, with the invaluable RB-X solution, the natural foods not only weren't wanted, but were not as good as those same starving artificial food syrups, for their digestive systems were ruined. In a day they were recovering, in a week they were moving about. When the next lunar noon came around, they were almost wholly recovered, enjoying once more the Castle, and mourning the friends lost. On February 22nd at sunset, the master switches were opened, the photocell banks brought in, and the locks closed behind them. The Relief ship, loaded now with the stores of hydrogen and oxygen, with instruments and documents, and the sad cargo of the dead, was ready. As the slow sun disappeared, the ship rose, and started back to Earth, a quarter of a million miles away.

The Garner expedition was ended. The frozen hell of the Moon was left behind. But an enormous thing had been accomplished. Thirteen men, by the might of their brains, and the work of their hands, had wrested from Luna a living, and more, comfort. Had they but known of RB-X solution, they need never have feared. They had established an outpost! The Castle! What memories of the great and the famous that stirs in our minds today? Duncan—Rice—Johansen—Murgatroyd—

In five years Luna was thoroughly explored, and the Castle was the base. Mines sprang up, other, and lesser, Castles appeared; and then the Lunar Government set the Castle aside as a National Monument. But before that Johansen had used it as his base for the trip to Mars, Murgatroyd had left there, never to return, but only to send back a ceaseless stream of messages from Venus, where he exiled himself, knowing he could not return.

Today it is open to the public, with the wonderfully fine murals Kendall left as an enduring monument to the Garner Expedition, with the same crude, but staunch and dependable steam engines Rice made, the same little rocket ship, and the same generator. From the great tankrooms came the fuel that carried Johansen to Mars, and Murgatroyd to Venus.

Today the Castle is as Duncan and Rice and their friends left it, save for a few more tunnels, a few new rooms. The pool is filled now, the tanks filled with their gases.

It is an enduring monument to the adaptability, the determined resistance of Man. On the lifeless, barren Moon, they could not find comfort, so they *made* it.

And by their example, made men follow!

THE END

THE ELDER GODS

CHAPTER I

LORD NAZUN, CHIEF OF THE Elder Gods, looked down at the city of Tordu, and sighed softly. Beside him, Talun snorted angrily, a pleasant dilute odor of drying kelp and salt sea eddying about him in the soft breeze. Lady Tammar chuckled and spoke softly. "It oppresses you more than usual tonight, Talun?"

"It's sure we'll gain nothing in this way. Nazun, tell me, what was in the minds of men when we appeared first?"

Nazun stirred uneasily, a vague, lean bulk against the midnight blue of the sky. "I know, my friend—but there was a certain fear, too, that we would not change with the changing times. Perhaps that is our flaw."

"And the greater flaw," the sea lord growled, "is standing by in idleness and watching the destruction of our people. The Invisible Ones are death—death not of the body, but of the spirit and mind. Where are my sea rovers gone? Dead and decayed. Fishermen—good, stout workmen though they be—lack the spark that makes the sea rover."

"We cannot attack the Invisible Ones by attacking, by taking over the minds of our people; that is the First Law," Nazun pointed out.

"No—and ye need a solid right arm to attack the Invisible Ones, which none of us possesses. But, on the same, we possess neither a solid thing that keeps us subject to material weapons such as a solid right arm may wield!"

"You'll turn no man of Tordu against the Invisible Ones. The pattern and movement of every Azuni is so set and known to the Invisible Ones, as to us, that he would be dead at the hands of the priests of the Invisible Ones before he moved half across Tordu," Lord Martal pointed out. "There are chances in the lives of men—but not when the Invisible Ones have time to plot out those chances first!"

"No stranger has reached these islands in five centuries," Nazu sighed. "Your sea rovers, Talun, rove as close by the shore as a chick by the old hen's feet. While they rove the shorelines of the continents, they'll never find Azun . . . and without wider knowledge of the pointing needle, no seaman ventures far. It will be a century yet before men wander the oceans freely once more."

Talun's sea-squinted eyes narrowed farther. "They wander," he said explosively, "where the will of the winds drive them, my friend. Now if ye want a stranger here on these islands, we'll see what the winds and my seas can do!"

Nazun stood silent, squinting thoughtfully at the sea beyond, and the town below. "One stranger, Talun—only one. One stranger, without background known to us or the Invisible Ones, is beyond calculation and the prophecy of the gods; half a dozen strangers, and there would be more factors on which to base foreknowledge—and defeat!"

"One then," growled Talun. "One good sea rover, with a spark and flame within him that these damned Invisible Ones can't read or quench!"

Lord Nazun looked down at the wilted form on the pebbled beach with a wry, dry smile on his lips, and a twinkle of amusement in his narrowed gray eyes. "A sorry specimen you've fished up for us, Talun. And did you need to cause so violent a storm as the recent one to capture this bit of drift?"

Talun's dark face knotted in a grimace of anger, then smoothed in resignation. His roaring voice cut through the dying whine of winds and the *broom* of surf on the beach below. "I never know, Nazun, whether you mean your words. The scholars that fathered you forgot me, and forgot to give me wisdom—a sad lack in this day. That washed-up thing may be a bit bedewed, a bit softened by immersion in good brine, but he'll dry out again. And he's a man, a real man! There's more than mush in his back, and more than jelly in his heart. These Azuni men that sail by the bark of a dog and the twitter of a bird will be the vanishment of me!

"By the sea, I'd say such a storm as that last was needed to net that man! There was courage in him to build his ship on the edge of the brine, and sail straight out from land! A man who uses land as a guide only to show him how to get farthest from it quickest has my liking, and my protection."

Talun's heavy brows pulled down belligerently as he looked Nazun in the eye defiantly. Then his gaze shifted back to the man uneasily. Nazun's deep-set, narrow gray eyes were friendly, twinkling with pleasant good humor, but there was in them a depth beyond depths that left Talun, for all his own powers, ill at ease and unsettled.

Lady Tammar laughed softly. "And while you argue, he dries out. Now, good Nazun, you have netted your fish, or Talun has netted him for you and brought him to this beach. What plans have you for him next?"

"He's been well stripped," Lord Martal grunted. He waved a muscle-knotted, stout-fingered hand at the man who was beginning to stir again on the lumpy mattress of hard quartz. "He has neither gold, nor sword to carve it out with, nor any other thing. I'd say he was fitted to take advice for his next move. He could have used a sword for defense, Talun. You might have left him that. By the cut of his figure, I'd say he would sooner fight than ask for help, weapon or no."

Talun scratched his bearded chin uneasily and snorted. The dying wind permitted the faint aroma of fish to cling about the bulky figure once again in a not unpleasant intensity. More a signature or card of identity than an offense. "Your favorite irons don't float," he said, half annoyed. "The man showed sense when he parted with that when his cockleshell went down. Now leave my works alone, and let me worry about my sea. I've done my task—a man, such as you asked, at your feet, stripped as you asked, but sound. You can find him swords and breastplates enough in the junk shops of Tordus, where your ex-friends have left them, Martal. My fishermen are still with me."

Lord Martal laughed. "Good enough, friend, and right enough. We'll equip him once again. There's a house, a small temple where men worship chance and probabilities, where I may find a way to help our new-found friend. Ah, he's getting up."

Weakly, Daron pushed his elbows under him, sneezed vigorously, and gasped. He looked about him at the empty beach. The pebbles that had left a faithful imprint on every aching muscle of his back and shoulders gave way to broken rock a hundred feet away, and that in turn became a rocky cliff. Daron turned his head wearily, heaved himself erect, and dragged himself over to the nearest good-sized boulder. He held his head firmly in place till the dizziness left, then looked about. The wind was dying away but the surf still made hungry, disappointed noises on the beach as it tried to reach him.

He looked at it resentfully. "You took my ship, and you took my crew, which seems enough. Also you took from me all sense of where I am, which was more than enough to rob me of. May the gods give that there are men somewhere near—though it seems unlikely. No men of sense would inhabit so unpleasant a coast."

He looked up the beach, which curved away somewhere beyond the rain mists into a gray, formless blank. Down the beach, the high rocky cliff dwindled away just before it, too, was swallowed by the gray, wind-driven mists. Overhead, the dull gray was darkened to night, and the dull gray of his spirits darkened with it.

He followed the line of the cliff speculatively, and looked at the smug, uplifted brow of it near him. There was no sense struggling up here if it fell away to an easy slope half a mile down the beach. He heaved himself up from the boulder and started, annoyed that he had not the faintest idea whether he was moving south, east, north or west. To his sea rover's mind it was a feeling of nakedness equal to the undressed feeling the lack of his sword gave him.

Half a mile and the cliff did give way to a cragged set of natural steps. Above, he found his dizziness returned by the effort of climbing, and the beginnings of a mist-obscured meadow of some wiry grass that thrived on salt-spray. He set off across it doggedly as the gray of the skies gave way to almost total blackness. The wiry grass clutched at his toes, and he felt too weary to lift his feet above it.

Resignedly, he lay down to wait for daylight. Half an hour later, the chilling, dying wind induced him to change his mind. He stood up again and started on. The wind had swept away the last of the rain mist, and presently he made out a gleam of light that came and went erratically. He stood still, squinting his eyes, and watched.

"It may be like the pools I saw in the Dryland, a dream of something I want, but again, it may merely be that trees are blowing in front of the light. In any case, it's something other than gray mist to walk toward."

He stopped a hundred yards from the little building and

watched more carefully. Strangers were not welcome in most of the world he'd known, but a rough gauge of the way an unknown people received a stranger lay in their buildings. Sticks and wattles—the stranger was apt to be the dinner. Good timber and thatch—the stranger was welcomed to dinner, usually roast sheep or lamb. Crude stone—the stranger was allowed to enter, if he could pay for his dinner. Finished stone—the stranger was shown the way to the public house.

It augured ill. The house was built of fieldstone, well mortared. But still—they'd be less likely to make dinner of him, even though they might not make dinner for him.

He knocked, noting, for all his weariness, that the door was singularly ill-kept. It opened, and Daron paused in measurement of the man who faced him. Six feet and more, Daron stood, but the man before him was four inches more, built long and supple, with an ease and grace of movement that spoke of well-ordered muscles.

But the face eased the sea rover's mind. It was high and narrow but broad above the eyes—strange eyes—gray and deep, almost black as they looked out from the warm firelight of the room beyond. The rugged strongly hewn features were keen with intelligence; the eyes and the tiny wrinkles around them deep with a queerly eternal wisdom.

"Your coast, yonder," said Daron, his mouth twisted in a grim smile, "offers poor bedding for a man whose ship is gone, and the grass of your meadows seem wiry for human gullets. I've naught but my gratitude left to buy me a meal and a night away from the wind, but if that be good value in your land—"

The face of the native wrinkled in good-humored acquiescence as he opened the door more fully. "It is a depreciated currency, much debased with counterfeit, a strange trouble of our land. But come in, we'll try the worth of yours."

Daron stepped in, and passed his host. Rather quickly he sought a chair made of X members supporting leather bands. It creaked under his weight as he looked up at his host. "My knees have yet to learn their manners, friend, and they seemed unwilling to wait your invitation."

"Sit then. How long have you been without food?"

"Some twenty hours—since the storm came up. It's not the lack of food, I think, but the too-free drinking of the last five of those hours. Wine has made my knees as unsteady, but I liked the process better."

"I have little here to offer you—a shepherd's fare. Tordu is some two days' journey away, beyond the Chinur Mountains."

"Hm-m-m . . . then this is some expansive land I've reached. Friend . . . but stay, if I may eat, the questions and the answers both will boil more freely. If you have the bread and cheese of the shepherds I know, they'll serve most excellently to sop this water I've imbided."

"Sit here and rest, or warm yourself nearer the fire. The wind is dying, but turning colder, too." The tall man moved away, through a doorway at the far side of the stone-walled room, and Daron's eyes roved over the furnishings.

There were simple things, chairs—stools of leather straps and wooden X's, some simple, wooden slabs—a table of darkened, well-worn oak. Some sense of unease haunted Daron's mind, a feeling of decay about the smoke-grimed stone of the walls not matched by the simple furnishings.

Then his host was back with a stone jug, an oval loaf of of bread, and a crumbling mass of well-ripened cheese on an earthenware plate. He set them on the table, as Daron moved over, for the first time observing closely the dress of his host. His clothes were of some blue-green stuff, loosely draped to fall nearly to his leather-sandaled feet, bunched behind his head in a hooded cowl thrown back between the shoulders now.

Daron's quick eyes studied the fingers that set out the food even as he reached toward it. They were long, slim, supple fingers, and the forearm that stretched from the loose sleeve of the blue-green cloak was muscled magnificently with the ropey, slim, deceptive cords of the swift-actioned man's strength.

Daron's eyes rose to the face of his host. The level, gray eyes looked down into his for a long moment, and Daron shrugged easily and turned back to his food. The eyes had regarded him with honesty of good intent—and the green-robed man was his host. If he chose to call himself a shepherd within his own house, to a stranger he befriended, that, then was his business.

"I am called Nazun," his host said presently. His voice was deep and resonant, friendly, yet holding within it an air of certainty and power that the sea rover had heard in few men before. One had been his friend, and had carved out an empire. None of them had been shepherds—for long.

"I am Daron, of Kyprost—which I think you may not know. I am afflicted with a strange curse—like quicksilver, I cannot long remain in any place, yet in all my wanderings I've never heard of land that lay halfway from Western world to Eastern. And—unless I swam back in five hours over the course my vessel spent twelve days laying—this is a land I never knew existed."

"This is the island Ator, of the Azun islands. Some few of our people have sailed eastward to the borders of the great continent from which you came, but not in many generations have the Azuni been the sea rovers they once were. They wandered here from the lands you know, long ago, but now they see no joy in roving. Azun is very pleasant;

they forget the old ways and the old gods, and worship new ideas and new gods."

Daron grinned. "Pleasant, is it? It was a hard, gray place I found. But for your light, it seemed I might find no more of it, for that the wind was cooling, I found for myself before I found your door."

Daron looked up again into Nazun's eyes, his blue eyes drawn to the gray. For an instant the firelight fell strong and clear on the sun-tanned face of the giant before him. The deep-sunk gray eyes looked into his levelly, from a face set for an instant in thought, a face of undeterminable age, as such strongly hewn faces of men may be. There was kindliness about it, but in that instant kindliness was hidden by overwhelming power. Daron's careless smile dropped away so that his own strongly chiseled face was serious and intent.

The gray eyes, he suddenly saw, were old. They were very, very old, and something of the chill of the dying wind outside leaked into Daron from those eyes.

The sea rover dropped his eyes to his food, broke a bit of bread and some cheese, ate it, and washed it down with the full-bodied wine from the stone jug.

The room was quiet, strangely quiet, with only the rustle of the fire to move the drapes of silence. Daron did not look up as he spoke, slowly, thoughtfully. His easy, laughing voice was deeper, more serious. "I am a stranger to this section of the world—friend. I . . . I think I would do better if you would give me some advice as to how I might repay you for this meal, which, at this time, is life."

Nazun's voice was soft against the silence, and Daron listened without looking up. "Yes, it is a strange corner of the world, Daron. Many generations ago the Azuni came, sea rovers such as you, and settled here. They found rich land, good temperatures, a good life. For a long time they roved the sea, but Azun was home. They built a peaceful country—there were no other sea rovers then to menace them—and prospered here.

"It was a peaceful home—they stayed by it more and more. Why wander in harsher lands? The Azuni have not wandered now in many generations. There is no need. And with peace, comes wisdom. They grew too wise to worship the old gods, and found new gods—you'll learn of them, the Invisible Ones, in Tordu, the capital of Azun—in new ways.

"But you will learn of this. Primarily, for safety and for pleasure here, remember this: the Azuni know more of minds and the works of the power of mind than any people of the Earth. This power may make things uncertain for you . . . but only some of the Azuni have the full knowledge now.

"For good reasons, friend, I cannot have you here the night. Go from the door straight out. There is a broken wall of stone some two hundred paces out, which you will see by the light of the moon—the clouds are broken to a scudding wrack, now—and beyond it is a cart road. Turn right on this, and follow it along. You'll find a public house along the road within the hour. And—if someone offers you a game, accept and you may have luck. Take this—it's a small coin, but planted well, it may grow a large crop."

Daron rose from the table. Turning as he rose so that his eyes sought the glowing fire. He slipped the small silver coin into his palm, tapped his hand, and the coin spun neatly in the air to slip, edge on, between his fingers and be caught. "Aye, friend. To the right. And—I will learn later, I think, how I may return this favor. Tordu would seem to be the goal of a sound man on this island of yours."

"To the right," Nazun nodded.

Daron stepped to the door, opened it, and stepped out into the night. The moon shone through rents in the shattered cloud veil. He went on steadily to the broken wall, crossed over, and turned right. He flipped the silver coin in his fingers and noticed to himself that the bright fire in the stone house no longer shone through the windows. For that matter, the moonlight shone through the ruined roof to make a patch of light in the room beyond the shattered, unhinged door.

Daron shrugged uneasily, and remembered the friendly creases about the deep-set gray eyes and tossed the coin into a pocket with an expert flip. He swung easily down the rutted cart road.

"Nazun," he said, and cocked an eye at the scudding cloud wrack. "Now the local people might know that name—and there are other ways than asking questions to learn an answer."

CHAPTER II

T HE WIRY GRASS GAVE WAY TO
scrub, and the stunted brush to patches of trees. The stone
inn house nestled in a group of the trees, half hidden by
them, but a signpost hung out over the road to rectify that
flaw; the traveler would not miss it. Daron fingered his
single coin and squinted at the signboard as the moonlight
flickered across it like the glow of a draft-stirred candle.

"That," said Daron softly, "means 'The Dolphin,' which
would be a right goodly name for such a place, so near the
sea; but that lettering is like to none I've seen before!" He
let it go at that, and went on toward the door, with a clearer
idea in mind as to the meaning of the name of Nazun. He
had, seemingly, acquired a new fund of wisdom, a new
language!

The voices of men and the laughter of a girl came
through the heavy oaken panels of the door as he raised the
knocker; and he heard the heavy, rolling tread of the host
as he dropped it down again. The man who faced the sea
rover now was no giant, but a short, round-bellied little man
with a face all creases, sprouting seedling whiskers of a red
beard as the only clue to what his vanished hair might once
have been.

"Aye, and come in, for though the night is bettering, it's
foul enough yet, my friend."

Daron smiled in answer to the infectious good humor

of the innkeeper. "And who knows better than I? Pray your drinks are better than brine, for I've had my fill of that, and your beds are better than the quartz the waves laid me out on. I've lost a ship, a crew, a sword, and all but one silver coin." Daron looped it upward so it glinted in the light of a hanging lamp and the glow of the fire.

The innkeeper's smile-creased mouth pursed worriedly. "Your luck seems bad, and . . . and your coin small," he said doubtfully.

"Ah, but you think too quickly, friend," laughed Daron. "Look, out of a crew of a dozen stout lads, I lived. You say my luck is bad? Out of all that I possessed, this bit of silver stayed with me like a true friend and you think it will leave me now?

"Now let us test this thing. Look; I want a bit of meat, a bit of bread, and perhaps some wine. You want my coin. Fair enough, but you say my luck is bad, which is a curse on any seaman. Let's see, then; we'll try this coin. If it falls against me, it is yours, and I seek another place for food. If it is the friend I say—"

The innkeeper shrugged. "I am no worshipper of Lord Martal, and I've no faith in the luck he rules. Go back through yonder door, and you'll find his truest worshipers in all Ator, I swear. They gamble away two fortunes in an evening, and gamble it back between 'em. But they gamble away my wine, and pay for that, wherefore they're welcome. Perhaps I should thank Lord Martal at that."

Daron chuckled. "By all means, man! He smiles on you, and the old gods are good protectors, I feel." The seaman swung across the little entrance room toward the curtained entrance to the main dining hall beyond. The smoke-stained oaken beams hung low enough to make him stoop his head as he pushed the curtain aside and looked beyond. A dozen men, some in well-worn, stout clothing bearing the faintly

sour, wholly pleasant odor of the sea, some with the heavier
smells of earth and horses, clustered about a table where five
men in finer clothes were seated. Three girls, in tight-bodiced,
wide-skirted costumes watched and moved about to fill the
orders of the men.

None saw him at first, as they watched the play of the
dice that leaped and danced on the dark wood of the table
top. Daron moved over, and some of the outer fringe looked
up at him, their boisterous voices quieting for an instant,
then resuming at his easy grin and nod. The ring of farming
people and the fishermen made way a bit, uncertain by his
dress, for, sea-stained and flavored, it showed fine-woven
cloth of good linen, worked in an unfamiliar pattern with
bits of gold and silver wire.

The seated men looked up at him, and back at the dice,
and rolled again. Daron leaned forward, putting his wide-
spread hands on the table. "My friends," he said seriously,
"I have an unpleasant mission here. My ship is lost, my
crew is gone, and all possessions left me save this coin." The
single silver bit clinked down. "Our good host has said my
luck is foul; I feel that it is good. Wherein does this con-
cern you? It is this; if I would sleep softer than the stones
outside, and eat fare tenderer than twigs, I must plant this
seedling coin and reap a harvest. I fear it is from your
pockets, then, the harvest must come."

The nearest of the players laughed, spun Daron's coin,
and nodded. "One stake, friend, and we'll finish the work the
seas began! A man with such a thing is hard put—it would
buy a bit of food, or a bed, but not both, and the decision
would be hard. We shall relieve you!"

"Now, by Nazun, you won't, I feel!" Daron laughed—
and watched their eyes.

The player shook his head and laughed. "Now by the
Invisible Ones, I know we shall. If you still put your faith

in outworn gods, it is small surprise they stripped you thus."

Daron relaxed, and nodded to himself. "We shall see."

"And," said the holder of the dice, passing them to Daron, "this is no field for Nazun, for there's no wisdom in these bits of bone. If the old gods appeal to you, why then Martal, I'd say, would be the one you'd swear by here."

"No wisdom in the dice—no, that may be. But wisdom may reside in fingers, thus?" Daron spun out the three polished cubes, and saw them turn a five, a five and a six. "What would you have me throw?"

"I'll take your stake," said the hawk-nosed player to Daron's right. "Better this.' His fingers caressed the dice, spun them, and shot them forth. They settled for a total of twelve.

"With two dice, I'd match it, with three—" Daron's roll produced fourteen. "But even so," as he picked up two silver coins, "we need some further crops. A bed and board I have, but Tordu is farther than a seaman walks. A horse, I think—Will some one match me more?"

A sword filled the scabbard at his thigh, and a good dirk was thrust in his belt, a horse was his, and money for a day or two when he sought his bed that night. He whistled a bit of a tune as he laid aside his things, dropped the thick oak bar across the door, and settled for sleep. "I'll say this for this land," he muttered, "very practical gods they have. Unique in my experience. They do a man very material good turns. Wisdom, it is, eh? I thought as much—"

The sun was bright, the air warm, but not uncomfortable, and the horse better even than the lamp's weak light had suggested in the night, when Daron started off. The cart road had broadened to a highway, and this to one well-traveled within a pair of hours. The scrub bush and sheep-dotted meadows gave way to farmlands bordered with fences growing neatly from the ground, well-barbed fences of some cactus bush for which the sheep showed sound respect.

There was little timber here, but under the clear sun, the meadowlands and farms stretched off into pleasantly blue-hazed distance, where the banking of the haze seemed to indicate a mountain range stretching off from east to west. The road led south, but like most farmland roads, seemed unconcerned with haste and directness. It visited from door to door and rolled aside when some small swale of land suggested climbing hills. The horse was sound and strong, seeming to have a nature as blithe as Daron's own, with little mind to bother a fair day about a change in masters.

Toward noon, the rising ground began to show some signs of timber, and the stone-walled farm cottages began to trail attendants in wooden walls, and sheep appeared again more frequently. The haze rolled up by the rising sun still banked to the south, but the shining gleam above it indicated that the haze had retreated to solid mountain fastnesses, with a snow-crowned peak above.

The sun was warmer now, and where a small stream trickled through a woodpatch, Daron dismounted, tethered his mount to a bush near the stream, and spread his food. He ate, and leaned back in easy contemplation and thought. The wandering breeze brought some faint hint to him of a visitor, and his swift thoughts placed his line of action before the odor was more than identifiable to him. He looked up with a smile as the footsteps of the newcomer crunched on the twigs nearby.

He saw a wind-blown, sun-tanned man, rather stocky and heavily muscled, with eyes squinting permanently from the glare of the sun on water. A sailor's cap perched solidly on his round, dark-haired head. A black stubble of beard showed on his heavy jowls and on his thick, muscular arms, and an impudent tuft thrust out from each ear.

"My friend," said Daron, "you're a way from the sea, which, by your gait, would be more homelike to you."

The stocky one seated himself with a grunt. "Aye, and the same to you. Those linens were never stained in a brook, and, unless you ride yon horse lying on your back, it's not the sweat of your beast.

"Bound for Tordu?"

"One I met last night named such a city. I am not familiar with this country—a remarkable land I find it—and it seemed the part of wisdom to seek the center of the place. And, by the bye, men call me Daron."

"Talun," grunted the stocky one, seemingly annoyed. "Tordu's a foul place for an honest seaman, though seamen of that ilk seem fewer with every season. The whole race of Azuni have grown soft and stupid, and the stupidest have gathered in Tordu to admire their overweening stupidity. They have no sense or judgment, and they shun the sea like the plague. Time was when the Bay of Tor was a harbor." Tahun snorted disgustedly. "They've got it cluttered so with fancy barges now no merchant ship can enter, and they've set a temple to those precious Invisible Ones of theirs across the mouth of the bay—they call it Temple Isle now; it used to be the finest shipyard in Azun—and their slinking Invisible Ones hang over the bay mouth till the good clean sea stays out in disgust."

"Invisible Ones? Hm-m-m. I'm somewhat unacquainted here, though I've heard a dozen times of these Invisible Ones—not including several references to them, both prayerful and annoyed last night, from certain gentlemen of the countryside I gamed with—but little explanation of them. Gods, are they?"

"Gods?" Talun snorted angrily. "They pray to them as to gods, and say they are not gods. The people of Tordu are fools and crazed ones at that. 'No gods,' they say. They scorn the old gods of their fathers, for say they, the old gods are foolishness—made in the image of men, and hence no more than projected men and the power of men's minds. The true god-being, these wise thinkers say, is certainly no man, a thing of force in form mere mortal mind cannot conceive. So they build themselves these Invisible Ones, and give them power, and curse the old gods.

"They're fools, and have no wisdom, and admire each other's mighty thoughts."

"The wise thinkers, eh?" mused Daron. "We have such thinkers in my land, and we have certain other thinkers who have one certain trait that sets them off—a remarkable thing. They think long, study much, and confess to those who ask that they learn steadily that they know little. Some think that a crabwise way to knowledge—but I am prejudiced; I learned from such a man."

Talun stirred uneasily, and his squinted eyes turned upward to the clear blue bowl of the sky. The blistering sun was burning down from it to his face, but as he stared upward a fleecy cloud formed, rolled, expanded and hid the sun. Talun settled back comfortably.

"Learning never appealed much to me. One of my friends—but not to me. The wisdom of the fools appeals not so strongly to the countrymen, nor to the sailors, and on that alone these Invisible Ones would gain no strength, for these thinkers are few, if noisy with their thoughts.

"But another thing has influenced them," continued Talun. "The gods, these deep thinkers say, should know the future—else what's the use of consulting gods? Now the old gods did not know—or did not explain, at least."

Daron sat more upright, looked harder at this stocky, hairy figure, the very image of a sailor or fisherman, from whom the shifting breezes brought a gentle tang of salt and fish and drying kelp. "Your gods, in this land, are most unique to me," said Daron softly. "Perhaps men have a certain reservation in their thoughts of gods in other lands—a thought that a god is some vague thing, whose statue man may carve, and to whom offerings may be made, but a remote being who does strangely little manifest for his worshipers . . . Now the gods of this country, I find, are most substantial beings—and most helpful. The Lord of Chance, of Contests, let us say: he wished me well last night, I think." Daron nodded toward the browsing horse. "Now if a people blessed by gods who have such usefulness complain, it would seem they set hard standards indeed."

Talun grumbled and rolled over. Daron cast an eye upward; alone in the blue vault of the sky the single white fleece of cloud remained motionless between them and the sun, casting a pleasant tempering shade. "Men want more than they have—and that, my friends tell me, is good, and the reason seems enough," answered Talun. "If a man be satisfied with what he has, why surely, he will get no more. If a man catch a dozen fish, which is enough to feed his wife and a child, and fish no more, I'd think little of his courage, or his sense.

"But now this knowing the future. It is not always good. These wise thinkers of Tordu, they put it that the gods should know, and the gods should tell men—and their Invisible Ones do. But the priests of the Lord of Wisdom, the wisest of the old gods, say gods should know—but should not explain all things."

"Why not?" asked Daron.

"If a god should tell you that this night you would wager your horse against a slave girl, and lose both girl and horse on a toss of the dice what would you do?"

"Why, sure I'd be a fool indeed to wager then!"

"Whereby, if you do not, you make a liar of the god," said Talun with a snort. "The god's prophecy of the future was not accurate, for you did not. Now such a prophecy the old gods made. 'If' might the priest report, 'you cast your nets at Seven-Fathom Bank, you'll snare a swordfish and spend three days mending nets.' Now the fishermen would not, but would lose a good day's fishing, and rumble that the prophecies were vague.

"But these Invisible Ones; they have no vagueness. They tell a man, 'As you walk home this night a horse shall kick and break your skull. Farewell, worshiper!'" And, that night the man is dead. He swears no horse shall come near him—they did at first—but the prophecy is right, of course. If the Invisible Ones read future right, then that must be his fate. If he has wit to escape that end, why then he's made a liar of the gods." Talun dropped one heavy lid, and his dark-blue eye speared Daron sharply. "And, young friend, old gods or new, no mortal man makes a liar of the gods!"

"That calls for thought," sighed Daron. "I see no joy in knowing my end if I have no hope of changing it."

Talun grunted and stretched himself up. "Nor did the country folk or fishermen at first. But try a human with that thought for long, and not even the gods will make him stand firm. Live a year beside a temple of these Invisible Ones, knowing every day that there you can find sure and absolute the day and manner of your death—No. Men are mortal, and they fear old Barak, the dread god of their mortality, but the sharp, itching bite of curiosity will drive them on. You've seen the countryman twist the ox's tail to drive it in the pen in which the ox can smell death? So curiosity sends men into that temple which they know means loss of hope."

Talun shrugged. "Once there—what man has courage and will to walk away? They sink like wine sots, drunk with future knowledge, giving up all strength and drive of spirit, for the Invisible Ones tell them what is coming—and they know it will come, try how they may, so you may be sure they do not try.

"Go your way, friend. I have business at times in Tordu, too, so I may see you again." Talun wandered off through the woodpatch and vanished behind a tree.

Daron lay back to stare at the cloud. It hung still precisely between the sun and the spot where Talun had sat. But it was evaporating rapidly now, and presently the blue vault of sky was clear. Daron chuckled as he untethered his horse and swung onto his back. Convenient, that trick.

His horse trotted on easily across the plain, passing a farm wagon here, neighing to a browsing horse along the way, and Daron sat straight and thought. A notion formed at the back of his mind that Talun had not altogether been a friend. That storm that took his ship and crew—

Well, it was evident he had a mission here, and surely no higher adventure had he sought than this! With gods like those this land boasted—they did not seem a stingy lot!

The day passed, and he stopped that night in another inn, the Sheath and Scythe, it was, and the men who drank the lank, cadaverous host's wine had no smell of sea or fish about them. The heavy, earthy smell that permeated the inn was thick to Daron's sea-trained nostrils.

Experimentally, he tossed the dice again this night. He lost three throws, won two, and knew his answer. What he needed, seemingly was his—but these gods did not take the spice of gambling from him by constant winning. He settled down then, and what Martal's help did not bring him a certain deftness of fingering did. The night grew fatter then, when he found that, somehow, this land had never learned the mighty magic of the three snail shells and the pebble.

Content, and more than warmed by good wine—his shells had betrayed him with clumsiness, else he'd have stayed longer—he went to sleep.

CHAPTER III

WITH A SAILOR'S INSTINCT, FOR all his hoofed carrier, Daron found his way to the docks of Tordu straightway—and snorted as he saw them. No smell of good fish and bad, no circling, wide-winged argosies of gulls. The broad, V-shaped Bay of Tor spread out, its mouth plugged by the Temple Isle, its waves showering familiar gold and diamond back to the blue skies and the sun. But the clean, salt-and-fish smell of any coastal sea was gone, buried, drowned away in a scent that reeked in the sea rover's nostrils. Incense! The bay was dotted with hoggish, bloat-belly barges, with white canvas mocked in pretty silks, good yellow cordage tinseled with golden threads.

The final insult to the sea was the crews. Girls! Golden-tanned pink skins, and dainty figures playing seamen! Slave girls with beribboned chains of gold pulling at the oars that drifted the silly barges out.

Daron groaned. The sailor's eye roved round the harbor, and his sea rover's soul writhed in anguish. High, granite-glinting cliffs, impregnable to any storm, formed a solid wall broken in two deep, sharp clefts, the twin mouths of the bay. Set like a grim, squat fort across it was the island, a grim, stanch island of black, pinnacled basalt bedecked with carved and spidery-lined temples, beflowered with beds of plants in artificial soil.

Here was a harbor the gods had made impregnable!

They'd set across its mouth such harsh defenses as no sea could smash, nor any force of men invade, for but a few score of good catapults could make those deep-cloven channels—wide enough for peaceful shipping—invulnerable to all assault.

Yet the great walls of granite fell away in rapid slopes so that the city of Tordu, at the head of the bay, straddling the Tor River, was on a level beach-front.

And barges—pretty barges mocking galleys with their silly, slim slave girls—monopolized this port!

Daron clunked his heels disgustedly against the stout ribs of his horse, and turned his back on the place. The horse *plop-plopped* away in an easy trot, while Daron's ire mounted within him. The horse, not Daron, avoided the rumbling carriages of gaily decked men and women, skirted the shore-side area of marble-fronted shops selling things for temple decorations and offerings.

Even the sound of this section of the city was unlike any Daron had known before. It rang with the voices of men and women, as any good town must, and the creak and *plop* of harness and horses' hoofs. But the ringing jingle of good steel swords, the strong, hard ring of vital, active voices was gone. The calls were vague, unimportant, even to themselves; the faces of the men were interested, but more from seeking interest than because they found interest in each small thing of life.

Daron drove westward across the city, away from the bay. The level of the ground swelled upward gently, and the street was bordered by high, plastered walls, tinted white and pale blues and greens and pinks, as pale as the life force of this silly city.

Then the ground dropped down again; and as it fell, the view of the bay was lost behind, and the large estates that hid behind those plastered walls shrank quickly. The

broad street split, and narrowed—and Daron began to look
about more keenly. The pale color of the walls gave way,
the pale, soft voices changed, the timbre of the city's sounds
changed, and the smoky, spicy scent of incense gave way
with it. From the east a breeze was sweeping the smell of
a true city, the odor of foods and men and the green of
growing things.

A good two miles back from the bay he found the sector
he sought. The men were taller, heavier; two women leaned
from nearby windows listening with hand-cupped ears to
the angry voices floating from a neighboring house. The
sweetly sour smell of wine floated out of a whitewashed inn,
and the smell of hay turned the horse's nose to the stable
yard as easily as the other turned his master's course.

Daron dropped the reins into the hand of the boy that
roused himself from whistling lethargy to split his freckled
face in a friendly grin. "You've seen a man become a fool
with the aid of wine?" said Daron gruffly.

The boy's eyes rounded. "My . . . my father runs the
inn—"

"A horse may do the same with food and water. Feed
the beast, but mind he's no more sense than you, so feed him
light, and water him gently." Daron grinned, and a coin
flashed suddenly in the air and winked into nothingness as
the boy's hand moved.

Daron swung from the courtyard to the street, and filled
his lungs with a grunt of satisfaction. The air had not the
tang of clean sea sweeps but the insult of the incense was
out of his nostrils. He blinked his eyes and entered the inn.

A half dozen townsmen, in loose armless cotton shirts
that slipped on over their heads, and woolen breeches falling
loose to their knees, contracting sharply to mold the shins,
looked at his different garb. The shirts were blue or green
or yellow, but all the breeches were brown.

Daron grinned. "You've a good eye for color, lads, but tell me this; is it good brown earth or dye that makes your breeches match?"

One of the townsmen looked casually round the room and chewed on something slowly before replying. "And where would you be from, stranger? It's clear you never heard of the Elder Vows."

"That might be, and that might be an answer. What is this Elder Vow? And is it the custom here, too, that the host so hides himself a guest goes thirsty?"

"No guest goes thirsty, but the host wears no more badge than does the guest." The man rose slowly, unfolding from behind his table like an endless python pouring from his hole. Lank as a ship's mainmast, he towered over Daron, his long arms dangling downward like wet rags hung out to dry.

Daron stepped back and eyed him up and down. "By Talun, now, you'd serve as jury-rig in any tall-sparred ship! If your drinks be as long as you, then there's good value for the money here! Give me something cool and wet that has less of the vinegar than the wine I've had since I landed on this shore."

The innkeeper grinned, leaned slightly, and plucked a cobwebbed bottle from a little door that sprung open at his touch, put it on the table and gestured broadly. "You've learned the trouble of the wines here quick enough.

"Now as to the color of our breeches; it seems small account of yours, but a long morning makes for easy talk, so sit. The answer's short enough, but there's little joy in short answers."

Daron smacked his lips and sighed contentedly. "Hm-m-m . . . a drink at last that wouldn't eat its way through marble stones! Let's hear this answer then, be it long or short. I'll leave when my business presses."

"I'm a fool," said the innkeeper sadly. "My friends"—
he waved his queerly flexible long arm— "are fools. My
foolishness—our foolishness—lies in this; we like to think
that what we strive for we get, and what we get we get by
striving for."

"A sound-seeming thought. Wherein lies the foolishness?"

The lanky one waved his arm again. "The street is full
of those who will tell you. The temples on the isle are full
of Invisible Ones and priests who will prove it for you.

"We go to the Older Gods. We wear these breeches to
save us headaches."

Daron cocked his head. "A curious custom. In the Dryland, where once I was, there was a race of men who wrapped a white cloth about their heads to keep it cool and save
them headaches, but this trick of wrapping the nether end
seems somewhat strange. Still, one cannot tell. It seemed
insane enough—that wrapping up the head to keep it cool—
until I tried it, after twice finding that the sun was no puny
light for man's convenience there. So I suppose you have
some logic in your acts."

The man on the innkeeper's left blinked his eyes slowly,
combed a full, spade-shaped beard of curly hairs, and patted
a pate as bald as an empty seascape. "We tried wrapping our
ears. The worshipers of the Invisible Ones still argued. So
we wore the brown breeches and simply knocked down those
who argued with us. A year or so—and they stopped argu-
ing."

"By Nazun, that's wisdom!" Daron laughed. "But still
I seek the explanation of the foolishness of striving for your
wants."

"I," said the innkeeper, "am Shorhun." He stopped and
chewed thoughtfully, looking at his sandaled foot.

"Daron, I'm called."

"If I go to the Temple Isle, the Invisible Ones will tell me whether or not the landlord of this place—who believes that I am a fool because I do not go—is going to throw me forth into the street. Incidentally, I'd be a fool in truth to seek an answer from the Invisible Ones on that; I know he is. But they might also tell me where I next will go, and whether I will prosper. Say that they say I will. The Invisible Ones prophesy always what *will* happen. Wherefore, if they say I will prosper, it will mean little to me what I do. It seems no prize of my good effort. If, through carelessness, I crack my plate on yonder doorframe, even that I prefer to think of as my own, my personally blundering act. If the Invisible Ones prophesy it—why, I have yet to crack my pate, and lack the satisfaction of cursing myself for a blind and imbecilic nitwit in the doing of it.

"Wherefore it is foolishness. I should go and learn my fate and then sit back to live it, like a twice-told tale, mumbling in my teeth as my pre-known date of death draws near.

"No, I prefer old Nazun. He deals in warning of things he well knows will not happen, I suppose—things I am warned against and, by avoiding, avoid trouble. Things—so the Invisible Ones say—I was not fated to meet in any case." Shorhun shrugged, a mighty thing that started like a tidal wave running up a narrow bay to crash in final jerkings at his head.

"I had thought," said Daron slowly, "to see the temples of the Old Gods. I saw none near the bay front."

Shorhun barked, a laugh that seemed half cadaverous cough. "Talun's Temple moved first. It fell to pieces one night with a mighty roaring and cursing, a sound that satisfied my feelings in its depth and originality, if it did disturb me next day in seeing his retreat."

"Eh? Talun was driven from his temple?"

"Aye. The old sea lord brought down a storm that ripped up every tree and all the nearly planted gardens of the Temple Isle, but that stubborn basalt was a bit too much for him. The isle stood."

"But what drove him out?" Daron asked intently.

Shorhun barked—or coughed—again. "Incense," he said lugubriously. "Before Tan Lormus, High Priest of the Invisible Ones invented that, old Talun came near to driving out the pretty barges of the rich devotees of the Invisible Ones. Talun, like the true Old God he is, was using only natural things—though the number of fish that died on the beach that year was natural only by a wide stretch of allowance."

Daron burst into a roar of laughter till the tears rolled down his leathery cheeks. "Praise be Talun! Now that was an idea well worthy of the sea rover's god, and may this Tan Lormus live again in a fish's body for his rupture of so fine a plan!"

"But Talun moved," sighed Shorhun. "And the others moved after him, one by one, till last of all sweet Lady Tammar moved. She lacked not for worshipers, even with the Invisible Ones, for, Invisible Ones or not, men and women yet must have love, and no fine thoughts or wise prophecy can satisfy in place of that."

"But—she moved? The bay, foul as it may be for a sailor's eye, might still, with a good round moon, be a goodly place in a lover's eye," said Daron.

"It was—it was. But Lady Tammar is strangest of the gods in many ways. Lady of Love, she is all loves, all things to all men. She is the strong adventurer's companion mate, as strong as he, and as faithful. She is the young man's first love, very young, and never wise. She is the mature man's wife—his ideal of her, understanding, wise, forever ready to aid him in his troubles. But—she is, too, the fop's simpering coquette, for she is the ideal of every man, however weak that ideal may be.

"So she moved back, back from the bay and its lack of common men in honest need. Lady Tammar had no joy in appearing thus to any man."

Daron sipped quietly at his wine. "I think," he said softly, "that I must see the new temple of Tammar."

Shorhun shook his great head slowly, and a little smile touched his face, changing it from the harsh look of weather-slit granite. "You can go—but Lady Tammar is wise. She does not appear to every man—for every man cannot find his perfect ideal, save in Tammar herself. And she is for no man. Once each month I go to her temple; three times she has appeared to me, and I go always in hopes. My wife is dead, and Tammar—

"But you can go."

"Are all the temples of the Old Gods near together?" asked Daron.

"Near together, yes. But some six miles beyond Tordu, six miles up the slopes of Mt. Kalun, looking out across the city to the sea."

"I think that I shall go there, then. There are inns near-by"

Shorhun shook his head slowly. "None nearer than Tordu. The Old Ones ruled it thus. Only the priests and priestesses and the temple people live on Mt. Kalun."

"Then this shall be my home. And—you have a tailor who could produce such fine brown breeches for me, per-haps?"

CHAPTER IV

DARON SNIFFED, AND HIS HEAD nodded approval to the easy motion of the horse. There was incense here, on this road up Mt. Kalun, to the temples of the Old Gods—but incense he liked. The smell of spicy pine tar, baked from the tall, straight trees in the hot sun. The high air here was clear and crisp as a sea breeze, cleared by the luminous green masses of the trees.

The horse stopped abruptly, blew through his nostrils vigorously, and looked back at his rider. Daron laughed and patted the arching, sweaty neck. "Enough, my friend? A bit of climb it is. Good, then, it's near high noon, for all we started early. Tammar's temple has stood these good few years, and will, I think, wait while we rest. And Tammar . . . well, Lady Tammar has lasted longer still. We'll stop—and there's a nicely sheltered place." Daron slid off his mount, threw the reins over the animal's head, and led him off the trail. A hundred yards to the right, the pine-needle carpet of soft brown gave way to a little clearing, green with grass.

From the saddlebags, Daron lifted a flask of wine, wrapped in a dozen layers of crushed green leaves, wilted now and somewhat dried. But the wine within was pleasantly cooled. A loaf of bread, and a cut of meat was food enough, and Daron settled comfortably. The horse was browsing at the grass, and blowing annoyedly. He was a lowland horse, it seemed, and the effects of some seven thousand feet of altitude were puzzling to him.

Hidden beyond the stand of straight-trunked pines, the road that led up to the temples carried a sprinkling of other visitors—hardy countrymen and tough-muscled seamen, the common men who had the will and muscle, too, to climb that narrow track.

No carriage road—those who came this way did not so from indolence and lack of other occupation, but because their minds and spirits drove them on. Daron, himself unseen, watched the steady, strong-backed walk of a man browned with the sun, hands dark with rich brown soil, bearing an offering of ripe, round melons slung in twin sacks across his shoulders.

"Now there," said Daron, his eyes closed down to slits of concentration, "goes a man who knows his mind. No fine-tongued orator would quickly move him to war—but, I would be loath to meet his kind as an enemy."

A pair of sailors, the breeze bringing even here the good, round talisman of their calling and proof of the god they'd worship, went noisily up the trail, blowing, laughing, rolling slightly in their walk, spurring each the other with insults of his weakness. Blowing like a hard north gale on this small slope? The wine had washed away his strength!

"Gods," said Daron to himself, "have little need of help in working miracles—but these gods of Azun be strange gods. Why might a god call on a man for help? Why, to lead and work with other men. A god is no doubt a mighty leader—but men and gods are different things. I'd fight for a god in whom I found just cause—but not behind such a one. There would seem to me a certain delicacy in the question. A man who leads against the enemy is credited not perhaps with skill, but in any case with more than jelly up his spine.

"But a god? An immortal god? Is courage needed for one who cannot die to face a deadly foe? And would such anomalous courage hearten those strong, if odorous, fishers? Why, the god might be courage itself—but still lack proof, where he cannot die or feel steel cutting!

"So—perhaps this is a certain question of leading men against those foppish ones that rule Tordu. Foppish—but from the nice-kept stable yards I saw, well mounted. And your mounted cavalry is a savage thing for simple farming men to face, no matter how ill-trained the mounted man may be."

Daron looked out and down. Two giant old pines, their trunks scaled like yellow-brown bodies of gigantic, uprearing serpents, had throttled out lesser competition to the northeast. Between their mighty boles, Tordu was visible, a sprawl of white and green and pastel blues against the green-brown farming land. The sparkling blue of the bay, with the white-crowned Temple Isle across its mouth mocked up at him with tiny, bright-ribboned barges plying slowly back and forth on languid oars, like water beetles crawling across a puddle.

Daron fingered a single coin tucked well down in one pocket, and looked out across the town. "Tammar I'll see— I think—for this bit of silver should be more than coin, keeping in mind its source. And gods do not favor mortals for naught, and if this Nazun, chief of Azuni's gods, sees fit to speak to me, why Tammar—"

He paused, his slit-narrow, night-blue eyes widening and easing away the straight furrows of concentration. Mixed visions swam before his mind—oval faces framed in spun-golden hair, with wide-opened eyes like sapphires staring out in seeming wonder, and black-haired heads, round and olive-skinned, with black-jet eyes. Tall bodies willowy slim, and lithe as temple dancers, figures strong and tall and fine, free-swinging, life-loving—

He shook his head and laughed. "No one—but part of all, perhaps. But Lady Tammar will know—and be, if Shor-hun tells me right." He leaned back, eyes rising to the vault-ed roof of interlacing, dark-green boughs.

A footstep near brought his eyes down, and his hand shifted half an inch to reach in one flashing drive, if need should be, the long, well-balanced weapon at his side. His hand fell away, his eyes narrowed, then widened slowly as a smile overspread his tanned face.

"You are too late, good friend. My wine is gone, my meat and bread consumed—and I cannot repay a meal of some few evenings gone. But my accomodations here are good in many ways. The seats are soft, the needles pad them well, and keep away the ground's damp chill. Would you be seated?"

Nazun's gray eyes smiled, and his head nodded easily. His lean, muscular body folded gracefully, till he was seated at the base of a mighty pine, facing Daron's curious eyes. Nazun's eyes flickered swiftly over horse, silver-mounted saddle, Daron's good and well-stitched clothing, and the jewel-hilted sword he carried. "A single coin has seeded well, since last we met."

Daron laughed easily. "One crop it raised—but the next night I found a planted pebble—planted beneath the shelter of three small snail shells—grew better still in the good soil of Azun."

Nazun's eyes laughed, and he nodded gravely. "Strange plants flourish well where the ground has not been sowed before. Yet the thing is very old."

"Perhaps," said Daron, "you could tell me its age?" He looked at Nazun's grave, unchanging face through narrowed eyes.

Nazun shook his head. "I've seen this earth somewhat longer than you, Daron, but that is older still. What legends of antiquity do your people know, Daron?"

Daron's gaze swung up to watch the bowing, swaying, stately dance of dark green boughs against a clear blue sky. His long, powerfully muscled figure looked relaxed and easy, his dark-green jacket blending here, and his gray-blue woolen breeches loose and floppy about well-corded legs. His face looked blankly easy—save for the eyes, where fine networks of tiny creases gathered about the night-blue eyes peering upward at the moon-blue heavens.

"Legends? Legends—and this Nazun is no mortal man, but Lord of Wisdom. Now legends are for children's ears, it seemed to me, but—but I am not Lord of Wisdom." Daron's thoughts flashed swiftly over years and nations—and legends. A pattern formed abruptly in his mind, a pattern he'd never seen before, and with his understanding, he started so he moved and looked deep in Nazun's eyes.

"Now by the gods!" said Daron, soft-voiced. "I've seen a hundred nations, and heard a hundred tales, and spent long nights around the fires to the music of the ballads and the thrill of long-drawn legends. I've heard how Bummeur of the Tutz nations defeated Lacoor of the Parrys from the Tutz balladeers. And, two nights later, heard how, in that self-same battle, Lacoor of the Parrys drew Bummeur of the Tutz to follow his retreat, and trapped him—from a balladeer in Par.

"But in the Tutz ballads, and in those of the Parrys, in those of every nation I have met, there is one common basis of ancient, ancient legend, stories older than the histories of nations. Once men were gods—and flew in air. And men were gods, to ride on fire, beyond the air, and spoke with the voices of gods, heard across all Earth, from nation to nation, and they had thunderbolts of gods.

"But men were men—not gods. They flew on their wings, and loosed their thunderbolts at one another, till each had stripped all godhood from the other. And—men were men, and grubbed in ground again, and rode the air no more, but plodded earth on old Shank's mare.

"Now a man may lie, and having taken council aforehand, a dozen men may lie, and lie alike. But when a hundred men, in a hundred nations, men who have never met, lie the same fine tale—there's more than lying there!"

Nazun's gray eyes twinkled, deep beneath their shadowing brows, and his head nodded lazily. "I've heard such legends among the peoples of Azuni—and one legend heard only here. That, when man stripped man of god-like powers, and the world rocked and heaved in torture to their thrusts, lands sank and new lands rose from the sea-beds. The island group that is Azun rose from the seas then, and some hundred peaceful men, who had certain wisdom of those things that made for godhood, took council. Now tell me, friend, if the nations tore like mad dogs at each other's throats and every nation was embroiled, and new lands rose from the sea—"

"I," said Daron, "would found a new nation on that untainted land."

Nazun nodded slowly, settled back against the tree and looked up to where a scarlet-breasted bird cocked wary eyes downward before he drew back his head to rap a resounding tattoo on the great trunk. "Now," said Nazun, looking upward, "let us think what wise men might do—in days when the world was mad with bloodlust and mighty powers. Say you were such a refugee that settled here on Ator, largest of this Azun group."

His eyes wandered down again to rest on a hopping bird fighting with a stubborn worm. "That bird there walks, but he can fly, thanks to a certain mechanism—a sort of machine that he was gifted with. Pity we have not that machine."

Daron cocked a squinted eye, and watched the triumphant bird gobble quickly, ruffle his feathers, crouch and leap into the air. "I've tried a thousand times to do the same," the sea rover sighed. "I've seen coasts no ship could reach, and no walking man could find. And the bird flew where I could not." He shrugged. "I could not make such mechanism."

"But once—men were, the legends say, near godlike —men might have had the wit for that, perhaps," suggested Nazun.

"Ah," said Daron softly, and watched the bowing, dancing, swirling limbs above his head. Thoughts flashed through his mind such as he'd never contemplated. Gods, or godlike, the legends said. But—if their godhood had rested in mechanisms, in cleverness of tool and trickery—that was a sort of godhood one could well strip away, as one force took the catapults of another, to leave them helpless, wandering in rout.

"They'd need," said Nazun's soft, almost dreaming voice, "most wonderful tools for that, no doubt. Better, finer tools than we. Springs, perhaps, of a steel better than we know, and mighty forges to make the steel."

The picture roiled and cleared in Daron's mind. That was the source of legend, then! They had been godlike, those men of old! But their godhood had rested in machines—and the tools to make the machines. Once smash those tools— and machines wore out, with no more tools to replace them—

"They," said Daron slowly, "had wit, perhaps, but, it seems, more trickery than godhood. Wit, knowledge—but no judgment, and wisdom is also judgment."

"Men's minds are strange, are they not, my friend? And little known. Had such ones, as these ancient legends speak of, known more of themselves, perhaps their godlike knowledge of the things they bent to toys might have made them gods indeed."

Daron looked closely at the pine-needle-strewn ground on which he sat, and thought. There was a story here—a further story. Gods did not speak to men to while away the time. There would be reward, perhaps, but also—when the affairs of gods were concerned, and mortal men were brought to enter—danger, adventure! "Had I escaped," said Daron softly, "from a world, and founded on an island, unmolested, a new city, a new nation, having some remnant of that godlike knowledge—I think I would forget it. I think, perhaps, more knowledge of myself would make life worthier to myself. How does man think—and how go mad? Some say a demon enters the spirit of the mad, and some say only that his mind is sick, like the belly with a colic. And some are only queer, and growing somewhat queerer, we say are mad.

"I know the thousand riggings of a hundred nations' ships—and know not how that knowledge lodges in my skull. I think, were I to build a new nation on the wreckage of that old, I'd learn myself a bit, before I tried the rebuilding of such powers as once destroyed men."

"And wait, before you learned again those things, till every man in all the race had judgment enough to carry burning brands through the granary of man without setting fire? Wait, as the ages passed, till there was not, and never would be again, a madman to loose the spark? Yes," said Nazun softly, "that would be—safe, at least."

Daron laughed, and nodded slowly. "Safe," he chuckled, "and stupid, as the turtle in his shell. We need—Oh!" said Daron suddenly, and looked at Nazun with a sudden, overwhelming understanding. "Man needs a *god, or godlike guide who acts, who interferes to direct man upward as he longs, and halt the downward settling of his urge!*"

Nazun moved easily, his long, blue-green-clad body rippling blithely to whipcord muscles under tanned and healthy skin. "Man needs his ideals personified, made real and given power. Given power enough, indeed, to stop the individual man who errs, but judgment enough to spare the man who sees ahead. One who is not man—for man is jealous of man, and unyielding to man's suggestions."

Daron sat very still, and concentrated on the soft brown mass of needles at his feet. "A mighty plan," he sighed. "And if man, through centuries, learned once to rule the rest of the world with godlike powers, perhaps through other centuries he might learn to rule himself. But how, I wonder, might it be?"

"The compass needle points to north, drawn by a thread of force unseen, unfelt by men. The brain of man is made of many tiny parts, working one against the other, millions on millions of them, by threads of force like the force that moves the compass needle, perhaps. A somewhat different force, more akin to the sparks that come from combing hair on cold, dry nights, it might be. If these small parts—these cells—act thus against each other, and it is their interaction, not the cells themselves, that is thought, then it is the force the cells generate, *and not the cells themselves,* which is thought."

"Yes," said Daron, his eyes narrowed and alert on those bottomless gray wells of Nazun's eyes. "And—the force that is the interaction is not material, as invisible as the fine thread of pull that turns the compass needle."

Nazun relaxed, and his eyes wandered from Daron's, as though the important story were told. "If these things were true, men might then learn to make those interactions that are thought self-existent, apart from the materials of the cells. A group of many men, wise and learned, might cause a concentration of such forces to take an independent existence, a self-thinking, immaterial thought. It would be—almost godlike."

"It would be the essence of man—his ideals, without his needs, his heights, without his weakness."

"And the minds of many men might mold and build it better, nearer to human kind, while yet it had the power to reject the wrong in men.

"With such—man might go onward safely, for such a guardian of man could guide and aid men."

"Why"—Daron halted, licked his lips with tip of tongue, and rephrased his thought. If Nazun wished indirection, there might be reason, must be reason here—"if such a thing should be attained, say—five centuries ago—"

"Perhaps seven and a half," suggested Nazun.

"—or so long as seven and a half centuries ago, then men so protected might advance that knowledge of material things once more in safety. It seems to me, they would."

"But if," said Nazun, "some twelve long centuries had passed since Azun first was settled, and twelve long centuries of vilifying those studies had established strong tradition— And does the young man choose the stony hillside, though it have rich and virgin soil beneath the rocks, when the proven, fertile soil of the valley is there?

"Daron, where would you start the search for facts that lead to knowledge that might make men fly again?"

"Why . . . with birds."

"There is a tradition, I have heard, handed down from the days of legends. It is very strong, and probably true. The way to flight is not the way of birds. The wings men fly upon must not move."

"I'd like," said Daron dryly, "to study this science of the mind."

"So many did. But that is gone—since the Invisible Ones came."

"These thought-force things might be invisible, might they not?"

"But, being thought," Nazun said, lazily turning to shade from the shifting sun, "might make themselves have form in man's mind."

"But any form!" said Daron softly, thinking suddenly of Lady Tammar, who was, so Shorhun said, every man's ideal, but not for any man.

"But why should they? These gods—men are men; they are limited as men, and cannot truly conceive of a god, can they? It is not logic. To imbue a god with human qualities is basic contradiction. They are more than human, and hence, by definition, not human. A human, then, could not conceive them. A god should see the future, and be possessed of absolute logic."

"The logic is sound," Daron nodded, eyes narrowed, "but the logic of a wise man of Tharsun, in the Tutz nation, was sound, too. It was logic that a heavy rock should drop much faster than a light one. It doesn't, incidentally. I had him show me, by test, the soundness of his proof.

"A god such as you describe might be a god! I could not know. But he'd be a poor neighbor, with his absolutes. The laws of nature are absolute, and logical. But I've seen a small child thrust its hand into the pretty glow of molten brass—and be punished with the absolutes of nature's laws."

Nazun shrugged. "I repeat the logic of the priests of the Invisible Ones. They have no root in human brain— though they draw their powers from the tiny generators of the force of thought that make up human brains. They live by the energies of the thoughts their worshipers give. But their root and existence lies within a . . . crystal ball, a thing some three feet through."

Daron stiffened where he lay. "That is material?"

"It is material, and may be crushed by a blow."

Daron knew, that instant, what his task must be. "Where might this crystal be?"

"On the Temple Isle—but no one knows. The Invisible Ones guard that knowledge—with certain reason. But it is not readily seen, nor wisely seen. The priests of the Invisible Ones, the Invisible Ones themselves—and the sphere itself. Three defenses make it safe."

Daron nodded, and shivered slightly.

"I . . . I saw a thing of similar nature. And thereby came near to being no more! A certain wizard of the Tahly folk showed me it, and, but for a friend, I'd be standing paralyzed before him yet! He learned, though, and taught me certain things. Hypnotism, where the mind is slaved!"

Nazun nodded. "Its strong defense, a final barrier. It was not meant so originally, but meant only as the basis of the Invisible Ones, its weaving lights their patterned thoughts, and, being mechanism, they are uninfluenced by anything but logic."

Daron snorted softly. "Cold comfort in such gods as that!"

"No comfort—but knowledge."

"Useless knowledge, if what I hear be truth."

"Useless—but satisfying, at times. To know the result of tomorrow's deeds. The Invisible Ones are there, that knowledge can be had. No good it can do, for, being truth, it can't be changed. But—a young man's wife is suffering in labor—and he can know the true result, two lives—or none! Or a child is sick, and the father sleepless with prodding fear, which might—and the Invisible Ones know—be needless.

"A day, you'll stay away, not caring greatly for that ultimate knowledge what day and hour Lord Barak has closed your book—but a month, a year, a dozen years. The knowledge is there—"

Daron nodded. "No man has will to fight such steady pull forever. And once indulged—the man's mind and will is trapped. Aye—that is logic, but lacks ideals. But—I wonder if the Invisible Ones"—Daron looked at Nazun's rugged face through narrowed lids—"could tell me when I shall die? Or—when they shall die?"

"They cannot. The course of a man is straight through time, from past to future, basing actions of the present on the memories and knowledge gained in the past. But a god acts on his knowledge of the past and future! That is chaos —and cannot be predicted. And those of men who associate themselves with gods—cannot be predicted."

Daron's eyes looked upward again. The lowering sun was casting longer rays, and the zenith sky was dark, deep blue, with the clarity of high mountain air. The darkening branches wove across the spot of sky, and whispered soft accompaniment to eager, anxious birds. A three-foot crystal ball with moving, weaving, hypnotic lights. A material thing that a blow could smash—but which, because it was material, no immaterial thing could harm!

Daron's eyes swept down—and widened sharply. The tree across the way swayed gently to the breeze, but Nazun was gone. There was a helmet where he had sat, a thing of woven wires of silver and gold, wires fine and soft as young lamb's wool, and five strange jewels. A blue-green, queerly luminous bit of stuff lodged at the front, a bit of stone that matched in color Nazun's garb. A bit of stone like agate, red-streaked and white, above the right ear, a bit of rose quartz above the left, and a sea-green crystal at the rear.

At the peak, a blob of utter night made solid was fixed in the fabric of the weave. "Barak, Lord of Fate and Death," said Daron softly. "And the others—Talun's sea-green, my Lady Tammar's rose, and Martal's streaked stone, Lord Martal's Stone of Chance."

Abruptly, as he settled it upon his head, it occurred to him that immaterial forces such as thought did not ordinarily move weighty gold and silver.

Slowly he caught up the reins of his browsing horse and mounted. Lost in thought, he nodded gently to the motion of the animal, and wondered further how it might be that clouds should form, and a howling storm move up at the behest of a wholly immaterial Talun. And puzzled at how much of a full, round truth Nazun had seen fit to gift him with.

A good hour later he roused, and looked about—and cursed himself for a fool. The horse, in natural course, had found the going easier down the mountainside. The temples, and Lady Tammar, were far above, and for this day, he must wait.

CHAPTER V

THE SUN WAS SET, AND THE moon well up, a round, pale lantern of lies, pretending to light the city of Tordu, when Daron turned down the cobbled street toward Shorhun's inn. The moon's light was a snare and a deception, as Daron well knew; it lied about the colors of the walls, saying that dirt-streaked muddy yard wall there was touched with silver paint, and that yonder wall was built of glinting gold. Daron well knew it was blue-tinged plaster, and the black tiled roof was bright green by day.

And the shadows, where only low voices and soft laughter originated, were people—though the moon would not reveal it. Deceptive. The glow of light on walls and streets, smelling with the faint and blended odors over which prevailed the queer, wet scent of water poured on hot stone cobbles and lawns at sunset. The little trees and sunken entrances casting shadows sharp and black, the narrow, canyon alleyways black gouges through the twisting buildings of the section.

Daron was deep in thought—but Daron had visited more nations than one, and in most, he'd found an eye that didn't sleep of more than slight aid for long and healthy life. The black shadow of an entrance arch, cut through a high plastered garden wall, spouted figures, two clumps of shadow that ran, topped with white blobs of faces, and lightening with moon-glimmer on steel.

The horse reared and screamed and twisted round in panic as Daron's sharp spurs raked his sides in a way he'd not known since this new master mounted him. He lurched and pawed forward—and the two shadows ducked aside from the sharp shod hoofs. Daron was off on the far side of the horse. The animal snorted once, and felt his rider gone. Startled, hurt, he clattered away. Daron was on his feet, balancing lightly in the shadow of the wall, while the two shadows turned to face him. Full moonlight struck at them now, while the wall's high shadow engulfed and blotted out clear sight of Daron's figure.

"Right!" said a low voice, and one of the pair leaped to Daron's right, the other to his left. They wore cloaks of some dark stuff, and cowls that snugged about their heads. The cloaks hung close about them, no hindrance now as they came on mincing, dancing feet, and lunged, a trained chorus that attacked from two sides at once.

Daron blotted out in shadow, and was behind the one as he spun on his heel. His cloak swirled loose at the hem, and the moon-glimmer of his sword reached up—and fouled in it. Moonlight silvered on his face, a lean, bony face with hollow, blackened eyes and line-thin lips that writhed in blazing anger. Daron's sword licked out, twisted neatly round the fouled weapon, and sent it flying, a glinting fragment of light, across the garden wall. Somewhere beyond, it landed with a ringing clang.

"Hold!" said Daron sharply. "I have no enemies here."

The second man danced forward, his face lifting in a smile of keenest pleasure as his blade darted under Daron's momentarily lifted sword. Daron's body shifted slightly at the final instant—and the blade bent double as it scraped on the thin steel plate beneath the sea rover's jacket at the breast.

The cowled man danced back as Daron's blade came down, a soft-voiced, vicious snarl on his lips. The second man was circling, his cloak stripped off in an instant's time and wrapped about his left arm, the glint of a dirk in his right hand.

"So be it, then!" Daron snapped. "I *had* no enemies here!"

"And," the sword bearer whispered, "you will have none —for the dead have neither friend nor foe!"

Daron slipped aside, backed toward the wall as he caught the other's sword on his own, the swift wrist play making the steel *thrum* and sing, and the close, keen following of blade on blade making scarce a click of contact. Daron danced and moved and wove, and watched the moon-whitened faces of his attackers. They were twins, twin meal-white faces with twin sooted, shadowed eyes. But one stood forth in lighter clothing, loose trousers gathered at the calf to tight stocking breeches, loose jacket hanging below the waist. But each arm carried an armlet of jewel-glinted metal, and across the breast was woven a pattern of spheres and many jewels.

Daron danced back and back, feeling out the swordsman, and knowing in the spring and slash of the blade he faced that this was one who'd handled weapons before and handled them well. He moved and danced and backed away, and the dirkman, short of reach with his small blade, circled helplessly.

Daron moved forward in a deceptive glide that scarcely seemed motion, and twisted as he moved. The long, thin blade lunged out, flicked once, and laid open his opponent's arm from wrist to elbow. A soft, thick inhalation of pain, and whispered curse; the cloaked one held his blade in his left hand, and charged in for revenge. Daron backed, circled left to avoid the lunge of the dirk. His twisting, glimmering blade lunged out once more and buried in the swordsman's throat. An instant's scream was throttled in a rush of blood, and the sword dropped down to ring on cobbled pavement.

Simultaneously, as Daron freed his blade, the dirk rang on the street, and the second man had swept up the fallen sword. Daron leaped forward, and in the engagement wrapped his blade about the base of the other's, and sent it flying. His own straightened out, and hovered near the jewel-sprinkled breast.

"Now how is this, my jeweled dandy, that you seek strangers for your murdering? Would not wisdom suggest you know your victim and his capabilities before you practice up on assassination? I have no knowledge of your laws here, but there is one of mine I think good. Who attacks me is an enemy—or gives good account of why he sought me out. Speak, and speak truth!"

The moon-whitened face was motionless, the thin, straight lips held shut. He faced the moon now, and the shadowed eyes were lighted, gleaming fish-belly white against the face. They shifted minutely—and Daron leaped aside and whirled.

The sword he had just thrown with his blade licked past his shoulder like metal lightning. The man whose throat Daron had spitted whirled, and leveled the blade for a second attack as the other swooped to retrieve the dirk, glowing like molten silver on the cobbles.

Daron cursed softly, and engaged the dead man's blade. It swept and swung and danced to meet every move. It glinted like a sweep of sunlit rain, a thousand lines of steel in place of one. Daron danced back, drew back his arm as the dead man lurched forward clumsily, blood bubbling through slow-formed words. "Stand still, fool; you die!"

Daron's arm swept downward, and his sword flew hilt-foremost toward the dead, white face. The dead man's sword swept up too slow, and the heavy hilt crashed true across his eyes, with all the strength of Daron's arm behind it.

The second attacker lunged in, grasped Daron's sword

before it fell, and reached out for Daron's dancing form. The dead thing squalled, raked at blinded eyes, and twisted vainly. Barely, Daron retrieved the blind thing's sword and danced away with skin still whole.

"Men," said Daron tensely, "I'll fight fair—but when the fairly killed come back again—why, there's an end to fairness!"

"You'll die," the rustling, laughing whisper of the other assured him. His cloaked arm reached, and suddenly, as the two blades engaged, grasped Daron's sword. Daron released the blade, dropped his hand to his dirk before the other, expecting a frantic pull, recovered balance. The dagger flashed, spun through the air, and buried in the bejeweled man's face. He screamed and stumbled forward, dropping the two blades he held to claw at the dagger.

Daron whipped up his own blade from the street, and slashed coldly at the fallen man's throat. The watchful sword rang against it, and sent it dancing down the street.

The thing stood up and stared at him with blank, dead eyes.

"You die," it said. "You must—for I cannot!" The words were whistling, nasal, but half formed. The slashed throat whistled and moaned as air sucked in and out.

"You cannot die," Daron agreed with cold, live things squirming in his belly, "but blind, you cannot see!" The sword he held danced out again, swept, parried, darted in—and in a second time. Daron stepped back, his blade lowered, to watch the blinded thing—and almost died on the lunging blade!

Desperately, the sea rover met the blade that danced and lunged and parried at his own, a dead, blind thing seeking out his every move and driving him back—back—with tireless speed, while lead flowed down Daron's veins and settled in his wrist. "Nazun—Lord Nazun," Daron whispered softly, "I ask no help in things I know, I ask no help in doing—but give me knowledge to stop this *thing!*"

The swords sang and danced and winked, and soft leather sandals scraped on cobblestones—and Daron felt the blade come nearer. Air whistled in the dead throat, and in his own dry throat, and he glanced sharply at the corpse that lay outstretched beside the dirk—and wondered when it would again rise!

Daron's breath sucked in in sudden understanding. For an instant, the leaden load of tiring muscles lightened with glimpse of relief. His defense grew bolder, then an attack that wrapped the dead thing's blade gave him the chance he sought. His own blade lunged forward again as he twisted— and laid open the dead thing's arm from wrist to elbow. The severed tendons dropped the blade, and as the other arm swept down, a slashing cut at the left wrist left it with useless fingers.

"You may not die, you may not blind," Daron panted hoarsly, "but those hands will grip no more!"

The dead man dropped like an emptied sack, lay limp an instant in the street and, as Daron watched, the limbs stiffened in rigor.

Cold gnawed at the sea rover's brain as he walked silently down the street, rubbing the tired muscles of his forearm. This section of the city was quiet as those men had at last become, the silvering of the moon alone remaining. The low voices and the laughter had vanished. Only far away across the still rustle of trees in the night wind came sounds of a city's movement, the restless, rustling tone that rises and falls and never dies while a city lives. The smell of flower gardens and fresh salt air swept from the bay on the wings of the inshore breeze. But no sound nearby.

Then, a block away, he heard the hesitating *clop-clop* of a shod horse's hoofs, the irregular rhythm of an unridden horse, uncertain of its way, feeling the weight of loneliness, lacking human guidance. Daron started toward the sound, loping silently, his mind skipping agilely, yet numbed withal, and bewildered mightily. His enemy was clear—for none but a god could make those dead things dance to their strings. But his friends—

Or had he thought that solution for himself? Had his own mind seen clear the ripped arm of the abandoned corpse, and the reason for its desertion? It was no more than he had done before—save that that dead, blind face opposing him with inhuman skill had frozen and numbed his thoughts beyond any experience he had ever known.

He thrust the thing to the back of his mind, and turned down a narrow street. His gray stallion tossed its head uneasily, and faced him, whickering uncertainly. "So, boy, it's easy now. I raked you then to save you from being spitted. Come, now—it hurt, I know, but a foot man does not fight a mounted man, but first his horse. Come—ah!" Daron swung up, and soothed the uncertain animal to an easy walk, and guided him once more toward the inn. But the sea rover's eyes kept sharper watch than ever they had at a good ship's bow.

CHAPTER VI

THE HANGING LAMP WAS DARK, with charred and smoking wick, and Shorhun's lanky figure draped uneasily in the fireside chair, asleep and snoring gently. His long, lean arms, like knotted ropes, hung loose beside the chair, his fingers half opened to the glow of the dying fire. Across the room, the boy was curled upon a bench, head pillowed on an elbow, and one long arm, a small duplicate of Shorhun's knotted cables, reached down to grip in lax fingers a dog's collar.

The dog looked up abruptly, with wide-opened eyes as Daron's horse *clopped* softly in the courtyard, and the creak and grunt of leather harness attested to the stabling of the animal. His quick eyes watched Daron enter the room. He snorted softly, and lowered his massive head upon his paws, eyes watchfully awake.

Daron rubbed his arm and smiled. Softly he stepped over to Shorhun and laid a friendly hand upon his arm. The lanky innkeeper moved and raised his head.

"Daron?" he said, his voice mechanical and toneless with broken sleep.

"Aye, Daron—and with a throat as dry as Fraka's plains. And—But get me wine, my friend."

Shorhun heaved up, and ambled toward his supply, to return with a bottle and a glass on a small tray. He set the lot before Daron, and slumped into his chair, resting his head within his palms.

"Ho, am I to drink alone? Come, Shorhun, another glass, and join me in it. And tell me, is it customary for this town that men should seek to murder strangers on sight?"

Shorhun raised himself, and fetched another glass. "No," he said tonelessly, pouring wine into the two.

Daron looked up into the lank, tired man's eyes. He was quiet for a moment as he watched the eyes, and watched Shorhun pick up the glass. Then his strong, brown fingers gripped Shorhun's wrist and stayed the hand. "Wait, friend. I think—I think your lamp needs oil, and I need light, I know. I would not drink until I see the color of my wine."

Shorhun moved wordlessly to the task, pulling down the counter-weighted lamp, filling the reservoir, trimming the wick and lighting it so that the room was warm with yellow light.

Daron's fingers were busy then with an aimless spinning of a bit of polished metal on a cord, a polished metal mirror that spun first one way, then the other. "Sit here," said Daron, as the innkeeper finished, "and listen, friend. I have a tale to tell."

Wearily, Shorhun sat down across the table and Daron began. His voice was low and soft, and he described his start that morning, following Shorhun's directions, and Shorhuns's sleepy eyes were watching the dancing, spinning mirror on the cord, and the swirling reflections of the lamp that danced with it.

"Once before," said Daron softly, in a sleepy voice, "I traveled such a hill-climbing road, to the dwelling of a wizard of the Ind people. I was tired as you are tired, and wanted sleep—as you want sleep—the rest and ease of sleep—sleep —sleep—"

Daron's voice was toneless, sleepy—but his eyes were bright and hard, and the mirror in the lamplight spun and spun, and hesitated to spin the other way at the end of its cord. "Sleep you need—sleep—" Shorhun's sleepy eyes sank lower, then abruptly tried to rise, his body seemed to struggle to rise, his head to turn from the mirror. "You hear only my voice, as you sleep—sleep—and forget all other things, but see the mirror that tires your eyes and makes you sleep. Shorhun, you hear only your friend, Daron, Daron who, like you, seeks only the Old Gods. You hear no voice but mine, and obey me in all things. You obey me, and only me, Shorhun!"

The tonelessness was gone, and there was the whip of sharp command in Daron's tone—and the mirror spun. "You will and must answer any question I ask. That is true!"

"Y-yes," said Shorhun.

"I am your friend, and friend to your friends."

"Yes," said Shorhun promptly.

Daron's eyes were tense and dark. Very softly to himself, he whistled a little tune, and thought. "Now this is clear; someone has been here and worked upon this man, and thanks be to old white-headed Barhamu for what he taught me in the hills of Ind! But what is the purpose? No god did this, for the look of his eyes in good close view was clumsy revelation. But a man—if Barhamu knew enough to match at all these god-making wizards of Azun—cannot make another do what that other would object to—such as murdering his friends!"

Daron thought deeply, then; "Shorhun," he snapped, "is this wine good?"

"Y-yes," said Shorhun, and stirred uneasily, his forehead careworn and weather-browned, wrinkling in a frown of childish puzzlement.

"Shorhun, there was a stranger here who laid commands on you?"

Shorhun's face worked, his mouth moved and knotted and fell still. Daron nodded grimly. "But that stranger, while no god, knew this mind art well. Now how to break that spell—"

A thought came to him, and he rose. "Shorhun," he snapped, "sit there, and do not move until I return." Then, thinking of certain things that lay upon a cobbled street— "Or," he added—"until the sun rises and the day is here."

Daron strode out the door, and sought down the road. It was half an hour before he returned, swearing softly, with a mewing cat in his arms. His clothes were torn somewhat, and stained with varicolored plaster dust from climbing many walls.

He set the cat upon the table stroking it. "Shorhun," he said softly, "I know. You can tell me, because I know these things already. The stranger came and talked with you, and laid command on you to forget. But you were to give me this wine, and do whatever was needed that I might drink it."

"Yes," said Shorhun, uneasily. "It is good wine. The flavor is better than my own."

"Watch," commanded Daron. He spilled a bit of wine, and forced some down the cat's unwilling throat. The cat mewed and spit and scratched, and, released, sat down and cleaned its fur. Daron waited patiently. Abruptly the cat jumped, doubled up, screeched in agony—then straightened down with ruffled fur to lick itself clean. Two minutes later it doubled up again, screeched louder, and writhed unhappily. The spasm stopped, to resume again within a minute more.

Within five minutes the cat was dead, in one last spasm wherein its cries were choked in a muscle-knotted throat, and its muscles convulsed so violently the broad abdominal muscles ripped themselves across in frightful spasm, and every muscle tore, so that the carcass was a loose bag of death wrapped up in skin.

Softly Daron spoke. "That is the wine you would have

fed your friend, Shorhun. That is the wine you would have drunk with me! That is murder in its foulest form!"

Shorhun shuddered, his face worked in knotted muscles, and his staring eyes twitched and danced. Abruptly he shook himself, and stumbled erect, "Eh? Daron! You here? Eh—it's night!"

Daron nodded, smiling. "Aye, it's night, my friend, and you may thank a man you never knew, one Barhamu, that you and I live now, and are not—that!"

Shorhun looked at the body of the cat, then picked it up and dropped it sharply in disgust, rubbing his hands as though they were contaminated by the contact. "What . . . what is this? And where is that dandied priest of the Invisible Ones that visited me here?"

"Ah, now the tale appears! I thought it might. Now listen to me, friend, and in the future look not so keenly at spinning mirrors, glittering jewels, or other tricks of wizards. I'll tell you something of a tale to straighten up that knotted hair of yours, but first bring me some wine—some wine of your own, and no more of this hell's brew. In the meantime, I sense a bit of trickery in your son's sleep."

An hour later, Daron was dreaming. Now even one with the easygoing conscience and the tough stomach that Daron had, dreams now and then, but no such dream as this. He dreamed, and, moreover, knew he was dreaming.

For that last hour before he went to bed, the helmet of woven gold-and-silver wire beside him, he had been thinking as he talked with lanky, grimly boiling Shorhun. With half his mind he'd told his tale, and explained many things to Shorhun that he had learned in a high, dry old building far up the slopes of the shattered mountains of the Ind. And with the other, deeper half of his mind, he had been thinking, stewing about one problem; the problem of the sphere.

The menace of iron and flesh and blood that was the priests of the Invisible Ones, he set aside. *That* sort of menace he had known before, and would know again—with luck! But the Invisible Ones themselves? That, it seemed, was in the immaterial, potent province of the Lord Nazun. But the sphere—

A single strong blow could smash it—but to see it was to be paralyzed. His keen, smoothly working mind was baffled, brought solid and firm against a thing that, he knew, was the one thing in all the world against which it could not fight effectively: itself. Too long and well had old Barhamu taught him for self-deception here. The trick of the Spinning Mirror and the Trick of the Winking Light were, alike, tricks that no mind could well resist—for they were tricks that turned that mind upon itself.

And then the dream had come, as he sought sleep. He stood before an altar of blue-green beryl, a mighty, perfect gem four feet high, by three feet square, his head bowed down in prayer. Behind the altar stood Nazun, his gray eyes deep as night, with unplumbed depths so vast that the lack of bottom made them black. The eyes drew up his bowed head, till his own blue eyes looked into them, and through them, swallowed by them—and saw with the eyes of Nazun!

His sight hurled out cross the night, driving through walls of blue-green stone, through the dark, whispering forests of the mountain, across the city, where Tordu lay dark beneath the setting moon, with only here and there some late light gleaming. The world was a painted map, luminous with moon-glow and the Bay of Tordu was a lake of quicksilver, marred by the black gash of the Temple Isle. For half an instant the world held in suspense; then, as though his point of sight had plunged like a falling meteor, the Temple Isle exploded upward, turned black and silver as buildings appeared, exploded outward, and his sight penetrated through. For an instant of time he was deep, deep within the heart of one, deep in a room whose black walls, carved from the living basalt of the isle's foundations, were lighted with a glow that seemed pure white.

A circle of warrior guards stood round the sphere, the three-foot sphere of crystal, like a fragile bubble floating in a three-clawed rest of gold. Uncounted myriads of pin-point lights circled in darting, swooping, patterned orbits, a mathematically precise involvement of inextricable cycles and epicycles, progressions and ordered, intricate orbits. The row of warrior guards stood firm about the sphere—but every back was toward it, and every guard stood with hand on sword and metal shield.

In a fraction of a second—then the vision was gone, chopped off with a hollow sensation of frightful fall that gripped and wrenched at Daron's mind and soul.

His mind retched and quivered in terror—then quieted as some vast thing of calm touched it, soothing, stilling. And Daron stood again before the blue-green altar gem of beryl. Lord Nazun stood behind it, and his gray eyes were tensed and tired; his strong-muscled hands leaned on the altar top, gripping it, it seemed, for support. The tanned, rough-hewn face of the Lord of Wisdom was white with strain and very tired.

Lord Nazun's voice was vastly weary as it whispered in the dream. "The Invisible Ones are wary; they cut off the vision soon. No further sight of that can I afford, for the cost is more than human mind could understand. But you have seen. Now—sleep again, and think!"

CHAPTER VII

D ARON SIPPED FRAGRANT FEYA, and with drowsy eyes watched the sun shadows play in the courtyard. The sounds of Tordu City were waking round him; the cries of women, the shrill voice of a small boy carrying on conversation with some friend two blocks away, the heavy creak of a laden ox-cart plodding toward the market, bearing round, green melons and green-wrapped ears of corn.

Behind the drowsing eyes, the vision of the sphere danced and spun and moved, the myriad lights flashed in their orbit there, and, despite the strong protection of Nazun's mighty will, half hypnotized him still. Slowly to Daron's inward gaze, one fact was forming from the vision. Those myriad points of light moved not aimlessly, but with an order more precise than the swing, ticking pendulum of the clock upon the wall. They looped and moved and danced —in ordered, plotted curves.

And abruptly Daron started. The drowsing eyes became alive, and the immobile face moved in a sudden, grim smile. He laughed softly, and swung to his feet. Shorhun, sitting silent at his table looked up, and opened sleepy eyes.

"Ten minutes more, my friend," the lanky innkeeper sighed, "and for all your concentration I'd have broken in. I have a question of some small moment I would ask."

Daron laughed, and swung his sword belt round to a position of greater comfort. "Then ask away, Shorhun, for one cactus-spined and triply damned question that's festered in my mind is solved. Perhaps I can solve yours."

The innkeeper unfolded upward and shrugged. "It was merely this. I live today, because your eyes do more than see, and your brain holds more than most. But—I know not your plans, of course, but if they do not include your death within some three hours, I'd advise you seek some other seat."

"Hm-m-m. My plans did not include quite that," Daron nodded. He cocked a half-closed eye at Shorhun's ugly, solemn face. "But why should this seat—a very comfortable one seeming—be so sadly dangerous?"

"The priests of the Invisible Ones know it's here. If half your tale of last evening be true, then you murdered one priest. If it be wholly true, then you did murder enough to bring down the wrath of all the Invisible Ones on a dozen men."

Daron grunted softly. "They are slow to anger, then. I'd act without thinking over the problem a whole night through."

Shorhun nodded. "They would. But King Elmanus wouldn't. And it's King Elmanus' word that's needed. He wakes at eight, has breakfast at eight and a half, and holds no audience before nine and a half. It's nine and a quarter now."

Daron looked up at Shorhun with interest. "Now if this King Elmanus has these haughty priests of the Invisible Ones trained so well to leave his sleep alone, he holds my strong respect. He is unique among the monarchs of the world I've seen; he can make a high priest wait as high priests should, until he's had his breakfast. What potent secret does he hold for this?"

Shorhun sighed. "Old Elmanus is near eighty years old now, and he's reigned for fifty-five. For fifty-five long years, the Old God's priests have howled in his left ear, and for fifty-five long years the priests of the Invisible Ones have shrieked into his right.

"It's reached a sorry state, where now he can hear very little in either ear, and not at all when he is sleeping. But he has curiously sensitive hearing to the wail of countrymen and seamen both. His nobles he hears continuously, wherefore he need not listen hard to them."

"I'd think," said Daron shrewdly, "the priests would have found another king."

Shorhun chuckled. "Old Elmanus has not the slightest fear of death. He's lived too long, and during that life the two sets of gods have grown apart and hatred grown between. Now each fears a new king more than they loathe the old."

"Has neither worked on the will of Elmanus' successor?"

"Elmanus has no son, and his daughter is a priestess of Lady Tammar—but no woman may hold the throne. His successor must be elected."

"He'd be a noble, and the nobles—so you say—are all besotted with the future knowledge of the Invisible Ones."

"He'd be no noble," said Shorhun sourly. "The nobles all know well that several hundred exceedingly tough seamen loathe their blood and bones and several thousand countrymen obey old Elmanus blindly because he's just."

"Hm-m-m. . . . it would make a throne as hot as the Sun's own fires! But—perhaps I'd best be on my way. Where would you suggest?"

"It depends upon your plans," said Shorhun, shrugging like a beaching wave. "If you intend permanent escape from Elmanus' guard I'd say your own land would be a sound place to seek. If for a day—start west, and I'll say north. They'll find you, though."

Daron rose, stretched mightily, and started through the door. "Call up that imp you name your son, and have him fix my horse. I saw a watchmaker's place two blocks away, and I have business there."

"I'll call my son, but my memory is short. He may remember long enough to bring the horse to Granner's place." Shorhun vanished through the kitchen door.

The sun was warm and the breeze that slid joyously down the mountainside was fresh with pine-laden scent, and the smell of many breakfasts pleasant to the nostrils. The cobbles, round beneath the feet, were easy walking, and Daron's eyes alert as he swung down the street. Two blocks away he came upon the little doorway that he sought, signed without by a huge wooden cog bearing the symbols "WATCHMAKING."

The place was dark, and still cool with last night's air, and the watchmaker who looked up at him a half-seen figure in the gloom. His head was bald and polished as the faces of his products, but fringed around with a halo of white hair so fine it floated in the air. His face was a wizened, dried up apple, split by a smiling mouth, and sharp blue eyes as old as the skies, and laughing with them.

"And what is time and a timepiece to one as young as ye?" he snapped as Daron entered.

"Father, I am touched by a strange malady. The malady is never fatal, I am told, but long enduring," Daron said solemnly. "The malady some call inventor's itch."

The bright-blue eyes speared up at him. "Huy-hu, now. Unless this thing you have invented is the size and crudeness of an ox cart, those fingers of yours will never make it."

"Alas, father, they won't," Daron sighed. "Yours will, though, I suspect."

"I've work enough with things I know, and things that

work, without befuddling my old head with foolishness. What have you in mind?"

"A thing about the size of a pocket watch, but of special and strange making. Now look you here, for all my handling of ships cordage, still my fingers have certain skill at drawing things, and this is what I'd need. I'll pay you for it with twice its weight in gold, and add another weight if it is done by the third hour of the afternoon."

Rapidly Daron sketched, and the old watchmaker's keen eyes followed him. A dozen sketches, and many special strictures and explanations were demanded, but at last the old man snorted understanding.

"That malady you call inventor's itch, we call more often madness. The thing is mad, and has no use, but I shall make it as you say. You'll have it by the second hour after noon."

"Good," said Daron. "Now here is proof of my madness, for I'll give you now the gold." Four round, hard coins he laid on the old man's desk and stepped outside, where Shorhun's freckled son lounged by his horse.

"My father says," the boy whispered softly, giving him the reins, "that guards are popping out of ash receivers, and springing up among the flowers. I'm going to the house of my grandmother for a week or so. Good-by."

Daron stood an instant in thought, then stepped around the corner of the building where the lad had vanished to take him on his way. Two legs scrambling over a roof top disappeared as Daron turned the corner, and the lad was lost.

Shrugging, Daron set off across the town, his mind busy with his plans. Deeper and deeper into the city he went, stopping once at an inn where he was not known. Two hours later—the loungers there had learned a certain respect for three snail shells and a pebble that made longer stay imprudent—Daron sought out a small tailor's shop, and took off his hands some misfit clothes that reeked in Daron's nostrils of earthy sweat. But, at least, they did not betray the seaman's origin.

For three long hours more he visited in armorer's shops, obscure secondhand places, seeking a shield. It was well afternoon before he found the place he sought, a tiny cubbyhole left when two haughty buildings had not quite met, a mere alleyway between them roofed over by some sad-faced individual with the salesmanship of Jeremiah.

"A shield," he sighed, and sat firm on the broken chair before his door, "I don't think I have many. What kind?"

Daron looked at him sourly. His beard was of the sort that prolonged and persistent laziness, not art, produces, and his hands stained not with the grime of toil but, it seemed to the sea rover, the dust that settles on anything long motionless. "A round shield," said Daron carefully. "A round, flat shield of good steel or of silver-plated bronze."

"Silver-plated bronze? I had one such—I think it's gone —but they are not practical, I'm told," he added hastily. "A shield of hard-tanned hide will turn an arrow, or stop a blade, and is far lighter. Tharmun's shop, two blocks from here, specializes in them."

"Aye, so?" said Daron patiently. "That's what I learned some five minutes past. Now look you, friend, your aura is that of a wild goat, increased in strength by your advanced age and greater size. The spiders have spun their webs between your feet, and how one so immobile has escaped a load of flowing fat surprises me. Or can it be that your colossal lethargy forbids you rising to seek food?

"Be that as it may, I'll see your shields, my friend, if I must prick your dusted hide to make you seek them in defense. Now move!" Daron's sword left its scabbard of its own volition, seemingly, and pricked the cadaverous, sad-faced one.

With a howl of anguish he bounced within his shop, with Daron at his heels.

The sea rover halted. The place was dark as the maw of some deep cave, and rank with lack of cleaning. Very slowly Daron's eyes made out its contents, while the whine of the proprietor sought to convince him he wanted none of the merchandise.

"Be quiet, or by Martal, I'll let that noise out through your throat," snapped Daron. "Now bring me that bronze shield you have. Is it not clear to you that I am mad, and not to be reasoned with?"

The shield was brought. It was bronze, a well-made shield that some craftsman had labored over, and in seeing it, Daron knew that chance had favored him. Unlike any shield he'd seen before, its face was absolutely flat and plain, without decoration save a very chaste and simple geometric pattern that inscribed a circle round the edge. The face was bronze, very thin, for lightness, but by its ring a hard, true melt. The back was crossed with a patterned grid of bars that made it strong enough to turn a broadax swing.

"Now by Martal, chance is behind me this day indeed," said Daron with satisfaction. "What price do you want, Goaty One?"

"Ten *thords* I paid for it and less than twenty I cannot take and stay in business," the merchant whined.

"Ten thords it is then," said Daron, dropping two golden coins, "and good day."

"No, no! Twenty, I said!"

Daron swung on his horse, and started down the street. Behind him he heard a long, sad sigh, and the heavy creak of the broken chair. The shield, he saw, was bronze, plated well with silver, and the price was fair. The silver was black as night with lack of care, and a dark, old bronze patina had coated over the gridwork at the back.

Daron rode directly to the watchmaker's shop, and entered. The old man looked up from his work and nodded. "Ten minutes more, son, and your madness will spin as gaily as you like. You are early."

"No," said Daron wearily. "I'm late. I needs must polish my shield."

The old man's sharp eyes turned on the metal shield and narrowed down. "Now, by Nazun, I know your wits have left you, or you've more strength than even those none-too-puny arms suggest. That thing may make a fine display—old Elmanus' guards once carried those, I think—but as protection, they're as light and dainty as a good stone wall."

Daron laughed. "I'm vain as the peacock of Ind, and must make a flashing display, father. Give me polish, then, and a bit of cloth, that I may dazzle those who look at me."

The old man bent, and drew out soft rags, and a cake of black-streaked rouge, and some white, moist paste. "Damp the rag at the pump yonder, rub on the rouge and mix the white paste with it. If there's any silver left, that thing should shine."

For half an hour more, Daron rubbed till his back and shoulders ached, and his new-old garments were stained with a dozen shades of red and black and green from the bronze. But when he finished, the old shield's face shone like the sun, with scarce a dozen bad scratches.

"So it's old Elmanus I've to thank for finding this shield, eh? I knew it was mad to hope to find so useless a thing, but this thing was what I needed, none the less."

"King Elmanus it was. He had a special guard of twenty men, who used those things. Elmanus found that a good spot of sunlight cast back by twenty mirror shields would stop men quicker, and with less stain of blood, than twenty swords. With those twenty shields, the guard could blind a man for half a week.

"Wherefore all Elmanus' enemies came at him after dusk, and found, of course, his twenty guards as well protected by those heavy shields as though they each were weighted down with chains. Elmanus lost three full complements of guards before he gave up those shields.

"You being only one, I'd think you had poor chance to learn wisdom—but that, my son, is your own task. It is your skin that shield is supposed to defend."

"Ah, yes, and so it is. Now tell me, is that thing finished?" Daron asked.

"Done. And here it is. I owe you also a coin, for, having an affection for those who are mad, I made it very light. Undoubtedly, it shows I am a kindred spirit, and mad as you."

"Mm-m-m," said Daron, holding the tiny thing, "it seems good enough indeed. I know good workmanship, and that is here. Keep the extra coin. Good day, father."

"Good day, and if you now seek Nazun's temple, he will cure your madness."

"I have no time. I have another appointment. Elmanus' guards are seeking me for certain questions involving the death of two priests, and I must find them."

Whistling, Daron went out, and the old man looked after him with shrewd, hard eyes. With sudden decision, brought on by overpowering itch of curiosity, the old man swung heavy shutters across his tiny window, barred them, barred the door, and hobbled off across the town. On his weak legs, it would take him some time to reach Elmanus' court.

CHAPTER VIII

On the highest crest of the rolling land that fronted on the bay, the palace of Elmanus set, overlooking the estates of the nobles. The avenue here was broad, and paved with bricks of well-baked, hard, red clay. Daron's horse trotted along easily and turned into the broad way that led up to the gate. A half dozen uniformed guards, in bright blue-and-white foppish cut, barred his way with neat precision. Daron stopped at their hail and demand of identity, and looked them up and down.

"Now, lads, for all that foppish rig, you've bone and muscle underneath, I do swear! Now let me—Officer, I should say by your stance, and the broadness of your palm, you've walked behind a plow and seen a furrow turn. And a good half of you knows the smell of drying kelp."

"Enough of that!" snapped the officer. "I ask no guesses as to whence we come, but whence you come. In the name of the king, answer, or you'll find time to answer in the keep."

"Now that, my friend, is no threat at all, for there be few places safer in this land. Further, your good king would favor seeing me. I understand certain of your brother guards have marched hot streets the whole day through seeking me. Men call me Daron, and my origin is something even I am not too certain of."

"Daron! Ho, forward, *round!*" The guardsmen moved

with perfect military precision, and with a smoothness Daron admired. He was instantly the center of a small circle hedged with good steel lance points.

"Daron, dismount, in the name of King Elmanus."

"Now softly, friend. What other purpose, think you, brings me here? Take down that hedge, and ease your nervousness. Good. Now, you of the infant mustache, take the horse, and feed him well. I'll want him back. Take sound advice, too. When your friends tell you that is not a mustache, but merely evidence of laziness, believe them. Either shave it off, or dye it dark. On your tanned face, the blond hair seems somewhat weakened, and like drought-burned grain."

The mustached guardsman's face turned red, and his eyes dropped, but he took the horse's reins, his young face sullen. The officer's eyes were lighting with a suppressed amusement and liking.

"Enough, Daron; I give the orders here. But take his horse, Kahlmur—and, by Nazun, his advice! Now forward. Elmanus has ordered your arrest."

"Your statement, officer—very incourteous officer, too, it seems. I know not your name, though you know mine— is exact. He has ordered my arrest; he does not want to see me."

"Pordan Holum, Daron. Holum, Pordan of the Outer Guards. Maybe his majesty does not desire to see you, but you may rest assured the priests of the Invisible Ones do."

The Inner Guards they passed, and to the doors of King Elmanus' Hall of Justice they were passed. Abruptly, there was an eruption of activity about Daron, and shouting officers. Priests began to appear from a dozen ways, priests in the flaming orange-scarlet of the Invisible Ones, and in the blue-green of Nazun, the deep, sea-green of Talun's temple, and the red-streaked white of Martal's retinue.

A tall, gray-eyed priest of Nazun first approached Daron, where he waited easily among the group of Holum's men. The priest was as tall as Daron, lean and thoughtful of mein, but there seemed some lack of fire in his eyes and face, a worried, tired and strained appearance round his mouth, and a crease between his brows.

"In the name of my lord, Nazun, I appear for you, Daron. The adepts of the Invisible Ones accuse you of murdering two of their neophytes within the streets of Tordu." There was a hasty, uneasy pressure to his words, and a curiously worried, uncertain tone in his voice. And, withal, a look of deep respect with which he regarded Daron. Very softly, so that only Daron himself could hear, he added: "Lord Nazun himself has ordered this appearance—but I fear their case is strong!"

Daron laughed. "I have no knowledge of the laws and rulings of this land, wherein your kindly aid is much to be desired, but none save Nazun himself and, perhaps, the Invisible Ones, knows more of this case than I. I think we may manage, and—if Nazun has given you some charge regarding me, perhaps he gave a charge to follow somewhat as I lead in my argument."

"Aye," said the priest uneasily. "He—Lord Nazun—takes interest in few men."

A priest in scarlet-orange, bedecked with gold and flaming jewels hurried up, a fat, round man waddling busily, with sweat-bedewed pate glistening in the light. "Pordan," he howled, "this man is armed. What manner of arrest is this! Take that shield, that sword and dirk from him. The man is a murderer; would you have an armed killer brought before our king!"

Daron turned to him, and bent a steady, hard-eyed gaze upon his fat, sweaty face. "Now by Nazun, my fat friend, you'll need no murdering. Have not your Formless Ones told you you'll die of bursted veins? And would you make a liar out of them by dying before your time?"

The fat-faced priest paled, and panted heavily. "You have no knowledge of that!" he gasped.

"So, I have not. I know nothing of what they say? But yet I do, it seems. Now, be that as it may, remember this. This is the house of King Elmanus, and your orders here are wanted no more than mine; in fact, I think, some several degrees less. I came to this place seeking justice, and of my own free will. Wherefore, my friend, Pordan Holum shows more courtesy than you.

"Now, Pordan Holum," said Daron, turning to the officer, "I give my sword and dirk and shield into your keeping, as an officer of the sea to an officer of the king's guard, to hold and protect with honor, till I may call for them."

"I take them as an officer, to hold and protect," replied Pordan Holum formally—with a gleam of satisfaction directed at the fat priest.

The great oaken doors, bound with mighty hinges of black wrought iron, before which they stood, swung slowly open, and a herald spoke. "In the name of King Elmanus, in the name of Ator, and the people of Azun, the Hall of Justice opens. Bring in those who seek justice before the king."

The crowd surged forward, and it was a growing crowd. A half score of priests in scarlet-orange, and a score in the assorted colors of the Old Gods flanked the little group of Holum's guards that marched with Daron toward the throne.

The room was vast and cool after the heat of outside, the light softened and dimmed. Great slabs of translucent milky quartz made the roof, pouring in the sun's light diluted and cooled. The walls were made of cool, green stone, and the floor was black basalt, soft and soothing to the eye. Great pillars of sea-green stone reached up, carved in intricate and graceful geometric designs.

At the far end of the long, high room sat King Elmanus, on a throne that narrowed Daron's eyes. There was a dais of red granite, and a backdrop of night-blue velvet behind. A ring of guards in that same night-blue velvet faded into it almost unseen, save for the flicker of their unsheathed swords, and their faces. Those faces were tanned and strong, and the men were big, broad-shouldered men with tapering build of speed and stamina. These were no city breed, but strong countrymen and seamen, every one.

But the throne itself! It was a chair of good blue leather, and deeply padded, without hint of gold or jewel, or any frippery. It was a broad, deep seat, with broad, comfortable arms, and the man that sat in it was broad and comfortable.

Daron's narrowed eyes slanted in a smile. Now here was a king who knew his dignity was beyond reproach, and sought the comfort aging bones enjoyed! Two slim, and pretty girls stood beside and slightly behind the throne, and Daron's respect increased. They were dressed in simple, easy-falling robes of some light linen stuff, and in the very simplicity of their garments Daron saw more the character of their master.

With neat precision the guards drew up and halted before Elmanus' throne, and behind them stood the fat priest of the Invisible Ones, and the lean and worried priest of Nazun. Directly before Elmanus, Daron halted.

Elmanus was old, his head crowned with a wealth of white hair that gleamed and shone against the backing of the night-blue velvet drape. He wore a simple jacket of white silk, on which was embroidered in golden threads and scarlet, a crest and coat of arms. And, beneath it, in the oldest language known to man, a brief motto. His breeches were

night-blue linen, with gold thread tracery, and in his hand
he carried a staff of pure gold, chased with a deep-cut formal
design. At the peak of the staff there gleamed a single,
monster sapphire, as deep as skies, and large as a man's
two fists.

Elmanus' face was tired, the dark eyes sunken in old
and leathery skin, his mouth creased about with the graven
lines of many years of struggle, but over all lay lines of easy
humor, and his eyes twinkled with good humor as they looked back into Daron's steady gaze.

"And this is the man you bring me, Tor Lamon, as
double murderer? I say with satisfaction, you are a liar or
mistaken." Elmanus snorted gently, and nodded to himself.
"What is your case?"

The fat priest quivered angrily. "The Invisible Ones,
your majesty, have stated that this is the man."

"Well, what say you for yourself . . . er . . . Daron, isn't
it?"

Daron shrugged, and smiled. "It is a matter of temperament. These two annoyed me. I was forced to remove them."

Elmanus' jetting brows of white, stiff hairs drew down.
"Annoyed you, eh? Are you given to these mad tempers,
then?"

"Aye, in case of such annoyance. One sought to spit me
on his blade, and the other tried hard with dirk and cloak."

Elmanus snorted and leaned back. "Annoyance enough.
What said the Invisible Ones of that, priest?"

"If this man's words be true, then why is it that, not
content with killing them, he coldly mutilated their corpses
so? One, Rehsal, a neophyte of two years' practice, was run
through the throat, and blinded too. Now if the man be
blinded, what need to run him through, and if he be run
through, why blind a corpse, save out of coldly murderous
temperament?

"And the other was yet more fiendishly mutilated! Shulthas was with us on the Temple Isle seven years, and was a man of good and even temper, yet his body we found run through the throat, blinded, and with the hands cut off.

"This Daron, I say, is a madman, a fiendish maniac. Give him to us, before this voyager from other, barbaric lands destroys more. He must be done away with."

Elmanus looked at Daron with lowered brows. "Your temper seems extreme, for even such provocation. What brought this thing about?"

"The power of the Invisible Ones, your majesty. These things I did; I ran the one attacker through the throat and he died as any good man should. I turned to face his companion—and the dead man rose and attacked me with a dirk. I blinded him—and he fought me with a skill he had not shown alive! Now such things I do not like, and it seemed the best thing was to make those hands incapable of grasping blade, and only then did that dead thing lie down as a dead man should!"

"Eh?" Elmanus gasped. "The dead fought!"

"The man lies to save his skin! The dead cannot move!" Tor Lamon roared.

Daron turned to the priest, and regarded him through narrowed eyes. "Now tell me this, priest, your gods can predict the future, can they not?"

"As every Azuni knows."

"And you can tell me the exact and final end to each and every power these gods of yours possess?"

"No, for they are gods, and no true god can be envisaged by a man," the priest replied haughtily, looking pointedly at the lean and worried priest of Nazun. "Their powers are unknown, and unknowable."

"Then," said Daron with finality, "they can raise their

dead neophytes to fight again. That may be unknown and unknowable to you; I saw them, you did not."

Elmanus leaned back, his old eyes brightening.

Tor Lamon sputtered. "The dead cannot rise!" he snapped. "It is preposterous, insane! No—"

"Man," said Daron firmly, "can envisage the powers of a god. So. I saw your Invisible Ones bring the dead to life. Go back to your temples now, and learn more about your gods."

"I think," said Elmanus, with a chuckle in his voice, "his point is very sound. Now on his testimony alone, I would not ordinarily have ruled that he was attacked, but since his arguments are so sound and his logic good enough to meet that of Tor Lamon, who seems sane enough, he must be sane. And if he is sane, he would not make an insane defense. The defense he has presented is insane, or true. If not insane, then it is true. We have shown him sane—sane at least as Tor Lamon—and therefore we must accept his statement and defense as true."

Elmanus leaned back with satisfaction in his sparkling old eyes, and watched the empurpling countenance of Tor Lamon. "I dismiss the charge. Daron is free."

"Your majesty," said Tor Lamon with difficulty, "there is a further vital point. I must accept your ruling that this outlander can murder—"

Elmanus' heavy brows shot down, and his finger shot out to stab at the fat priest violently. "I said the charge was dismissed!" he roared, in a voice that blasted at the great room's roof, and set Tor Lamon back in shock. "You deny my ruling by that statement."

"I—I retract my words. I . . . I spoke without due thought. But, your majesty, there is a further trouble this outlander brings."

"Speak then," snapped the old king, his deep eyes sparkling.

"The predictions of the future that our whole country depends upon today—"

"And more fools they," said Daron softly. Elmanus lips twitched.

"—are upset by this outlander. These predictions are based on a knowledge of all things that enter into life upon this empire you rule. Now this outlander has appeared, and injected a new and disturbing element, an element not in the orbits of the peoples of Azun, and upsets the prediction of the longer range."

"Your gods are strong," said Daron softly. "They are mighty, beyond the understanding of man. One man upsets their powers, which is, indeed, beyond the understanding of man, as far beyond his understanding as that a heavy ox cart be upset by a single grain of dust. Strange are the ways of the Invisible Ones."

Tor Lamon purpled with rage. "As much," he ground out, "as the power to predict the future is beyond your comprehension."

"The man's point," said Elmanus mildly, "is well made. It does seem strange." Elmanus relaxed back into his chair with a deep satisfaction. This was, beyond doubt, one of the most excellent examples of priest-baiting he had seen in fifty-five years of weary tending to dry and wordy cases. This Daron was a man to have around!

Tor Lamon's cheeks paled from their fat-bleached dusky red to a cold, white rage. "If a man have two children, and each of these children have but two, and these in turn have no more than two, there will be sixteen then, in the course of one man's lifetime. Now if the man—and his children like him—be an active man, given to killing neighbors who annoy him, at the rate of two in four days, such a family may have profound effect. In fact, it would appear, but some four generations of such men and we would have no more Azuni left in our empire!"

"That sounds somewhat improbable, but still seems a point possible of argument," said Elmanus weightily. "Surely you have asked the Invisible Ones when this man shall die?"

Tor Lamon writhed, and Daron, who had studied more than one useful art, spoke softly. "The Invisible Ones could not give him that answer, for their powers are strangely limited, but they could, and did, tell him this; Tor Lamon dies here, this day!"

The paleness of Tor Lamon's face became ghastly, his lips and eyelids became blued and purpled slowly as he stood, and stark fear shone in his eyes, all rage dying out. "You . . . you cannot know!" he gasped—and screamed as he said it, doubling up and clutching at his heart. He rolled, and fell at Elmanus' feet, dead.

A dozen lesser priests sprang forward, and knelt by the fallen Tor Lamon's side. Slowly they straightened. "Tor Lamon knew that he would die here," they acknowledged.

"How," asked Elmanus uneasily, "did you know this? Are you some newer god still, another god to plague my people here with death?"

Daron shook his head slowly. "There is a vein in the neck, even so fat a neck, and a swelling at the base of his neck, even beyond his fat, and many other small signs that the skilled may learn. I learned those signs. If the man's brain be exposed, there may be found a small but fatal leakage of blood. It may be, though, that the bursting of the great vein of the heart did this. The man was doomed, and being given to anger, doomed him doubly."

"Your majesty," a scarlet-orange robed priest said, "we ask one thing. This man should die; his very presence has, now, three times taken Azuni lives."

"Through defense against attack, twice, and only by the over-weening anger of Tor Lamon, the third time. The man lives, "said Elmanus decisively.

"Then, in the name of the Invisible Ones, let this man be taken for study to the Temple Isle, that he may be fitted into the pattern, that the knowledge of the future may not be disrupted."

"With the proviso that one month hence, the man be returned to me, healthy, whole, and sane as he is now, that seems a fair request." Elmanus looked at Daron.

"With that proviso," said Daron distastefully, "and the additional one that I be given time to see the sun and breathe the air, I suppose I must agree."

"So be it then," Elmanus nodded. "Take him and all his possessions with him, save his horse, to be returned to him when, one month hence, he returns here before me."

Daron looked slowly at the silent priest of Nazun. The man looked worried, tired, and wearied by his worry. He looked baffled, too, as he looked into Daron's eyes and saw therein a deep total satisfaction!

CHAPTER IX

DARON STOOD MOTIONLESS, weaponless, helmetless, before the scarlet-orange robed high priest of the Invisible Ones. This temple room was small, its walls pure white marble, their decorations a bas-relief of symbolic scenes in the creation of the Invisible Ones. Behind the high priest stood a block of basalt as black as the pit, streaked and grained with flaming scarlet-orange veins in lightning darts of brilliant color.

There was no other thing in the room, and light that entered came through plates of pure white marble shaved thin as heavy paper, diffused and softened, shadowless. But above that altar there remained a feel of vast and angry tension, a straining, malignant drive that sought to reach and tear at the mind of the sea rover standing between four heavy-thewed and brawny priest guards.

Priests those four might be, but by the ripple of their scarlet-orange cloaks across their broad and heavy shoulders, their training had come in larger degree from the hilt of a sword and the grip of a shield than from the pages of a book. They gripped their silvery needle swords now with an easy sureness that spoke conclusively of confidence in handling them.

But confidence was gone now from the face of the high priest; his brows were contracted in a frown of futile anger, his eyes blazing with rage, and his lips strangely tense with fear and lack of surety.

"Who are you, outlander? Was that aged fool, Elmanus, right in naming you some new and potent god, a god both material and of force, too? The Invisible Ones shy off from you, cannot reach and touch your brain. Speak, what are you —man or god?"

A slow, easy smile of complete and easy satisfaction touched Daron's lips. "Now that, friend priest, it seems to me, is the purpose of my being here; you seek to find that answer. Sure it seems, Elmanus gave you thirty days to learn, and me no orders to inform you.

"This I will say; you'll know before the thirty days are gone—but not from my lips." Daron's smile changed to a solemn frown of thought. "But hold. You and your priests have maintained that no true god can appear as a man. A god, you say, by very definition is non-human, beyond conception of a human mind. Now that is a point I would not agree upon, but your own definition shows you, it would seem, that I must be a man, and no god."

"Why do you dispute that definition?" snapped the priest. "It is clear that a man-thing is no god, for, by very definition, a god is superhuman."

Daron laughed. "True enough, and sound logic that may be. But you have lost, here, it seems, the principles of logic. Have you heard, perhaps, of the 'undistributed middle'? Look you, a fish swims in the sea."

"Aye."

"I swim in the sea. Therefore I am a fish."

"And of what importance is your false and silly sophistry?"

"A god is more than man," said Daron pointedly.

"By definition, that is so."

"And more than man's conception can hold. Wherefore you limit his powers stringently in one thing; whatever he may be, it must be unfamiliar, he cannot appear a man. So—and, swimming in the sea, I am a fish."

The high priest cursed softly to himself, and glared at Daron's mocking eyes, and cursed again at old—but potent!—King Elmanus.

"Your mind is a maze of silly, tricking traps and nonsense thoughts. The Invisible Ones appear in any form they choose; watch now the altar top, watch closely, see the darkening there—the slow darkening and condensation—see it grow, grow darker, more solid, a vague cloud at first—solidifying, strengthening—forming to no normal man but a winged being of luminosity—a glowing, slowly forming thing—"

Daron smiled and nodded to himself, and stole a sideward glance at the four priest guards who stood beside him. Awe and fear were growing on their faces; and in Daron's mind a dry old voice repeated an old refrain in the liquid, fluent syllables of the Ind: "No mind but yours can rule your thoughts, no mind but yours can control your inner self. But your mind will, if you permit it, follow after any other mind, and see and feel and be as that other mind desires—if you will let it! I can make you see the flower or the tiger, smell the perfume or the acrid breath, but it is your mind, not mine, that does that thing."

And Daron looked at the empty altar and smiled at the futile mouthings of the fat and sweating priest. His hands moved and waved in futile gropings, and Daron let his mind laugh at the futility and pay no heed at all to all the high priest's exhortations.

"Your men," said Daron softly, "see wondrous things. I see an empty altar. Cease your foolish mouthings, and get on with what you seek to do."

The high priest's eyes blazed in exasperation, and he

collapsed from mighty dignity like a pricked bladder of air. "Wake!" he snapped fretfully. "You see no more."

Four priest guards started, their eyes blinked rapidly, and their mouths gaped foolishly at empty air. With the white calm of incandescent fury, the high priest spoke again. "Take this accursed outlander to the South Wing of cells, and keep him there. I'll search him later."

Angrily the high priest turned away, and vanished through a door that seemed a part of the marble wall. Daron turned to the awed guards, and looked at them through lowered lids, a broad grin splitting his face. "Remarkable! These Invisible Ones are invisible indeed. You seemed to see something there?"

"Quiet!" snapped the leader of the four. "March, and step along."

Daron followed easily, his mind busy with his thoughts. For one thing old Barhamu had said was true; no mind but his could touch his inner self. And one thing he had said was not true of these Azuni—they could trick the minds of many men, a mass of worshipers!

Down from the upper levels of the temple they went, and through corridors hollowed out in black basalt that formed the foundations of the isle, then across half the width of the isle it seemed, to rise again into a building of gray, hard granite, and huge oaken, iron-bound doors. A guard in dull-blue cloak and well-worn leather turned a huge iron lock and passed them through, accompanying them, to use his key again upon another door.

The passageway before them now—walled and floored and ceiled with hard gray stone—was lined with heavy doors, iron bound and locked. It was a narrow passageway, so that but two men could walk abreast, and at the far end an open door opened into a guard room where four blue-caped and

well-weaponed guards lounged at their ease, to straighten
into interest as the men came up the hill.

"In the name of the high priest, Shor Lang, we bring
this prisoner. By King Elmanus' given order, one month he
stays, to be guarded, fed and kept in health. And these are
the orders of Shor Lang," said the scarlet-orange garbed
leader of the priest guards formally.

One of the blue-caped prison guards, his head covered
by a good steel helmet, worn at a jaunty, carefree angle,
nodded, grunted, and tossed a heavy iron key to the priest
guard. "Number three, down the way. If he's the howling
menace to peace of mind that stinking fisherman we just
threw out of there has been, you can have him back and
welcome."

Daron's swift eyes took in the room. Two benches, two
chairs, all hard and made of slabbed wood. One table, with
a good and comfortable chair. A paneled case on one wall
filled with bound volumes with a thousand titles—all reli-
gious. The table was littered with a dozen stacks of a dozen
different forms, ink and pens, and odds and ends. As Daron
turned away, the captain of the guards was filling in one of
the forms.

"Where's his equipment, or does he walk the streets
as naked of blade as he is now?" he asked.

"His materials will be brought to you for storing in the
locker room. Elmanus ordered all returned to him one month
hence. A shield—and it's one of those mirror things old
Elmanus finally got sense to dispense with—a sword, a dirk,
and a helmet of gold and silver wire and phony jewels."

"Wire?" The captain of the guards looked up, and then
looked toward Daron's retreating back. "A fool. If he had
gold and silver, he could get good steel and leather. I'll hold
this form till the things arrive. Here's receipt for your man.
Hm-m-m, he rolls like a seaman but his garb stinks of earth."

Daron stepped through the oaken door to his cell. The walls were gray granite, too tough it seemed for even prisoners' patient scratching of names and decorations. One cot, one chair of hard oak slabs, and little other furnishing. The door closed behind him with a *thunk* of very sound and solid oak, and the lock turned with an oily grate of heavy steel.

Daron paced the room with eyes keen in observation. The door was no flimsy thing, but it was pierced by a spyhole with a little sliding plate that let the guards look in whenever they might think of it, but left the prisoner blind as to passings in the corridor.

A window, high on the other side of the tiny cell, was barred with inch-thick wrought iron, blackened by weather, but resistant to rust. They were let into a granite block of size and strength that echoed clearly: "No—not this way, my friend."

Daron lay down to pass the time and think a bit. A month he had to plan his way—which should be time enough. An hour after he came, a guard came down on feet so soft they made no noise through thick oak panels. Only the sudden *clank* of the sliding spy-hole plate, and the gleam of a weirdly unsupported eye apprised Daron of his coming. Daron grunted. With that sudden sort of inspection, there'd be no safe working out of tools within this room.

Restlessly, he went over to the spy-hole again. Six close-spaced bars of metal stopped it from the inner side. Bronze, though, and Daron eyed them speculatively. Daron carried a dirk-blade without handle beneath his clothes, a handy thing, he'd found.

The light died out of the high window, and the cell was dark. Daron slept.

With morning, the door was opened by two guardsmen, accompanying a single small and worried man in a greasy apron. The small and worried man edged nervously into Daron's room, and offered him a tray of wood, bearing two bowls of food.

The sea rover laughed. "My friend, I eat men only when most direly hungry. Keep me well fed, and your bones are safe enough."

The little, gray-haired man's lips pulled aside in a mechanical and nervous smile. "Yes. Yes, yes, oh yes. Food. Yes, sir. I—"

Daron looked at the grinning guards. "Has some one been frowning at him?"

"There's a fisherman with hair and strength enough to be old Talun himself down the way, and this goat-eared thing that calls itself a cook has been underfeeding him. Drathun, our fishing friend, swears he'll eat him yet," said one of the guards.

"Why, if I know seamen and their ways, there'd be peace and safety for him if he'd feed him," Daron commented.

"Eat up yourself, and get ready," said the guard as the little man danced nervously through the closing door. "Old Elmanus, so they tell me, ordered exercise and air. And Shor Lang says the gardens. So . . . so you'll learn some gardening in an hour more."

An hour later, the little man was back to pick up the empty bowls. The food was bad enough, but fairly plentiful, so Daron felt easy as he strolled out to the passageway. Six guards were there now, and the captain of them was going down the hall, opening the great cell doors one at a time, with a huge brass key. A dozen assorted prisoners came out, some seamen, browned and smelling of dried kelp and fish scales, some farming men, with brown-stained hands, and shambling, easy walk, and one man with the mold of lumbering.

Daron watched the process keenly. The corridor was lined up all one side with cells, and heavy doors that opened outward into the passage. Two cells opened from the other wall. At one end of the passage—the end but two doors from his own cell—there was a heavy oaken door that let out to the main building. At the opposite end was the guardroom's ever-watchful doors.

As Daron stepped out into the corridor the men from the cells nearest that outer door were already waiting. One, a massive, squat chunk of a man with bearlike arms and legs, and bearlike forward-slanting neck, looked up at him from deep sunken eyes beneath enormous bushy eyebrows, black as charcoal marks. His body, through torn and salt-stained jacket and breeches, was as hairy as an animal's.

But the little, far-sunk eyes were twinkling with good humor, and the mouth was wide and strong, the creases round its corners slanting upward.

"So," he said, in a gentle rumble, like a starting avalanche, "this be the outlander then? I'm Drathun, fisherman because no other of the scum of Nozos have the guts to sail beyond a dog's bark or a birdie's peep. What are these other lands? As big as Azun, then?"

"Nozos?" said Daron. "Hm-m-m, that's on the Isle of Eran, is it not? Ah yes. As to the outer world. There's more sea than land, man, but there's far more land than ever you've seen. What brings you here?"

"Catching fishes in the isle's shadow!" he boomed in laughter. "They feared their pretty barges would smell of good, clean food."

"So they teach you now the beauty of the little pansy and the delicacy of the rose's sweet perfume? A new trade for you then?"

"Gardening!" Drathun snorted. "And two more months

of that. Solmun, my helper—aye, the lad with midget mustache on his lips—goes free in another week."

"Quiet," roared the guard captain. "Now, *march*!"

He led them to the door, worked at the lock with his great key, and the little troop was led outside, down an angling corridor to stop before another oaken door. Three guards remained with them, and three stepped through the doorway as the captain unlocked it with his key. Racked tools occupied one wall, and on the other, Daron's sharpening eyes saw a miscellany of possessions. Nets and clubs and hats and—a silver-plated bronze shield, a long, strong sword, a jewel-hilted dirk, and a familiar helmet of gold and silver wires and curious jewels.

A heavy mattock in his hands, Daron followed quietly to the gardens outside. A tangled mass of weeds and tough-rooted creepers sprang from an uneven plot of newly imported soil that lay upon the barren basalt rock. Two lanky farming lads, Daron, and Drathun, the chunky fisherman, were set to work, watched by one crossbow-armed guard.

The sun was hot, the air was still, and the roots were tough. The position of work was one Daron was not accustomed to, and his muscles ached before the day was done. He slept that night with the heavy, solid sleep of exhaustion. And—of contentment. He had a month.

CHAPTER X

DARON SAT DOWN WITH HIS back to a tree, and the heavy odor of new turned, sun-baked earth in his nostrils. Only faintly the salt, clear scent of the sea swept in, and he looked with sour eyes at the glint of sun on wind-ruffled waters.

"Drathun, my friend," he sighed at last, "that, and not this stubborn land, is the place for men. Now a plant belongs in soil, rooted and fixed, unchanging itself in a never-changing stuff. But for a man to grow—and growth is change—he needs must live where change is constant on the sea."

"Aye—and a month, a week, and two more days before I get back to it." Drathun's deep-buried, twinkling eyes looked saddened.

"I think," said Daron softly, looking up through the tracery of an ornamental tree, "that we might leave these people here without their full consent. If you don't roar it out like a captain calling the bow-watch in a storm."

"Eh?" said Drathun sharply, in a much reduced bellow. His powerful, blocky body tensed.

"Do you," asked Daron, "like our aid and helper there, Tarmun, the farmer?"

"He's a solid ox, but good enough."

"Tarmun!" called Daron, turning toward the farmer lolling under a hedge, a floppy hat of straw across his face.

The gangling farmer raised his head, and the hat fell

away. His face was long and sad and brown, and the man himself was long and sad and brown—and only Daron had the strength of arm to equal that of the slow-moving farmer.

"This shade is cooler here—and our brief hour of rest draws to a close. Come nearer, friend. I want to know that triply distilled essence of vegetable evil the next time I pull its root. That—what is its name?"

"Snake-bite root," the farmer roused himself gradually, stretched, and ambled over. "You can tell it," he sighed lugubriously, "by the purple veining of the root, and"—his voice fell as he sat near them, and farther from the guard still munching on his lunch in the shade of another tree— "you're a liar, my friend. You know it well after one bite, being above the wit of a hog, which learns likewise, in one good sting. What do you seamen want of me?"

"You like it here, perhaps, in the Temple of the Invisible Ones, my friend?"

"I loathe their rotten ways as heartily as you men of Talun do, as you well know."

"Then, my strong-armed friend," said Daron easily, staring up through the tree to the free blue sky, "do me the favor of tying this lumpy one in a goodly running bowline as the guard puts us in the cells this night. You know perhaps an insult or two to sting a seaman's hide?"

"Oh, the seaman's good enough in his place, but the place has too much smell. That stinking merchandise that Drathun would have us think is food, makes right good nourishment for plants, when well rotted at their roots."

Drathun's deep-sunk eyes grew somewhat brighter, and his wide, friendly mouth grew harder. "My oxlike friend, you learn your wit and knowledge from the horses you nurse about your farm. I'll knot those hawser-things that you call arms with greatest joy tonight."

"Aye, so?" said Tarmun sadly. "But then, Daron perhaps knows better why and when and where this thing should find its working out."

"In the passage before our cells, when all but we have been locked away. Drathun, your cell is nearest to the door, on that same side on which my cell is placed. Tarmun, your cell is across from my own. The cell on your side nearest to the outer way is unoccupied. We three will be last to be put away. If you would fight—"

"Aye," said Drathun. "We will, but, friend—" His brows drew down in puzzled wonder, and his tiny, deep-set eyes looked up at Daron from under paint-brush brows.

A guard stood up, stretched leisurely, and roared a call to work. The three beneath the tree moved apart reluctantly, Daron's voice rising slowly in "—know the accursed rope next time I spot it, and I'll fry it slow and happily."

Tarmun yawned. "Do that, seaman, and you'll learn that plants have better protection than your brainless fish. Fry it, and the vapors will give you such an itch on all your body as you've never known, nor ever will forget. Drop that—it's mine. It's lighter."

"Yours, you mud-footed farmer, that tool is mine!" roared Drathun, grabbing at the mattock angrily, well knowing it was his, and Tarmun knew it, too.

"Let loose, fish-skin. You'll never swing a mattock like a man, and that will bring more aches than results, with your soft-muscled flesh."

"Why, you horse-faced flounder of the land! Let go that hold, before I try the mattock blade in that dried clay you call a head! I'll—"

"You," said a bored guard, "will drop that thing, seaman. If your friend, the ox, wants to play with it, let him. Sure it fits his hand better than yours, but I'll try a rope's end on your back if you prefer to argue."

Growling, Drathun picked up another mattock, and swung to his work, his brow-hidden eyes darting at the shambling, long-armed farmer.

From a dozen ornamental trees about the gardens, Daron collected bits of exuding gum, and chewed them placidly, to moisten his work-dried mouth. The guards sat comfortably in the shade, and joked at the laboring men, and kept the water bottles handy.

Twice through the long, hot afternoon the stubby, bear-like seaman and the horse-faced farmer came near blows, and twice the bored guard captain stopped their angry voices. With sunset, the dozen men were gathered together, and marched back to their cells, placed before their doors, and one by one locked in.

The captain locked away the fourth from last, and turned to Daron. In a slow, drawling voice the lanky farmer spoke. "Was it," he asked of Drathun gently, "your mother or your father that was the bear? For surely you cannot be full human with such a pelt as that. You should use a currycomb more frequently, and comb the stink of fish from it."

From the gray granite floor, Drathun swung a calloused fist toward the farmer's heavy jaw. With the slightest, slowest movement possible, Tarmun moved aside. His long arm reached out, grabbed Drathun's fist, and in an instant the two were rolling, struggling on the floor.

The captain of the guard looked down with exasperated boredom.

Daron roared in laughter. "Ho guard, give me that key! They've been wanting to fight this out all day; we'll let 'em try it for a night."

Grinning, the captain released the key, and Daron, with a mighty heave of his foot, sent both the struggling pair into the vacant cell, and locked the door on them, to toss the key to the captain. He stared through the peephole slot, till the guard captain shoved him aside.

"Now my fine buckoes, you two can fight the whole night through," said the captain sourly, "if such be your mind, or you can learn the part of men and stand up here. Your supper will be in your cell, but by the Invisible Ones, there'll be no scrap of food in that place you've got now."

Sullenly, the two men rose, eyeing each other angrily. Equally sullenly, they came out, to be locked in their separate cells, as Daron stepped into his. In Daron's closed palm, however, was an impression on the gums he'd gathered of that master key that turned all locks in this whole wing!

And in Daron's mind—lest the Invisible Ones be seeking to read his thoughts and plans—was a turmoil that defied their every effort. And that, too, was thanks to the old wizard of the Ind. Daron was trying to remember places, people, and happenings he had forgotten, and since most forgetting is caused by a subconscious barrier to remembrance, both conscious and subconscious minds were in a fine fog.

Under the tree, the next noon hour, Daron and Drathun sat, and at long and patient calling, Tarmun at last came over, mollified. He sank down beside Daron, well away from Drathun, the half-amused, half-bored guard captain watching Daron's laughing eyes as he smoothed their anger down.

"And now, since Drathun plays with closed fists, I have an eye two shades darker than the other," sighed Tarmun, "and no good reason for it. I like the man—and he's as slippery as one of his own eels. What was the reason for this?"

"An impression in a bit of gum. I've a design of that magic bit of metal called a key our guard captain conjures our doors open with. Within another pair of nights, I could carve out a key to do the same—but for that thrice-accursed peephole in my door. But—I've a mind to block it up."

"The guard," said Tarmun sourly, "will approve of that."

"He will," laughed Daron, "when he sees my block! Now Drathun; you say your assistant was held less blameworthy, less punished for the crime of fishing in the bay?"

"Aye. The Invisible Ones are touchy on the score since old Talun sent droves of dying fish to pollute the bay, and drive the noble pretties on their way."

"He goes in two days, I think?"

"Aye."

"Now if I were a fisherman released from this place, I'd go to Talun's good temple on Mt. Kalun, and give thanks to him. And, if I were released at such a time as this, I'd tell the priests of Talun that the fishing fleets might well be here—following a heavy run, perhaps—when next the moon is dark. Say five days hence."

"Aye, would you now? Daron, you seem to me a man of sense; I'll tell the boy your good advice." Drathun's deep eyes looked uneasily at Daron's immobile, placid face. "A run of fish, the whole fleet would follow willingly—if Talun would grant such things at any man's request."

"And were I released, a seaman, now, after seeing Talun's temple, I'd seek the fishing fleet, and tell them of my strong dislike for this prettied isle, and this misused harbor that has beribbon-decked girls for sailors. I'd even try to urge them to sail in here in force."

"Their reluctance would not be overwhelming—if they saw a reason there," remarked Drathun.

"Now," said Daron, "if such things had been suggested to you, as a fisherman, and it had been mentioned that, if Talun approved, a run of fish would come—would you follow such a run, and enter the harbor?"

"And every man of Nozos, and every other fishing port as well!" Drathun answered.

"And," said Tarmun lazily, "you might mention that idea to a farmer here and there. Who be ye, Daron? Man or god?"

"There'll be small loss, however it may fall, if no run of fish appears to tell of Talun's approval," said Daron with finality.

"None," agreed Drathun, stretching mightily, and standing up. He wandered off to settle heavily beside his young assistant, a hundred yards away.

Daron was wandering about, picking up some bits of wood and twigs. Presently the guard called them to work again.

The captain of the guard walked down the row of cell doors on soft feet, mechanically slipping open the peepholes of the doors to glance at the men within. He came to No. 3, leaned toward the peephole and slipped the plate aside—and jumped back with a howl of dismay—

Abruptly from within came a roar of echoing laughter, and the captain of the guard looked again, heard the running feet of the guardsmen down the corridor, and cursed luridly.

"By the Invisible Ones!" he roared, "that triply-damned slot nipped out a piece of my thumb as neatly as you please. Go on back, ye fools. I'll fix the thing."

Angrily he unlocked the door and swung it open as his men turned back. He stepped inside the door, and pulled it halfway shut behind him. On the cot, doubled up in the light of his lamp, Daron was laughing soundlessly now.

He wiped his eyes, and looked up at the furious face of the captain of the guard. "By the gods, captain, do me this small turn; leave up the thing, and let your men bite as hard as you! So it nipped your thumb, eh?"

The captain glared at him. "Nipped my thumb? Blazes, no, as you well know, fish-skinner! It stuck its leering face out into mine when I slid that peephole cover aside, and I liked to jump out of my sandals with the startlement!"

Daron laughed silently, and through his laughter managed: "My respects, captain! Ye've a mind that works fast."

The captain snorted softly and turned toward the door and its peephole. "And have my men make me a laughing stock for crying 'Guard! Guard!' for fright at a silly jack-in-the-box—though, by the god's, a more obscene face my eyes have never laid on before! What is the cursed thing?"

One of the light bronze bars had been twisted from the peephole grate to make room for the contraption of paper, twigs and strings. A knotty root supplied an evil, tiny face with hideous, wormy beard, held on a springy twig that had been compressed behind the peephole plate to thrust the startling obscenity of the twisted root in the captain's face when the plate was moved. A bit of luridly red paper supplied a body of snakelike form, a wholly startling thing.

"A root!" the captain grated in disgust.

"A root!" said Daron, shaken with laughter. "Let not this art be sacrificed with but one showing, friend!"

In silent anger at his own stupidity, the captain closed the door, and slipped the peephole shutter back. He could hear the scratchings as Daron fitted up his contraption again.

He walked on his rounds, and so did not hear the further scratchings as Daron carved, from the removed bronze rod, a duplicate of the captain's key that had been hidden against his belly when the captain opened the door.

An hour later, there was another howl of terror, a moment's silence, and a lurid cursing of a nipping slide. Daron, in silent laughter, stared out the hole into the red and foolish face of the guard. In determined silence the guard replaced the trap, and Daron returned to his carving. Slow work, for even good hard steel does not make fast progress on well-tempered bronze. But the key was shaping.

CHAPTER XI

"MAYAN'S A FOOL—HE NEVER brought in more than a thousand pounds of fish at once in his life—but he's agreed to do it tonight. And Tarmun will be ready." Drathun whispered as he passed Daron. The guard snapped something at him, and he turned into the cell.

Thirty seconds later, Daron was locked in his cell, and within an hour, the last meal of the day was gone, and the little timid man had collected the bowls of their food.

Then: "Guard! Ho, guard!" Tarmun was roaring.

The guardsman walked down the corridor lazily. "Aye, what is it?"

"The Captain gave me permission to wash the earth from my jacket this evening. Let me down to the washroom."

"Captain, Tarmun, the farmer, wants to wash his jacket down the passage."

"Let him go," called the captain boredly, "but keep an eye on him."

Daron heard the click and scrape of the heavy key in Tarmun's lock then the heavy tread of the farmer, passing by his door.

"Hey, guard!"

"Aye, what now?"

"I be going mad of sitting here in one small room. In the name of the gods, will you let me get something to read, at least?"

"Captain! Mayan, the fisherman, wants something to read. Shall I send him down."

"Now by the Invisible Ones! I didn't think the fool had brains enough! Aye, send him down the hall, and if he must read, he'll read of the true gods."

Again the great bronze key scraped in a lock, and the heavy hinges creaked as the door was forced open. Mayan's rolling steps echoed down the stone-walled hall.

Mayan's cell was but one door beyond Daron's and on Daron's side of the corridor. Tarmun's cell was directly across the corridor. With the two men out of their cells, one walking by the guard down to the washroom, the other bound down the long hall to the guardroom—

With a single flowing motion, Daron was up and at his door. The five remaining bronze bars behind the peephole clinked in Daron's hand, and noiselessly, the peephole plate slid back. Through the hole, Daron saw what he had prayed for. With both men out of their cells, their great oak doors stood open—open into the narrow passageway from opposite sides, completely cutting off the view from the guardroom! And the guard was watching Tarmun wash his jacket.

Daron's long arm snaked out through the peephole, reached down, and thrust the key he'd carved into the lock of the door. It scraped, stuck a bit, turned—and the door opened. Instantly, Daron's arm was back, the five bronze bars were refixed in the peephole, and the contraption of roots and paper blocked the hole again.

Daron swung through the door, and as the door closed soundlessly behind him, he stiffened in horror.

"Ho!" came the roar of Tarmun's great voice down the passageway. Daron had the door half open again, and was darting through as the voice roared on.

"—on a fair spring day,

"When the snow's away,

"We'll plant the seed and pull the weed,
"And wait the harvest's sway—ay—"

Daron cursed weakly, and stepped out the door again. The lock clicked to behind him, and the key was in his hand again. Two steps, two motions, and Drathun's door swung open, and the squat, powerful seaman moved soundlessly out. Two steps more, the door was shut and locked behind him, and the outer door swung open. Instantly Drathun was through, then Daron, and that door too, was locked tight behind.

"Left," whispered Daron, and the two were off on soundless, shoeless feet—each, at Daron's strict order, thinking furiously of things they could not remember! Left, and down, and across a deserted corridor, and the key slipped in another iron-bound oaken door. The unoiled hinge creaked softly, and Daron cursed beneath his breath, then they were in.

From beneath his jacket, Drathun pulled a stub of candle, lit it, and the door was closed behind them. In the light of the candle's glow, the locker room was ghostly with hunched things, unnamable and unrecognizable. Two tense-nerved men danced lightly on their feet as each made his way to his own things.

Ten seconds later, Daron was out, and Drathun close behind. On Daron's head sat now the gold-and-silver wired cap of Nazun, and in his hand he carried his own good sword. Drathun, behind him, had a helmet of good round steel he'd looted from some temple guard, and bore a sword like a good ship's spar for length and mass.

Daron's mind went blank for just an instant's time, as he sent a frantic prayer to Nazun for guidance—then something smashed into his mind, and exploded in his brain. In the instant it came, it died—but left its trace on Daron's mind.

"Remember forgotten things," Daron whispered to Drathun, and the squat seaman nodded, his deep-set eyes blank with thought. Daron took his arm, and jerked him to motion down a side corridor.

In that instant's flash of understanding, a map of the entire Temple Isle had been engraved upon his mind—and the room of the sphere he knew! On fleeing, soundless feet he set out, with Drathun's shorter legs rolling fast and noiseless behind. Down long gray corridors of granite he went, then down a stair that led to black basalt corridors.

The candle flickered in the lightless gloom, and shadows writhed behind them and before. There was an odor of musty dark, and the faintly sour smell of sea-washed rock about them. Through long, long tunnels they fled, till they were far beneath the main temple of marble.

"There's something pricking at my mind," Drathun whispered.

As he spoke, Daron felt the first strange tingling of the cap he wore, and a soft, dim glow of bluish lights like the lights of the winter sky in the far north, played round his head. Simultaneously, Daron was turning off and down, along a horizontal corridor of black basaltic rock, then down a stair. Another corridor branched off, turned, and descended once more. But now the black basalt of the isle was not fine enough. This run was lined with white marble blocks.

The candle was out, and far ahead Daron heard the stir of men, and excited voices. A light sprang into being ahead, and the two dropped aside in a branching corridor to wait.

A pair of scarlet-orange cloaked priestly guards ran by, their voices tense and angry, bearing a crystal lamp. Behind them another pair appeared. Then the lights were all upon the way the seamen had come. They started on, had made a hundred yards, when from a black tunnel mouth two guards sprang out with roaring cries that mouthed and mumbled down the bore, and lost all semblance of voices to become vague animal cries.

"Their hands!" snapped Daron, "Take off their hands— or these things will not die!"

Drathun snorted, and his broad mouth opened in a grin. The great sword he bore he twirled like a staff of wheat, his great thick wrists untiring in its lightning glimmer. It struck the priest guard's lighter weapon, twisted, flung the thing aside to clatter on the floor—and drank at the man's heart. The figure in scarlet-orange slumped, fell forward, and measured its length on the floor. Drathun turned to find Daron engaged with a left-handed opponent now—and gasped as the man he'd killed stabbed up at him from the floor, dead eyes white and ghastly in the light of the lamp the priests had carried.

"They can't die!" the fisherman gasped, his blade slowed by his very fear of this unholy thing.

"No, fool—their hands, take off the hands, and dead or alive, they can't grip blades!"

Two minutes lost, two handless corpses behind, they pressed down the corridor. The men they dodged were ranging back now, their shouts and cries an echoing confusion down the corridors. Daron ran on, eyes grim and determined, Drathun beside him sweating cold with horror. This thing was new to him, and none too old to Daron.

"Two turns more, Drathun, and we reach the room. Look not within, or you fall paralyzed. Believe me there, as you did not believe what I said of those undead guards. I'll go within; you guard my back, and look not in the room until I call. Hear?"

"Aye. I'll wait outside."

They turned a corner—turned another, and met a dozen guards, looking this way and that to locate the source of echoing calls that resounded endlessly in the halls. The two were in their midst and through them to the doorway before they well knew they'd come.

And at that doorway, a sheet of livid lightning struck, struck—and held! Blue curling flame, that writhed and danced and shrieked! A scarlet-orange guard backed away in leaping panic of the thing at his back, and Daron tripped him with a flying foot. The man stumbled, twisted, shrieked as he touched the wall of flame.

Then he fell through, but was not consumed. Instead, he wavered slowly to his feet, as guards and attackers stopped alike in fascination. The man stood up, and his face was blank, his lips lax, his arms helpless, flabby things that swung at his sides. He laughed and chuckled, and the chilling sound rattled loosely in the corridor. He laughed, and the laughter grew in Gargantuan reboundings, thrusting fingers of madness in their brains.

Then the soldier-priest was dancing, dancing, skipping down the hall, and the men drew back and let him pass.

Daron stiffened, and his face went white and tense. "Nazun!" he called—and leaped toward that sheet of waving flame.

He touched it, and the helmet on his head grew warm while icy pricklings tore at his scalp. A shrieking hell of warring forces danced and sang and shattered in crystalline trumpetings about him, his body ran in crimson flame, blue laced, and wrapped in the blue lightnings of the Invisible Ones, a sheath of flickerings that blinded.

Warring things struggled there, with low mumblings of sound and silent fury that underran the root of their blasting. Then slowly, from the very peak, where the dead, black stone of Barak, Lord of Fate reposed, a veil of black welled out, a heavy, clinging smoke of night that rippled, spread out, and overran, tumbling down about the figure that stood paralyzed, a helpless point on which two unseen forces concentrated.

The black lapped out, and drank the blue curtain of flame, drank and pulled and grew, and the howling hell of lightning died down, weakened, till only the mad, maddening mutterings remained, and even they grew weak. The icy pricklings left his scalp; the crimson cocoon of fire withdrew—

Abruptly he was through the doorway, and in the same instant that the cloaking cloud of blackness vanished, Daron pulled from a hidden pocket the little mechanism the watchmaker had made for him, and clamped it in his eye, a monocle of mechanism. He touched a button, and it whirred, softly, swiftly. Behind him he heard the roar of fear-struck guards coming again to life and action, and the clang of Drathun's mighty sword. Before him, in the same instant, he saw the circle of guards.

A dozen picked fighting men, men in cloaks of pure white wool, with harness of creamy leather, studded heavily with silver fittings, leaping toward him who faced at last the three-foot globe that was the root and being of the Invisible Ones!

There was fear and stark amazement on the faces of the guards, a fear and unknowingness that hampered their minds, and slowed their movement. This huge and bearded warrior who stood before them, with one blue eye closed and a monocle of whirring mechanism mounted in his other eye, this—man or god—who passed the veil of madness!

Daron's silver shield swept up, and every warrior of them looked to it, as any trained and instant-reaction warrior must—

And every man of them slowed, stiffened—and became a rigid, useless thing, eyes fixed and glazed, staring at the image of the thing of mystery that they had never seen! In the polished, perfect mirror of the shield, they stared into the mystery of the whirling, circling, patterned lights, the lights that boiled and raved and twisted now, as though some maddening thing was driving, hurrying, forcing them on.

Daron moved forward, two slow steps. His heavy blade came up—and fell.

A high, clear and piercing note sang out, a sweet, cloying sound of exquisite tone, as from a mighty, perfect bell. Again the heavy blade came up, and fell. Louder rang the note—but perfect still.

The silver shield moved, streaked forward, and clanged in brazen wrath—and the silver sphere exploded in a mighty blast of light, a shrieking, howling tornado of more-than-sound, a light that seared and darkened eyes.

The sphere was gone.

Daron snatched the whirring mechanism from his eye, opened his closed eye—and had by that one eye the advantage of every other. The twelve white-cloaked guards were down, down in limp and broken postures that told the warrior's eye a tale of ultimate defeat.

These men were corpses—and had been!

The power that animated them—the Invisible Ones—was gone!

Daron turned. Drathun was standing, half leaning against the doorway, holding a streaming wound in his left arm. "They fled when that bubble burst—and all shrieking furies of the world fled by me, too! By Talun and Martal, men, what deadly stuff is this we battered into?"

"That was the death-howl of the Invisible Ones, my friend," said Daron grimly. "Now we've a rendezvous above, I think."

"The fishermen's ships!" Drathun gasped. "The Invisible Ones are gone!"

"Come up—they'll need guidance, they'll need to know!"

Along the winding passages they ran, passages that seemed like veins of some dead animal now, drawn of all life, dead things that had been living. The guards had fled; they saw no men, but far away they heard the howling, shouting clamor of men in terror and in pursuit.

They vomited from a sloping ramp, and stood in a garden torn and trampled now, a score of corpses, dead and useless things—with no mark to show their death! Fallen, Daron knew, in the instant that the crystal shell that was the root and basis of the Invisible Ones was shattered.

Daron charged across the gardens toward the main entrance to the vast, snowy temple of the Invisible Ones. A line of blue-cloaked guards was fighting, holding back a horde of howling, rough-clad seamen. And at their very head, roaring in a voice of thunder, stood a rough and hairy figure, a very squat giant of a man—

"Talun!" roared Daron, and charged forward. "By Talun and the Old Gods all, they're gone, ye seamen, they're gone! The Invisible Ones are fallen! Their power is broken for all time to come! Take back your harbor, seamen! Take back your island, too!"

"Ah, Daron!" the mighty, squat, old figure roared. "Come on, lad—fight, don't waste good breath in idle talk! Drive out these scum! We'll bring the good, clean sea back to Tordu, and drive that stink of incense out forever!"

CHAPTER XII

Daron looked up and ahead, where, in the early sunlight, the topmost parts of Nazun's blue-green temple loomed above the trees. He halted momentarily, and breathed deep of the clear, crisp mountain air.

Drathun, panting, looked up at him. "Ye be a determined man, Daron. This air is thin. Now while you rest and get a bit of breath, give me one more bit of fact. You drive me mad, friend! What was that whirring thing ye wore in your eye last night as you broke the sphere?"

Daron laughed, and pulled the little thing from his pocket. "Here, Drathun, look at it. Look through it, and press this button here."

The seaman did. A hole drilled through front and back, covered by smooth glass surfaces, was darkened suddenly as a plate of metal began to revolve, passing in front of it, then circling back. Swiftly it gained, till the moving metal was but a blur, a haze that slightly dimmed the clear sight through the pierced hole.

The seaman grunted and passed it back. "A hole, with a bit of metal revolving past so fast it is not seen. A blur—no more. Now what is the magic of this thing?"

"In the lowlands of Looz Yan, in the land of the West, I saw a similar thing. They have there great windmills, and this thing they call a *strobe*. Now the magic of the thing is this: if you peer through this at a whirling thing, that thing seems to stand still! When I looked through this at the ordered whirling of the lights of the sphere—the lights moved slow, and lost all order, and made no sense. The magic of their power was broken, just as my view of them was broken by that metal plate. Yet, because they did not whirl in ordered circles, I could see them move in normal lines."

"Hm-m-m, there's more magic in simple things than I thought. Now, one more thing—"

"We climb the mountain now," laughed Daron. "And while you go to Talun's temple, I pay respects to good Nazun—and visit Lady Tammar. Up, my friend."

Drathun grunted. "Aye, up. My bones grow wearied, for I've had no sleep this night, and action enough for a dozen nights. I'm no young man such as you, or those who seem to be following us."

Daron looked back for the first time. Below them, a rushing crowd of men and women struggled up the path, panting, calling, beckoning. Daron smiled.

"I think the Old Gods have gained in popularity, with the death of the new."

"So the wine-sot turns to water when his affliction is withdrawn," Drathun growled. "Half those who worshiped at the Temple Isle could not stay away, though they willed it. Well—we have given them sound cure for that! A hundred tons of fish were offered there to Talun this night, on the red-orange altar of the Invisible Ones!"

Daron walked on, steady and slow, as the mountain man must, who would gain his goal in health. The high hills of the Ind had taught him that, as well as other things. "The fools will kill themselves in running up that mountain."

A voice, a shade more piercing than the rest, reached up to them. "Daron—Daron—wait there!'"

"Eh?" Daron turned. "Someone called my name."

Drathun laughed, a deep roar of amusement. "Are you

fool enough to think that name unknown after this night!
All Tordu calls your name now!"

Daron shrugged. Again the call came up, clearer now,
and the speaker, a long-legged youth, blowing like a spent
horse, shouted out again. "Wait there for us, Daron! We've
need of you!"

Daron turned and looked up at the tops of the temples
above, clustering in the long-slanting rays of the risen sun.
He looked back at the crowd, and the youth, and said to
Drathun: "I'll wait, or the young fool will run his heart out."

"Elmanus"—called the youth. He slowed now, gulping
deep breaths of air, and stumbled nearer, to throw himself
on the pathside grass. "Elmanus is dead!"

"Eh?" snapped Drathun. "Old Elmanus gone?"

"Aye—he died this night."

A half dozen other men were struggling up, blowing
hard. Long-legged farm men, and a seaman with rolling gait.
The seaman laughed and panted all at once, and stuttered
out the tale.

"Aye, the good old king is gone—may the gods protect
his name—and gone happy, at that."

"What struck him down?" Daron asked. The king had
been old, but seemed strong and well for all that.

"Joy," panted a horse-faced farmer. "And foolishness."

"He had a wine bottle in one hand," the youth panted.

"And a slave-maiden of his on the other," the seaman
managed, between a laugh and a gasp for air.

"And the old fool danced a jig! At his age! He was
howling in glee, and dancing round, and the girl had more
sense than he!"

"She tried to stop him," the seaman nodded. "But he
was howling praises on your name, and curses on the vanished Invisible Ones, and shrieking—"

"—that," the farmer interrupted gleefully, "he didn't

give a damn what gods were gone, so one set or the other
was destroyed."

"Ah," said Daron, a half-smile tugging at his lips. "Too
much release from pressure—and he exploded."

"Aye, he tried to dance, and tripped and fell. His leg
bent under him, and broke his hip. He was old and drunk
with wine, and the shock killed him two hours gone."

"But," the seaman panted, "as he died, he was conscious
again, and he said to his ministers, "Bring me that Daron!
Bring him here! He's the only one in all this land with force
enough to be a king!'"

The crowd was growing, surging, panting all around
them now, and shouting out to Daron. Suddenly they parted,
and an officer in old Elmanus' livery came up, panting hard,
his face red and sweating. "I near killed my horse, I fear,
Daron, and these seamen and farmers beat me even so. King
Elmanus is gone—gone from joy, and gone demanding that
you take his place."

"I—" said Daron, and looked about the crowd. Every
hot and sweating face looked up at him eagerly. Abruptly,
he spotted one face that was cool, and slightly smiling, a
round, rough-hewn face, with dark and heavy brows, and
leathery, tanned skin.

Old Talun shut one eye slowly and nodded to him. Beyond, behind him, even, Daron saw a tall, lean man in blue-
green robes.

"Now this land," said Daron with a sudden laugh, "is
a broad, and right good land, and one thing I like about it.
It has good gods, gods who act and do, and fight for what
is theirs! And, better, these gods pay those who help them
in their own way, and show no stinginess!

"So be it then; not for King Elmanus alone, but if ye
people—fishermen and farmers both—want me there—why
there I'll go!"

There was a roar of cheers that washed up about him like a pounding surf, and a hundred hands laid hold of him. Before he well knew what had happened, he was riding down the mountainside on the shoulders of a howling, cheering crowd.

His roars and protests went unheard, and, at last, he grinned and accepted it. But, back across his shoulder, he looked toward Tammar's temple, glowing rose-quartz vanishing behind, gleaming in the sun.

He'd reach that temple yet!

THE END

FINE SCIENCE FICTION AND FANTASY TITLES AVAILABLE FROM CARROLL & GRAF

- [ ] Aldiss, Brian/LAST ORDERS $3.50
- [ ] Aldiss, Brian/NON-STOP $3.95
- [ ] Amis, Kingsley/THE ALTERATION $3.50
- [ ] Asimov, Isaac et al/THE MAMMOTH BOOK OF CLASSIC SCIENCE FICTION (1930s) $8.95
- [ ] Asimov, Isaac et al/THE MAMMOTH BOOK OF GOLDEN AGE SCIENCE FICTION (1940s) $8.95
- [ ] Ballard, J.G./THE DROWNED WORLD $3.95
- [ ] Ballard, J.G./HELLO AMERICA $3.95
- [ ] Ballard, J.G./HIGH RISE $3.50
- [ ] Ballard, J.G./THE TERMINAL BEACH $3.50
- [ ] Ballard, J.G./VERMILION SANDS $3.95
- [ ] Bingley, Margaret/SEEDS OF EVIL $3.95
- [ ] Borges, Jorge Luis/THE BOOK OF FANTASY (Trade Paper) $10.95
- [ ] Boucher, Anthony/THE COMPLEAT WEREWOLF $3.95
- [ ] Burroughs, Edgar Rice/A PRINCESS OF MARS $2.95
- [ ] Campbell, John W./THE MOON IS HELL! $3.95
- [ ] Campbell, Ramsey/DEMONS BY DAYLIGHT $3.95
- [ ] Dick Philip K./CLANS OF THE ALPHANE MOON $3.95
- [ ] Dick, Philip K./THE PENULTIMATE TRUTH $3.95
- [ ] Disch, Thomas K./CAMP CONCENTRATION $3.95
- [ ] Disch, Thomas K./ON WINGS OF SONG $3.95
- [ ] Hodgson, William H./THE HOUSE ON THE BORDERLAND $3.50
- [ ] Leiber, Fritz/YOU'RE ALL ALONE $3.95
- [ ] Leinster, Murray/THE FORGOTTEN PLANET $3.95
- [ ] Lindsay, David/SPHINX Cloth $17.95

☐ Lovecraft, H. P. & Derleth, A./THE LURKER ON
   THE THRESHOLD $3.50
☐ Malzberg, Barry/BEYOND APOLLO $3.50
☐ Malzberg, Barry/GALAXIES $2.95
☐ Moorcock, Michael/BEHOLD THE MAN $2.95
☐ Cawthorne and Moorcock/FANTASY: THE 100
   BEST BOOKS Cloth $15.95
☐ Pringle, David/SCIENCE FICTION: THE 100
   BEST NOVELS $7.95
☐ Siodmak, Curt/DONOVAN'S BRAIN $3.50
☐ Sladek, John/THE MULLER-FOKKER EFFECT $3.95
☐ Sladek, John/RODERICK $3.95
☐ Sladek, John/RODERICK AT RANDOM $3.95
☐ Stableford, Brian/THE WALKING SHADOW $3.95
☐ Stevens, Francis/CITADEL OF FEAR $3.50
☐ Stevens, Francis/CLAIMED $3.50
☐ Stoker, Bram/THE JEWEL OF SEVEN
   STARS $3.95
☐ Sturgeon, Theodore/THE DREAMING JEWELS $3.95
☐ Sturgeon, Theodore/VENUS PLUS X $3.95
☐ Sturgeon, Theodore/THE GOLDEN HELIX $3.95
☐ van Vogt, A.E./COSMIC ENCOUNTER $3.50
☐ Watson, Ian/CHEKHOV'S JOURNEY $3.95
☐ Watson, Ian/THE EMBEDDING $3.95
☐ Watson, Ian/MIRACLE VISITORS $3.95
☐ Wolfe, Bernard/LIMBO $4.95

Available from fine bookstores everywhere or use this coupon for ordering.

Carroll & Graf Publishers, Inc., 260 Fifth Avenue, N.Y., N.Y. 10001

Please send me the books I have checked above. I am enclosing
$_____ (please add $1.00 per title to cover postage and
handling.) Send check or money order—no cash or C.O.D.'s
please. N.Y. residents please add 8¼% sales tax.

Mr/Mrs/Ms _____
Address _____
City _____ State/Zip _____
Please allow four to six weeks for delivery.